BROKEN DREAM

BROKEN DREAM

HELEN HARDT

This book is an original publication of Waterhouse Press.

This is a work of fiction. Names, characters, places, and incidents either are the product of the author's imagination or are used fictitiously, and any resemblance to actual persons, living or dead, business establishments, events, or locales is entirely coincidental. The publisher does not assume any responsibility for third-party websites or their content.

Copyright © 2025 Waterhouse Press, LLC
Cover Design by Waterhouse Press, LLC
Cover Images: Depositphotos

All Rights Reserved.
No part of this book may be reproduced, scanned, or distributed in any printed or electronic format without permission. Please do not participate in or encourage piracy of copyrighted materials in violation of the author's rights. Purchase only authorized editions.

ISBN: 978-1-64263-412-9

To the two therapists who helped me when I needed it

PROLOGUE

If I can't have you, I'll make sure no one else ever does.
    She never heard me say the words out loud.
    But they live inside my mind.
    I watch.
    And I wait.

CHAPTER ONE

ANGIE

Today's the day.

Anatomy lab begins.

And I'm feeling a little...nauseated.

This is a huge part of a medical student's education, and I knew it was coming. Still...

The room is chilly. It has to be, so the cadavers won't rot.

Yeah, more nausea.

"How can you not be more excited?" Tabitha Haynes, a bubbly blonde and my assigned lab partner, asks me.

She and I met briefly at the mixer at the beginning of the first semester, but we haven't been friendly. I haven't been very friendly with any of my fellow students, to be honest. I'm kind of an introvert. I was popular in high school and college simply by being one of the "awesome foursome," which consisted of my twin sister, Sage, and my cousins Brianna and Gina. We're the youngest in our large family, so we've always hung out together. Sage, Bree, and Gina are all extroverts, so I tagged along, and they brought me out of my shell.

But I'm alone here in Boulder, Colorado, as I begin my second semester of my first year of medical school.

"I'm going into psychiatry," I tell Tabitha. "The thought of dissecting an actual human being kind of makes me want to barf."

My comment doesn't seem to faze her. "I'm going into surgery, so this is huge for me," she says.

I wrinkle my nose. "Don't you ever think about the ethics of it? Like, what if we recognize him? Or her?"

"Now you're just being gross," Tabitha says. "Besides, we've only been in medical school for a couple of months so far. You may really enjoy this lab. You may decide you don't want to focus on psychiatry after all."

I shake my head. "My aunt is a renowned psychiatrist. She's retired now, but she's amazing. If I can be half the psychiatrist she is, I know I'll contribute something wonderful to the world."

Tabitha rolls her eyes at me. "Dr. Melanie Carmichael Steel. We all know who you are, Angie."

Yeah, everyone knows I'm a member of the Steel family. I may not carry their last name, but my mother, Marjorie Steel Simpson, is sister—and the only female sibling—to the three Steel brothers.

"I don't flaunt my family ties," I say.

"Did I say you did?" She purses her lips. "There's been talk, of course. I'm not saying I've been talking, but there's been talk."

I should be surprised, but I'm not. There's always talk.

"About what?" I ask.

"About you and your hefty Steel trust fund. About why you're even bothering with medical school when you have enough money to last your entire lifetime and more."

"God." I let out a huff. "I'm so sick of this kind of shit. I got it all through college, too. Maybe I should've gone to medical school somewhere on the East Coast where no one has ever heard of the Steels."

"Calm down," Tabitha says. "*I* haven't been talking. That I promise you. Frankly, I think anyone who has the drive and perseverance to get into medical school—which is not easy, as you know—and the desire to heal should be here."

I nod. "I have that. I've learned so much from my aunt over the years. I want to help people the way she does."

"Then you totally should." She crosses her arms. "But I'm just saying, don't count out surgery, because once we cut into this cadaver, you may find you like it."

I force a smile at Tabitha. Maybe we could be friends. She's cute, with her blond hair and light-brown eyes. She's half a head shorter than I am, but I come from tall stock.

"So what should we name him?" Tabitha asks, looking down at our cadaver covered with a thick white sheet.

I drop my jaw. "You want to *name* the dead guy? I'm still on 'what if we recognize him?'"

She smirks. "Are you kidding me? These bodies have been soaking in formaldehyde for years. Have you had anyone you know die and leave their body to science in that time?"

Ugh. I don't want to think about that. "We don't know whether we're going to get a male or female," I say.

"So we choose an androgynous name, then. Like Jordan or Morgan."

Is she kidding me? "Don't you think we should see what he or she looks like first?"

God. Soon we'll have to look at it.

She lets out a laugh. "You are too funny! You don't want to do any of this, but you want to wait until we *see* the cadaver before we give it a name?"

I grimace. "Hey, if I had it my way, there would be no

name. There would be no anatomy lab."

"Then why didn't you just pursue a doctorate in psychology? Why bother with med school at all?"

"Why wouldn't I?" I shrug my shoulders. "Psychiatry is a medical profession. I happen to think the link between physical health and mental and emotional health is very important."

"Okay, okay... Simmer down." She punches me gently on my upper arm. "If you want to get through med school, though, you're going to have to pass anatomy lab. We're going to be doing this for four years, and probably more during internship and residency. Well, at least during internship for you. If you stick with psychiatry, that's where your residency will be."

"Thank God," I say under my breath.

Then Tabitha grabs my arm. "Fuck," she says. "Check out our instructor."

I look to the front of the room, where a tall man is walking in.

Make that a *really* tall man, with gorgeous dark-brown hair, black stubble on his sculpted jawline, and the most piercing emerald-green eyes I've ever seen.

Oh my God.

He may just be the best-looking man I've ever laid eyes on, and I grew up in a family of famously handsome men.

"Who is that?" I hear another student whisper.

Every woman in the room is staring at him, and quite a few of the men as well. And I don't think they're all gay. He's just *that* good-looking.

"Good morning," he says. "I'm Dr. Jason Lansing, and I'll be your instructor for this semester's anatomy lab. Please call me Jason." He gives a dramatic scowl. "*Dr. Lansing* makes me feel about a hundred years old."

Laughter echoes throughout the lab. I simply gulp and try not to stare at my professor's magnificence.

He looks around the room. "You'll get to meet your cadavers soon. First, some preliminaries." He paces up and down between our tables. "You're very lucky to have only two students per cadaver. In normal years, there are four per cadaver, and even sometimes six. The school received a hefty donation this year, so we're able to do two per cadaver."

Hefty donation.

From my mother and father, of course. But no one needs to know that, though I'm sure they all suspect.

He looks up and down the lab, pausing on each individual face. "You may be feeling a mixture of anticipation, excitement, maybe even a bit of nervousness. That's all normal. Today, and over the next few months, you'll begin a journey of understanding the human body in ways that can only be taught here."

He pauses a moment. Is he going to ask if we have questions? He doesn't. He simply clears his throat and continues.

He gestures to the sheet-covered cadavers. "These are not just bodies. They are people who made the thoughtful decision to donate themselves so that you could learn. They've given you one final gift—one of knowledge. Every time you approach these tables, remember that you're not just studying anatomy. You're honoring a life."

Another pause.

What's with all the pausing?

"Over the course of this semester, we'll be covering different regions of the body, moving from the thorax to the limbs, and eventually to more delicate areas. Each lab will build on the last to give you a complete view of how interconnected our bodies truly are. For many of you, this will be the most hands-on learning you've ever experienced. It will be challenging and at times uncomfortable, but also incredibly rewarding."

He takes a few steps closer to the nearest table—which happens to be Tabitha's and mine—and places a hand on the edge.

He's so close.

So close that I can smell his scent over the chemical aromas of the lab.

He smells like the outdoors—crisp pine and the faint smokiness of a fire that's long since burned out. It's rugged and raw, as if he's part of the wilderness itself, untamed and irresistible.

"Remember, this is a privilege, and we are here to learn—not only from books but also from these individuals. They teach us the complexities of human life, health, and disease in a way no lecture can. Each scar, each variation you'll see, tells a story."

A few students exchange glances.

"Let's also be mindful of each other," Dr. Lansing adds. "Some of you may feel overwhelmed today or in the coming weeks, and that's perfectly okay. We're in this together, and I encourage you to support each other, to ask questions, and to take breaks when needed. This lab is a safe place for learning and growth."

With those last words, he's talking directly to me. At least I feel like he is. I seem to be the only apprehensive person in the room.

"Before we begin," he says, "I want to go around the room

BROKEN DREAM

and have each of you introduce yourselves. You've been in school together for a few months now, and if you're like most new medical students, you've been spending all your free time hitting the books, and you haven't gotten to know each other." He crosses his arms. "But medicine is a collaborative practice. For the rest of your careers, you'll be working with other physicians and depending on them as they will depend on you. We'll start with you two." He meets my gaze, his hand still resting on Tabitha's and my table.

I swallow as I try to breathe.

When I finally open my mouth—

Tabitha beats me to the punch. "I'm Tabitha Haynes," she says, "and I'm from Denver. My undergrad degree is in microbiology, and I'm hoping to become a surgeon."

"Good to have you here, Tabitha," Dr. Lansing says.

He deepens his gaze at me.

God, those eyes.

Like a bright-green flame.

I feel like he's melting the clothes off my body.

I clear my throat. "I'm Angela Simpson. Call me Angie. I'm from Snow Creek on the Western Slope. My undergrad degree is in biology and psychology, and I'm interested in psychiatry."

Jason's lips tremble a bit.

Seriously? Is he trying not to laugh at me?

No. I'm reading far too much into it. He's our instructor, and all medical specialties are valid. He knows this as well as I do.

"I see, Angie." He presses his lips together. "Any particular reason for choosing psychiatry this early in the game?"

No way. He didn't interrogate Tabitha about her choice.

"My aunt is a renowned psychiatrist, and I truly respect what she's been able to do during her career. Psychiatry is my calling."

He slowly nods. "I'm sure your aunt is very proud of you."

Is it my imagination, or is his tone kind of dismissive?

Before I can consider it further, Dr. Lansing moves to the next table.

And then all I can think about is what he might look like without a shirt.

It's sure as hell more appealing than thinking about the dead person lying in front of me.

CHAPTER TWO

JASON

There's one in every class—a student who thinks he or she is going to save the world from the current mental health crisis.

A worthy goal, for sure.

But an impossible one.

I'm living proof of that.

And of course for this lab, she has to be the most beautiful woman in the room. She's tall, slender, with a gorgeous head of dark hair pulled into a ponytail, beautiful brown eyes, and full pink lips.

I listen with one ear as the rest of the students introduce themselves.

Once everyone is done, I move back to the front of the room. "Are you all ready?"

I get several resounding *yeses*.

Nothing from Angie Simpson, though. She looks like she's about ready to lose her breakfast.

I take a steadying breath and look around the room, making sure every student is focused and ready—or as close to ready as they can be. This first encounter is a memory they'll carry long after they've left this lab. I still remember the day I saw my first cadaver.

I knew then I'd be a surgeon.

I just didn't know how short my time as a surgeon would turn out to be.

"Let's begin." I move to another table in front. I can't be so close to Angie Simpson. Something about her makes me feel things I've long forgotten.

The cadaver at the next table lies covered in a heavy sheet. "We'll start by uncovering just the thoracic area, the upper chest," I say. "This way, you'll see just a section of the body, not the whole, which helps keep our focus and eases us into this process."

I reach down and slowly lift the top of the sheet, just enough to reveal the shoulders and upper chest.

The room is silent, filled only with the soft sound of fabric moving.

"This is the thoracic cavity," I say. "In here, we have the heart, the lungs, and vessels that carry life to every part of our bodies."

I pause and look around the room. Some students' eyes widen, others look deeply thoughtful. "Now, reach out, place your gloved hand gently on the sternum here, at the center." I demonstrate, pressing lightly. "This is the core of the chest. From here, we'll feel the ribs, the borders of the thoracic cavity. Take your time, feel the shape, imagine the movement that once filled these lungs with breath."

I walk around the room. From some students I sense curiosity. From others, astonishment. From a few, boredom. All normal.

Then I lock eyes with Angie Simpson. No boredom there. Definitely no curiosity. Maybe a little astonishment.

Mostly she seems to be giving off a mix of dread and determination. Her hands are as white as the sheet covering the body in front of her. She looks like she's holding her breath, as if the weight of the moment might overwhelm her.

Her lab partner has uncovered the chest and is probing it with her gloved hand.

But Angie hasn't touched anything yet. She's only now snapping on her gloves.

"You doing okay?" I ask.

She clears her throat. "Why wouldn't I be?"

"Because you're pale as a ghost," I say.

Her cheeks redden, and my God, she's beautiful. She's the most gorgeous woman in the room. Her lab partner is pretty as well, and on any other day, I might say she was the prettiest girl in the room. But she's girl-next-door pretty, while Angie...

Wow.

Just wow.

"I'm fine. I assure you." Angie drops her gaze to the floor.

"We're not going to cut today," I tell her.

Angie's lab partner lets out a disappointed huff.

"Of course I know that," Angie says. "I mean... You wouldn't let us cut right away."

She won't meet my gaze, and she's stumbling over her words.

It's adorably cute.

I return to the front of the room. "Open your anatomy books to page seventy-five and take a look at the thoracic area in the diagram."

I wait while they shuffle their textbooks open.

"See how everything has a proper place?"

Murmurs of agreement.

"Don't expect everything to look like that when you cut into these cadavers. What looks perfect in a textbook looks very different in a live body."

"Don't you mean *dead* body?" a guy says from the back.

I let out a chuckle. "Touché. What you'll see in these cadavers are organs that have been preserved. No blood flows through them. But don't expect all the organs to be in a tight little group the way it looks in your textbooks. Every human being is different, and while most humans have their organs in roughly the same area, it doesn't look the same as the diagram."

"So when do we get to cut?" the same wise guy from the back demands.

"It won't be too long," I say. "Remind me of your name again?"

"Garrett." He flashes me a goofy smile. "Elijah Garrett."

"Right, Elijah Garrett. You're interested in cardiothoracic surgery, if I recall correctly."

"I am."

About half the students mentioned some kind of surgery as their focus. I hate to tell them that only about ten percent of them will make the cut. Not the time or place.

"I understand your excitement," I say. "I remember when I sat in this same lab many years ago. I couldn't wait to make my first incision. It will be something you will never forget. But if you continue in surgery, Elijah, wait until you make your first cut into an actual living person." My heartbeat quickens slightly. "That's an addiction that will never go away."

Elijah smiles, nodding.

Yeah, that kid *will* be a surgeon. I see it in his eyes.

I couldn't wait to sink a scalpel into flesh, even dead flesh. The thrill of discovery, the responsibility that weighs heavy in your hands, the sheer awe of unraveling the mysteries held within the human body... It isn't for the fainthearted.

BROKEN DREAM

I glance back at Angie, who's still looking kind of sickly. I think her lab partner—Tabitha, if I remember correctly—senses it too. She gives Angie a pat on her arm.

"All right, everyone." I raise my voice to regain their attention. "Look at your gloves and observe how clean they are. That will change very soon."

Laughter—some of it nervous—echoes throughout the lab.

"And when it does," I continue, "you'll realize that you're not just here to learn about parts and pieces. You're here to learn about life and death, about beginnings and endings, about the delicate balance that keeps us breathing. This is not just an anatomy class but a life lesson. What we start today will shape you as individuals and as medical professionals."

Elijah raises his hand.

I nod to him. "Yes?"

"How will we be graded?"

I chuckle. "There's always someone who asks that. You can find all of that information on the school's learning management site on the page for this class. Copies of my syllabus as well as my grading rubric are readily available to you there." I move to the side and lean against my desk. "Let's take a break for ten minutes. Use this time to get yourself acclimated if you need to. When we return, we'll dive deeper into the thoracic cavity."

A collective exhale fills the room, followed by some hushed chatter and movement. Most of them make their way out of the lab, but a few remain behind, huddled in small groups or studying their textbooks.

Angie Simpson makes her way toward the door. I stop her. "You seem troubled," I say.

She inhales. "I'm fine."

"Take a break. Join your classmates. You'll feel better."

"None of this matters," she says. "I'll never see the inside of an OR. Psychiatry is my calling."

I tilt my head. "Are you sure about that?"

I want her to say she's not sure at all. That psychiatry is nothing to her.

Because it sure as hell is nothing to me.

But she raises her chin slightly. "As sure as my name is Angela Daphne Simpson."

Angela Daphne. A gorgeous name. Daphne was a beautiful nymph pursued by Apollo. She became a laurel tree to escape him. Angela, of course, comes from *angel*.

She indeed looks like an angel.

I rack my brain for a diplomatic way to get my thoughts across. "If you don't like the lab portion of medical school, you could have pursued a doctorate in psychology. You don't need an MD to practice."

"Tabitha just said the same thing to me." She rubs at her forehead. "Why doesn't anyone get it? I want to be able to heal the physical as well as the mental. I want to—"

"Then you need to be here, Angie," I interrupt her. "You need to understand the physical in order to adequately address the mental. The mind and the body are naturally linked, and you can't hope to heal one without understanding the other."

My words surprise me.

I believe them wholeheartedly.

I just don't believe psychiatry is the answer.

Angie stares at me for a moment before she nods. "You're right," she says quietly. "I'll manage. It's just... It's a lot more real now than it was on paper."

BROKEN DREAM

I smile, resisting the urge to give her a reassuring pat on her shoulder. "Don't worry. You'll get used to it. And remember, it's okay to feel overwhelmed sometimes. That's part of being human."

She gives me a small smile, turns, and leaves the room.

I turn toward the wall to discreetly adjust my groin.

Fuck.

CHAPTER THREE

ANGIE

I've been in medical school for a couple of months now, and I don't feel close to anyone.

I'm okay with that.

I spend my days going to class, my evenings studying, and my weekends doing lab work and studying some more. Some of the students have outside jobs to pay for school. For the life of me, I don't know how they do it. They must not sleep.

I spy Tabitha talking with Elijah Garrett, the guy in the back who seems hell-bent on cutting into his cadaver. I walk up to them cautiously.

"Hey, Angie," Tabitha says. "Have you met Eli?"

"I don't think so." I hold out my hand.

Eli shakes it. "Tabitha's been telling me you're a little grossed out by all of this."

I resist rolling my eyes. Great. Pretty soon the whole class will know I'm the one who is squeamish about cutting into dead bodies.

In a way, it doesn't make any sense. I grew up on a ranch. My family raises cattle for food, and I enjoy steak as well as anyone. Especially those from my family's ranch—the best beef in Colorado. Some say in the country.

Of course, cutting into a cooked piece of meat is a lot

different from the body of a human corpse. It's a lot harder to separate yourself from the situation when a dead person's eyes are staring at you the whole time.

"Nice to meet you, Eli," I say. I give Tabitha a side glance, my eyebrow raised ever so slightly.

She giggles, covering her mouth. .

Eli just smiles, his eyes sparkling with amusement. He's tall and thin, and his raven-black hair falls over his forehead, contrasting sharply with his pale complexion. He reminds me of Edward Scissorhands.

Ha!

Scissorhands who wants to cut.

"Looks like we'd better get back in there." Eli gestures toward the crowd of students walking back in the lab room.

I nod and walk back into the room, trying not to stare at Dr. Lansing.

Jason.

Jason Lansing.

What a nice name.

Until a fresh wave of formaldehyde hits me. I swallow hard, trying to keep my stomach at bay. Around me, students chatter. Tabitha takes her place next to me, our cadaver still covered except for the exposed thoracic area.

"Okay, let's get back to things," Dr. Lansing says from the front of the room. "As you know, you won't be cutting today."

A big groan from Eli and a few others.

He holds a hand up. "This isn't something you go into without your eyes being wide open and without your stomach being tough as nails." He looks around the room, his gaze homing in on me.

Great.

"This isn't for the faint of heart. If you can't handle this"—he gestures to the sheeted forms on the tables—"then maybe it's time to reconsider your career path."

Seriously?

My eyes are wide as Jason stares straight at me. Again.

He just told me how I need to be here if I want to heal the physical and the mental.

Now I feel like he's telling me to get the hell out.

I don't look away.

No way will I let him scare me out of medical school.

He clears his throat. "Now that we've got that out of the way, let's talk about what we're dealing with here. Anatomy isn't just about knowing what's where. It's also about understanding how everything works together. As we progress, we'll look at how diseases affect these systems. You're going to see firsthand how a lifetime of heavy smoking ravages the lungs, or how cirrhosis changes the liver. You're going to see the effects of untreated diabetes on the eyes, kidneys, and blood vessels. You're going to see what heart disease does to the arteries."

I take a deep breath, trying to ignore the sharp smell of formaldehyde that seems to be embedded in my sinuses now. I glance over at Tabitha. Excitement is evident in her wide eyes.

Eli looks like he can't wait to get his hands dirty. He's clenching and unclenching his fists, his knuckles white against his fair skin.

"This is a serious undertaking," Jason continues. "We're not just studying anatomy. We're studying the history of a person's life, their choices, their circumstances, everything that led them to this moment. Our cadavers were not just specimens but human beings who lived, had experiences, felt joy and pain."

With those words, I feel like Jason is speaking directly to me.

More than that, I feel his eyes trained on me, as if the emerald-green fire is burning two holes in my flesh.

My nipples are hard, and I don't dare look down because my unlined bra is going to show them protruding through my T-shirt.

He's right.

These are people.

Like I said to Tabitha in the beginning. What if we recognize someone?

She's right, of course. The bodies will be unrecognizable.

"I see how excited some of you are, how ready you are to cut. But something you need to learn—I'm talking to all of you, not just our future surgeons—is that you can't ever cut into a human being without thinking things through first."

"But these are dead people," Elijah says without raising his hand.

"Let me open up to you guys a bit." Jason rakes his fingers through his gorgeous black hair. "This is my first time teaching anatomy lab."

I can't help my surprise. Jason seems so sure of himself, so exact in what he says, how he wants to make us feel about these cadavers who donated their bodies to science.

"I'm sure you're wondering why I'm telling you that. Some of you may be thinking, *Oh great, a new guy. He doesn't know what he's doing.* Or some of you may be thinking, *Great, a new guy. An easy A.* Let me assure you that whatever you're thinking about me, you don't know the whole story. Let me tell you this..." He begins to pace across the front of the lab. "When I became an attending general surgeon years ago, I made many mistakes. All young surgeons have by the time they complete their residency." He stops pacing and gazes out the window. "At some point, and sooner than you may expect, you *will* take a life. You won't do it on purpose, of course, but one day, a mistake you make will take the life of another human being." He returns his gaze to a now silent class. "You will have to live with that. You will have to learn from that. And you will have to move forward from that. You'll carry that weight with you every time you walk into an operating room, every time you pick up a scalpel."

A hush falls over the room.

"But remember," Jason continues, softening his tone, "at the end of the day, you are human beings trying your best to save lives. It's called the practice of medicine for a reason. You will never be perfect. Yes, there will be losses. But do not let them define you. Learn from them, and seek comfort in your victories."

He looks around the room, his gaze landing on each student before moving on to the next.

"As for me," Jason adds, "I still feel the weight of my mistakes. They're a part of me now, as much as my training and my skill. But they made me better, and I hope they will make me a good teacher." He turns away to reach for something on his desk. When he turns back, he's holding a small box. "This," he says, "is one of the most important lessons you will learn here."

He opens the box for us to see. Inside sits a scalpel.

He holds it up to the light. "This isn't just a scalpel. This is your connection to another person's life. It's a symbol of trust and responsibility, an instrument that you must wield with careful precision and utmost respect."

He walks around the room, allowing each of us to catch a glimpse of the scalpel gleaming under the fluorescent lights.

I glance at Tabitha and then over my shoulder at Eli. They both look enthralled by Jason's words and the object in his hand. As Jason walks by Eli's desk, Eli reaches out, nearly touching it before thinking better of it and retracting his hand. Jason gives him a nod before moving on.

"Every incision you make," Jason continues when he returns to the front of the room, "is a life changed. Every stitch you sew is a wound healed. And every mistake you make... Well, we've already talked about that."

Jason places the scalpel back into its box and sets it onto his desk with a click. He turns back to face us. "But remember," he says, "you're not alone in this journey. You have each other to learn from, to support, and to challenge. You have your teachers, who are here to guide you, and we have the memory of every patient we've lost who has pushed us to be better."

A beat of silence passes before he continues. "Tomorrow, we will begin our first dissection. It'll be a test of your knowledge and your skills, but most importantly it will be a test of your character." He pauses once more, his words hanging in the air. "I want each of you to take time tonight to reflect on why you chose this path. Remember that passion when things get tough. Remember the responsibility that comes with each decision you make."

He turns back toward his desk and begins shuffling papers around, signaling the end of the lecture. As students start filing out of the room, I feel a strong urge to stay back, to talk to Jason, to understand more. I observe as Eli and Tabitha leave and disappear into the hallway.

The room is almost empty when Jason finally looks up

from his task, surprise visible in his eyes. "Still here?" he asks with a small smile.

"Yes," I answer, swallowing the lump in my throat. "I just..."

God, Angie, get a grip.

I clear my throat. "Your words really struck a chord with me."

It's not a lie. Jason has a respect for the learning of anatomy that I find...interesting. I never wanted to dissect a cadaver, but now I'm rethinking that stance.

Not like I have a choice if I want to get through med school anyway.

Jason's smile widens a fraction before he moves away from his desk and leans against it casually, crossing his arms.

"Medicine isn't easy," he says, "and I won't lie to you or sugarcoat it. It's going to test you in ways you can't even imagine." He gives me a sarcastic laugh. "Even those of you who choose never to wield a scalpel. Even psychiatrists."

CHAPTER FOUR

JASON

Angie turns and walks out of the room.

Yeah, my bad.

I shouldn't have made that snide remark about psychiatry. This woman obviously has a calling, and who am I to try to change her attitude?

Just because psychiatry didn't work for me doesn't mean it doesn't work for millions of others.

She mentioned an aunt of hers.

For a moment I think of calling her back in, getting the name of her aunt, looking into her work.

Then I realize something.

I don't give a rat's ass who her aunt is or what she may have accomplished in her life as a psychiatrist.

I'm simply looking for excuses to pull Angie back into the room with me.

God, she's fucking beautiful. A classic beauty, with nearly perfect features—large and long-lashed eyes, high cheekbones, full pink lips. Her figure...

Long luscious legs, broad shoulders, succulent tits.

Her nipples were showing through her T-shirt.

Every guy in the room noticed.

I didn't like them looking at her.

But I'm a teacher. I'm *her* teacher. Trying anything with her would be unethical. Besides, she can't even be twenty-five years old. And she's probably younger, if she went straight from college to med school. That would make her only twenty-two or twenty-three—at least a twelve-year age gap between us.

Plus... She stands for everything I hate about medicine. Psychiatry.

Psychiatry fucked me over. Cost me a lot more than anyone knows.

I clench my fist around the pen in my hand, a futile attempt to control the storm inside me. It snaps in half, blue ink splattering across my hand and the desk.

Shit.

I grab a tissue to clean up the mess.

I look up. The door to the classroom is still ajar. I watch Angie retreat, her brown ponytail swaying against the small of her back, until she disappears from view. It somehow feels like losing a part of me—a part I didn't even know existed until today.

The silence in the room is overwhelming, each tick of the clock on the wall echoing in my ears.

Hmm.

Angie's voice clouds my mind. Her words. About psychiatry being important, about it being a way to heal people. Even though I know she's wrong about it in my case, maybe she's right overall. Maybe I'm being too harsh.

Until an image slams back into my head.

My own experience with psychiatry, the countless sessions spent on a leather couch, dissecting my dreams and fears, only to be left more confused and lost than before. The constant popping of pills that dulled my senses but never soothed my soul. And the loss...

No, psychiatry didn't help me.

It only made things worse.

I rub my forehead with my ink-stained hand, hoping to ease the headache that's beginning to pulse in my temples.

Angie's face flashes in my mind once more—her eyes filled with conviction, her lips curved into a defiant smile. I can't help but feel drawn to her. Something about her passion for psychiatry captivates me, regardless of my own contempt for it.

As much as I hate to admit it, Angie has sparked something in me.

Something I haven't felt in a long time.

I sigh, leaning back in my chair and massaging my temples. The headache is only getting worse, but there's a part of me that likes the pain. It's an annoying throb that just feels real.

Teaching anatomy lab was certainly never my calling.

But it's what I'm stuck with now.

A surgeon who can't cut.

A surgeon who can't cut is like a bird that can't fly, a fish that can't swim. It's a paradox, an anomaly. I let out a bitter laugh.

I open the box and stare at my scalpel—a memento from an era when I had the power to heal with my hands. I close my eyes and remember the OR. The metallic smell of blood, the steady beep of the heart monitor, and the adrenaline rush that came with every cut.

Then a knock on the cracked door.

I snap my eyes open.

Standing in the doorway is Angie, her face flushed from what must have been a hurried walk back to the classroom.

"I forgot something," she says softly, avoiding eye contact. She walks over to her desk and picks up a small notebook.

"Angie," I begin, unsure of what to say next.

My mind is a whirlpool of thoughts and emotions that threaten to swallow me whole. Something about this woman pulls at a thread inside me and threatens to unravel the tightly woven defense I've built over the past years.

She pauses, her hand still clutching the notebook. "Yes?" Her voice is light, but there's a slight tremor in it.

I won't read anything into it. She's embarrassed. That's all. She left her notebook, and I'm her professor.

I want to apologize for my insensitivity regarding her chosen field. But the words don't come.

Instead, I settle on, "You left quite an impression today."

She turns to face me, her eyebrows furrowed. "Do you mean that in a good way or a bad way?"

"The jury's still out on that," I reply, leaning back into my chair.

"Oh," she says softly, her face falling.

Silence stretches on uncomfortably long.

Until I can't help myself.

I stand, close the distance between us, pull her to me, and crush my lips to hers.

The world around us seems to fade as I lose myself in the taste and feel of her. Her lips are surprisingly soft. They melt against mine with a slight hesitation.

But only slight.

Within a few seconds, she's kissing me back with a fiery passion. She wraps an arm around my neck.

Heat rushes through my veins, burning away the icy wall I've built around myself. My heart hammers.

How long has it been since I felt this alive?

I inhale. She smells of something sweet. Apples. Blossoms. Simply Angie.

I'm dizzy with longing.

But as quickly as the kiss started, reality comes crashing down.

What the hell am I doing?

I pull away from her and break the kiss.

Her cheeks are flushed, and she's breathing just as heavily as I am.

"Oh, God," she whispers, her eyes wide and stunned as she takes a step back and shakes her head. "We... We shouldn't have done that."

"I know." My words come out in a rough rasp.

My stomach is knotted with guilt.

But damn...

Her taste lingers on my lips. I reach up to touch my mouth.

She looks at me, her eyes wide and confused, the notebook clutched in her hand. She takes a deep breath, composes herself, and without another word, she turns and marches out of the room.

What the fuck have I done?

Three years earlier...

"Jay," Lindsay yells to me, "don't forget the frog!"

Of course. Julia just turned three, and Lindsay's mother got her this ridiculous stuffed frog. She takes it everywhere. Calls it Fwoggie.

"Where's Fwoggie, sweetie?" I ask my daughter, holding

her on one hip.

She points.

I follow her finger and find Fwoggie stuffed underneath a pillow on the couch. Julia's not a big talker yet, but she's the most observant kid in the universe. She knows where she leaves everything.

I grab the frog. "Daddy's got a big surgery, and he's going to be late." I push the frog into Julia's hands. "Let's go, sweetheart."

"Love you!" I call to Lindsay.

"Love you both!" she calls back.

And I'm out the door, where I quickly secure Julia in her car seat and start my SUV. It's raining. Ugh. People around here don't know how to drive in the rain.

Lindsay is a teacher, and she has parent-teacher conferences today. Julia stays at the daycare center at my hospital most days, but today I'm taking her to Lindsay's mother's house for a day with Grandma.

She'll probably give her another ridiculous stuffed animal.

My high-risk Whipple procedure is scheduled for nine o'clock sharp, but traffic is a mess, and I'm so not in the mood.

I go over the steps of the Whipple in my head.

First, the incision—a deep cut across the abdomen, which gives me full access to the pancreas and the surrounding structures. I pull the edges apart gently. The head of the pancreas comes into view.

I begin by separating the head of the pancreas from the nearby tissues. I visualize each connection—vessels, ducts, and nerves that must be delicately severed, each one carrying life to and from these organs. Next, I move to the duodenum, where I divide and remove a portion. The bile duct is next, disconnected from the pancreas so it can be rerouted later.

I work meticulously, envisioning the margins, making sure every section is clean and free of any tumor cells. It's a slow, deliberate process, moving piece by piece, unraveling the—

The tires skid.

Hands tight on the wheel.

Too tight.

Can't stop.

Can't steer.

Rain streaking the windshield, blurring the road.

Brake.

Why isn't it stopping?

The car spins. My heart pounds, slamming against my ribs.

Everything moves in slow motion but too fast.

Control slipping.

Can feel it slipping.

This is real. This is happening.

Impact coming. Can't stop it.

I brace. Muscles locked. Shoulders tense.

Hold on. Just hold on.

Flashes. The crunch of metal. Shattering glass. The scream of something breaking—inside or outside, I can't tell. Body jolting. Air forced from my lungs.

Is this it?

Julia! Julia!

My mind screams a thousand things, but only one thing really matters.

Julia!

CHAPTER FIVE

Angie

My lips are stinging.

A good sting.

I've been kissed before.

Not as much as Sage, but I've had my share.

But this...

Jason's not a college guy.

He's a man.

A full-fledged doctor.

And he's my anatomy professor.

Tabitha waves to me. "Angie, come here. Eli, Ralph, and I are going to get lunch. You should join us."

I swallow. Lunch. Right. After thinking about cutting up dead bodies.

I'm supposed to eat now?

I nod, trying to find a smile for Tabitha. She's oblivious, her eyes sparkling with enthusiasm, as if nothing has changed.

But everything has changed.

"Sure," I manage to croak out. "Lunch sounds great."

Great? My stomach churns at the thought of food.

Is this what it feels like to be in love? Or is this just horror at the realization that I've kissed a man who spends his days elbow-deep in cadavers? Who's also the most gorgeous man

I've ever laid eyes on?

We make our way to the cafeteria. The smell of stale coffee and fried food hits me like a punch to the gut. Yeah. Not helping my nausea.

God, I need time alone.

Eli suggests we get a table first while Tabitha and Ralph get in line for food. We settle for one in the corner of the room, away from the buzzing crowd and the harsh cafeteria lights. I sink into the cold metal chair.

Eli is saying something about some new surgical technique he read about, but his voice fades into the background as my mind wanders back to Jason. His cool demeanor in the lab, his respect for the dead who gave their bodies to science, the way his eyes softened when he looked at me.

Tabitha returns, thrusting a tray of food onto the table. "Go ahead and get your lunch, Angie."

"I'm not hungry," I say as I look at the sandwich on her tray. It's a little wilted.

"You have to eat, Angie." She narrows her gaze to me but then turns to Ralph. "Oh! I haven't introduced you two yet. Ralph. Angie."

I look up at Ralph, getting my first real look at him. He's nice-looking enough, with dark hair, a strong jawline, and brown eyes. He's a little older than the rest of us—the slight silver at his temples and laugh lines around his eyes give him away. I'd peg him for mid-thirties. He might even be older than Jason.

But he wouldn't be the first person to start medical school in his thirties. Lots of people decide to shift careers around that point in their lives.

"Nice to meet you," I eke out, offering Ralph my hand.

He eyes my hand a moment before taking it and limply shaking it. "Likewise."

Ralph doesn't appear to be a man of many words. At least it seems that way at first, until he starts talking about an article on forensic pathology he read, which I couldn't care less about. I'm here, but I'm not here. My body is present, but my mind is miles away.

With Jason. Jason's lips. His obvious arousal as he pressed into me.

I look around the cafeteria absentmindedly. Students, professors, some nurses and doctors from the adjoining hospital...

Everyone else's life goes on as if I didn't just kiss my professor.

Then I see him.

Jason.

He's sitting alone at a table in the corner with his laptop open. When did he get here? How long was I wandering in bliss from his kiss before Tabitha grabbed me for lunch?

Jason takes a bite out of an apple and then shifts his gaze.

Our eyes meet.

An electric jolt runs through me, and everything else blurs. He raises his eyebrows and smiles. Not a big, flashy grin, but a small, private one. Just for me.

My heart stutters. I forget to breathe. Warmth floods my cheeks.

I rise. "I guess I'll get some food."

"Take this." Eli shoves his salad at me. "It's got arugula in it. Can't stand the stuff."

Oddly, Eli's offering looks appealing enough to distract me. I start shoveling it into my mouth, not tasting it.

"Angie? Did you hear me?" Eli's voice.

He said something?

"No," I say quickly. "I mean, sorry. What was that again?"

Ralph raises an eyebrow. "You okay?"

I nod quickly. "Yeah. Just... I guess my mind wandered off. Anatomy class affected me a little more than I anticipated."

Ralph narrows his eyes at me. "I'm sure."

Not getting a great vibe from Ralph. But maybe it's the age difference.

I look over at Eli. "What were you saying?"

He pastes a weird smile on his face. "Study group tonight. Pizza. The four of us."

Study group?

I study alone.

I glance toward Jason.

The thought of being alone at home with my thoughts doesn't seem so appealing. I won't get any studying done if my head is wrapped around Dr. Jason Lansing.

So I nod to Eli and force a smile. "Sounds great!" I say a little too enthusiastically.

Tabitha looks up, clearly surprised at my eagerness. I meet her gaze and smile.

Ralph nods from across the table. "No anchovies," he says.

Tabitha and Eli agree, so I don't bother telling them that I personally love anchovies. Sage says they're disgusting, calls them stinky, hairy fish. She won't let me get them on one half of a pizza because she says they pollute the whole thing. I've been getting my own personal pizzas since high school.

I risk another glance toward Jason, but he's no longer at his table. I spot him by the cafeteria exit. He glances back over his shoulder. Our eyes meet once more.

Then he's gone.

A sense of emptiness fills me, like he took something away with him when he left. My appetite vanishes, and I push my tray away. Eli's discarded salad was disgusting anyway.

"Angie, are you sure you're okay?" Ralph's voice breaks through my thoughts.

I glance at him, taking in his furrowed eyebrows and concerned eyes. I force another smile. "Yeah, I'm fine." The lie tastes bitter on my tongue. "Just not very hungry."

"I swear this cafeteria food gets worse every day." Eli grimaces at his half-finished sandwich. "I don't blame you for not wanting to eat, Angie."

I laugh weakly. Eli, of all of us, looks like he could stand to gain a few. He's skinny as a rail.

"You'd think they might have more organic offerings," Tabitha says. "I mean, what if I were vegan?"

"Are you?" Ralph asks.

"No, and it's a good thing." She thins her lips. "Though I don't eat a lot of meat."

I glance at her half-finished sandwich, which appears to be turkey.

I say nothing.

Eli starts talking about what we should study tonight, but my thoughts are consumed with Jason. His smile, his touch, his kiss—every single moment replays over and over in my mind.

"So what do you think, Angie?" Tabitha asks me.

I jerk back to reality. "Sorry. What?"

"For study group tonight. Pizza. What about your place?"

"My place?"

"I've got two roommates, Eli lives in his grandmother's basement, and Ralph—"

BROKEN DREAM

"I live in a tiny studio where I can barely turn around," Ralph interrupts. "Where do you live?"

I guess it's time to admit that I live in a gorgeous townhome a mile away from campus that I purchased on my own. Except not on my own. With my trust fund. It's got three bedrooms and a tiny yard for my miniature schnauzer, Tillie.

And yeah, it will be perfect for our study group.

"Sure. My place is good."

"Where is it?" Tabitha asks.

I rattle off the address.

Ralph widens his eyes. "That's in Breckenridge Knoll."

"Yeah," I say.

"It's a gated community," he says.

My cheeks burn, but why should I be embarrassed that I live alone in a gated community?

"It is," I say. "Is that a problem?"

He doesn't respond.

"Sounds perfect," Tabitha says. "What time should we pop by?"

I check my watch. "How about six? We can make the pizza our dinner."

"Does that work for you guys?" Tabitha asks, nodding to Eli and Ralph.

"Sounds great." From Eli.

Ralph stays silent.

I know the look on his face. I've seen it before.

He doesn't like rich people. He thinks we're all entitled snobs.

But he can think whatever the hell he wants. I got over those prejudices long ago.

CHAPTER SIX

JASON

Kissing Angie was a huge mistake.

An even bigger mistake is stalking her online.

Her socials are pretty straightforward. She has a sister named Sage, brothers named Henry and David. Tons of aunts, uncles, and cousins, and damn...

She's a member of the Steel family. The Steels pretty much own the Western Slope of Colorado. And here she is living in Boulder, going to medical school.

A rich girl. A trust-fund baby.

Everything I certainly never was.

I paid my own way through medical school and ended up six figures in debt. It's paid off.

From funds I would gladly give back.

I'm feeling something, though.

Something I haven't felt since Lindsay.

Whatever it is, I need to flatten it now. She's a student, and I'm her teacher.

Not only would I risk losing my job if I got involved with her, but my own ethics won't allow it.

Which doesn't explain why I'm stalking her on her socials right now.

I don't like the way she made me feel.

BROKEN DREAM

Yet I yearn for the way she made me feel.

It's been so long.

I close my laptop. Enough of this shit. Besides, I have an appointment.

Thursday afternoons—or evenings, depending on my schedule—I always go to the same place.

It's a chilly January day, but that doesn't matter to me.

Nothing will keep me from visiting my wife and daughter.

I put on my down jacket, my muffler, my leather gloves, and I leave the medical school and get into my car.

I drive a Prius. I've never been the ostentatious type. Even when I was a sought-after general surgeon, I put most of my money away. We did splurge on a beautiful two-story home, but I sold it after...

It didn't feel like home anymore.

Now I live in a townhome. And I no longer have a sought-after surgeon salary. I'm a professor. Good job, to be sure, and I have a lot to teach my students.

But it's nothing compared to cutting.

God, I miss it.

A light dusting of snow covers the ground as I get out of my car and enter the cemetery.

I stopped bringing flowers. They just die.

I've seen enough death.

The headstones aren't ostentatious either. Lindsay would've hated that.

They sit side by side, gray markers designating where the ashes of my wife and daughter are buried.

Lindsay Davis Lansing, loving wife and mother.

Julia Lindsay Lansing. Only a babe on earth, but now she flies with the angels.

Three years old.

Three fucking years old, and it's all my fault.

I kneel on the frosty grass and gently brush away the snow that covers their names. It's too soon for them to be washed away, even by weather. With my gloved fingers, I trace the letters and numbers etched into the stone.

I sigh, watching my breath float out in a misty cloud.

And I let myself remember.

Innocent laughter ringing through the house, the scent of Lindsay's perfume drifting through the air wherever she walked, Julia clutching my hand with her tiny fingers.

Guilt tightens its grip on my heart.

I've become accustomed to the guilt. It's kind of like an old friend now because I can't remember Lindsay and Julia without it. It's always there, hovering like a houseguest who you wish would leave but in a weird way you know you'd miss if he did.

Icy winds whip around me. I'm used to the chill. It's been my companion for years.

"I'm sorry," I whisper into the wind, hoping the words will somehow reach Lindsay and Julia. "I'm so sorry."

How many times have I said it before? How many more times will I say it in the future? A lifetime's worth of apologies will never erase my guilt. I sit in the cold, the silence around me heavy with the weight of my regret.

Finally I rise. Snow has started to fall again. Soon it will blanket the two graves. It's beautiful and tragic at the same time.

As I walk back to my car, I leave behind a part of me with Lindsay and Julia. The part of me that still hopes for redemption. The part that yearns for their forgiveness.

Forgiveness that will never come because they are no longer here to give it.

Dr. Morgan used to tell me I had to forgive myself.

As if I ever could.

Fucking psychiatry...

I scrape the etching of frost off my windshield, get into my car, and begin the drive. I almost wish for traffic, anything to stall my return to the silent townhome that's now my existence.

I turn into my neighborhood. A family—a dad and two kids—plays in the snow.

A pang hits my chest.

I look away quickly, but the image is already seared into my mind. Such a sight should make me happy, but all I feel is sadness, regret, envy.

That was supposed to be *my* life.

Julia would be six now. Old enough to help me build a snowman, have a snowball fight.

Six.

At school already. Learning to read. Maybe playing soccer or T-ball.

She'd most likely have a sibling. Lindsay and I talked of filling our house with children.

Tears prick at the corners of my eyes.

Julia used to love the snow. She'd laugh when snowflakes hit her face. She would have loved building a snowman.

Winters were always cozy. I'd sit with Julia and read her favorite book. She loved when I did voices for the characters. That always sent her into fits of giggles.

Lindsay would watch us from the kitchen as she loaded the dishwasher. When she was done, she and I would put Julia to bed together, each of us kissing her good night and always remembering to leave her night-light on.

"So the monsters don't get me, Daddy," she'd say.

I'd give her belly a squeeze. "Daddy will never let any monster hurt his little girl."

And she'd giggle as I closed the door, leaving it open just a crack.

My ghost of a life.

And the promise of something that will never be.

The monsters *did* get her. Just not in the way she feared.

I drive up to my townhome.

And there it is—the sense of dread. Every moment here is a constant reminder of their absence.

I pull into my garage and then walk around to pull the trash cans in.

And I hold back a breath when I see her.

Angie Simpson, a few homes down.

She's pulling in her own garbage can.

Does she live here?

She's a first-year medical student. Has she lived here since the beginning of the school year and I've never known?

I watch as she wrestles with the bulky bin, a stray strand of hair escaping from her ponytail. Her cheeks are flushed from the cold.

I lift a hand to wave to her.

She doesn't see me at first, but then she looks over at me. Her eyes widen.

"You need some help?" I ask.

She quickens her pace. "No, I've got it!"

Yet as she pulls at the handle of the bin with small, gloved hands, it's clear that she doesn't. Or maybe she does. If she's lived here a while, she's obviously dragged her garbage can into her garage many times before now.

I take a few steps toward her and—

She stumbles backward, losing her grip on the large trash can. A soft gasp escapes her lips, and in that moment, she reminds me of my Lindsay—that shimmer of stubbornness in her eyes, her unwillingness to give in or give up.

"Are you sure?" I ask again, already moving toward her before she can answer.

She stares daggers into me. "I'm sure."

She lugs the large bin into her garage and then closes the door.

And that's that.

Angie Simpson lives three doors away from me.

And I never knew it.

Fuck.

CHAPTER SEVEN

Angie

My heart is beating a mile a minute.

Dr. Lansing? Jason? Jason, who kissed me like no man has ever kissed me before?

He's my damned neighbor?

How did I not know this?

I'm not the neighborly type. I didn't go knock on doors and introduce myself, and no one came to my home bearing homemade cookies or a casserole.

I don't have time to think about it. I need to clear up the clutter because my study buddies will be here in half an hour for pizza.

Which I should probably order.

Tillie scampers into the kitchen, sniffing at my feet. She gives me an inquisitive look. She can tell I'm unsettled.

I kneel and scratch her ear. "It's nothing for you to worry about, girl."

I also should've listened to their discussion about pizza toppings. All I remember is Ralph's no-anchovies edict.

Everybody likes cheese and pepperoni, right? Tabitha said she's not vegan, and her sandwich had meat on it. Ralph and Eli also ate meat. Pepperoni and cheese it is.

I put in the order on a food app and then go into my

bedroom. I pull my hair out of its ponytail and brush it out, letting it float around my shoulders. Then I change out of my jeans and T-shirt and into leggings, a long sweatshirt, and fuzzy socks. My usual study attire. I see no reason to change my habit just because three classmates are coming over.

I walk back out, hang up some coats that are just lying around, and then head to the kitchen to clean up in there.

I'm startled by a knock on the door. Tillie starts barking.

"Coming," I yell. "You guys are early."

I lead Tillie to the back door and let her out into my backyard. I then open the door without looking into the peephole. After all, I know who it is.

But I let out a gasp.

What was I thinking? Of course it's not Tabitha and the guys. Security would have called me.

It's someone else. Someone who lives in the neighborhood. Jason Lansing is standing there.

Looking amazing in a leather jacket. He was wearing down before, but now it's leather and what looks like a cashmere scarf—could be Burberry—his cheeks ruddy from the cold.

"Oh," I say. "Can I...help you with something?"

He sighs. "I just wanted to apologize. You know. For today. For..."

Kissing me?

The words are on the tip of my tongue, but I can't get them out.

"I didn't mean to cross any boundaries," he says.

One could say that his showing up at my front door is another crossed boundary, but I don't want to mention that.

A tiny part of me isn't upset that he's here.

His gaze is steady now, serious, and filled with an intensity that has my heart fluttering.

"We're good," I say hastily. The last thing I need is for him to feel awkward around me. He's my professor. And my neighbor. God, this is a mess. "Don't worry about it."

He lets out a breath with a cloud of condensation. "Good. That's...good."

Should I invite him in? It's cold, after all. But I'm expecting people. And the house...

"Would you like to come in?" I finally say. "I can make some coffee...or something."

He puts his hands up in front of him. "No, no. That's okay. I guess you know now that I live here. It's a quick few steps to my place." He narrows his eyes. "I didn't realize you lived here, Angie."

"Since September." I kick absentmindedly at the floor. "I guess you didn't see my brothers and cousins hauling all my stuff in."

"I was probably working."

"Yeah. Right." I blink a few times. "Of course. You're a surgeon."

He looks down. "I wasn't doing surgery."

"Oh?"

"No. I mean... I don't operate anymore."

"Why not?"

He takes a deep breath in. "That's a long stor—"

Before he finishes the word, Tabitha walks up onto my stoop. "Hey! Dr. Lansing, what are you doing here?"

"Jason, please," he says. "It turns out that Angie and I are neighbors."

"Sweet!" Tabitha flashes a grin, her eyes wide as she takes in the exterior of my townhome. "This place is amazing, Angie."

"How did you get through the gate without calling?" I ask.

"I told the guard you were expecting me. He let me go."

Great. A guard who lets a flirty young woman bypass the rules. No harm done, of course, but the neighborhood management will be getting a call from me.

I swing the door wider so Tabitha can enter.

She breezes past me, her rosy perfume wafting in the air around us.

Jason takes a step back, nodding at her as she passes. "Nice to see you, Tabitha," he says.

"You too, Dr. Lansing," she replies with a flirty grin. Probably not unlike the one she gave the security guard at the gate.

"I guess I'll leave you to it." Jason steps away from the door. "Good luck with your studying."

"Thank you," I say, my voice more detached than I mean for it to be.

He smiles once more before turning and walking down the path leading to his place.

I close the door behind him and lean against it. The smell of Tabitha's perfume is strong in the air, and I hold my breath for a moment, desperate to let Jason's scent linger.

"So..." Tabitha begins, plopping down onto my couch and kicking off her shoes as if she's been here hundreds of times before. "When were you planning to tell me that hunky Dr. Lansing is your next-door neighbor?"

I raise an eyebrow at her. Are we supposed to be besties now that we're lab partners...and apparently study buddies? "I didn't realize it myself until today."

Her eyes widen. "Seriously? How can you not notice a man like that living next door?"

"Easy," I reply, making my way to the kitchen. "By being too absorbed in my studies to bother about who's living next door. And besides, he's our professor, Tabitha."

"Well, yes, but he's also hot." She follows me into the kitchen. "And single, as far as I know. I didn't notice a ring on his left hand."

I guess I'm not the only one who made it a point to check out Jason's ring finger.

"That doesn't matter." I pull plates out of a cupboard, trying not to let talk of Jason make me tingle so much.

She pouts at me from where she's perched on one of the bar stools. "Spoilsport."

I roll my eyes at her as my phone rings. I grab it. "It's security, probably calling to let me know the guys are here." I put the phone to my ear. "Hello?"

"Ms. Simpson, it's Derrick at the gate. I have an Elijah Garrett and Ralph Normandy here."

"Thanks. They're fine."

A moment later, the doorbell rings. I open it to find Ralph and Eli and two bottles of wine.

"Hey, Angie," Ralph says. "We brought wine."

"Not sure how much studying we'll get done with that," I reply, stepping aside for them to enter.

Eli waltzes past me, the woodsy scent of his aftershave replacing Tabitha's rosy perfume. Thank God. I'm not into floral scents. They give me a terrible headache.

"Somehow I knew you'd be a killjoy," Eli says with a laugh.

"We're here to study, not to drink," I remind him.

"But where's the fun in that?" Eli walks into my living room. "Where should I put these?"

I gesture to the kitchen when the doorbell rings again.

BROKEN DREAM

Pizza. I've got my food apps on the security list, so they don't bother calling me each time.

I grab the three pies and bring them into my kitchen.

"Where's your corkscrew?" Eli asks.

I open a drawer, fish it out, and hand it to him.

"You like red?" Ralph asks.

I glance at the bottles and widen my eyes. "Oh! Yeah, I love it. Would you believe my cousin makes this wine?" I peruse the label. Steel Vineyards Ruby. The wine is named for my uncle Ryan's wife, Ruby Lee Steel. Uncle Ryan used to run the winery, but he retired, and now my cousin Dale runs it.

"Really?" Eli wrinkles his forehead. "You're related to the Steel family?"

"Yeah." I swallow. "Marjorie Steel Simpson is my mother."

Ralph frowns. "Fuck me. That explains the gated community."

I grab four wineglasses out of my cupboard, turning so they don't see my eye roll. I get it. Ralph doesn't like people with money. He sure seems happy to eat pizza on my dime, though.

When I turn back around, Eli has joined Tabitha in the family room, but Ralph is still in the kitchen, standing very close to me.

"Uh...did you need something?" I ask.

"Just this," he says, and presses his lips to mine.

CHAPTER EIGHT

JASON

Once I'm back at my own place, I strip off my coat and gloves and turn on the gas fireplace.

I'm chilled.

But not so much from the weather.

From the effect Angie has on me.

I just visited the graves of my wife and daughter, and the guilt is still eating at me.

Only more so.

Angie's a student.

And...

Angie's not Lindsay.

I pour myself a glass of bourbon, the liquid burning a slow path down my throat. The guilt, the sorrow—none of it washes away.

The room is quiet except for the low hum of the gas fireplace and the clinking of ice cubes in my glass. My gaze falls on the picture of Lindsay and our daughter that sits on top of the mantel. A wave of melancholy washes over me.

They were my world once, and now they're not.

Angie.

She's not Lindsay, indeed.

Lindsay was my first love. My only love. We met in

college and hit it off right away. She had dated some awful creep in high school, and I was the first guy who treated her the way she deserved to be treated. She got a job teaching high school social studies while I went to medical school. It wasn't easy. Our marriage suffered, and it only got worse during my internship when I was on call during all hours. We'd go days without seeing each other.

Then my fellowship year, Lindsay got pregnant with Julia.

We laughed at the time. About how we never saw each other, so how could it have even happened?

But we were thrilled.

And by the time she was born, I had an offer to be an attending general surgeon at the university hospital, and I had authored several papers. When I got an offer to present one of them in Switzerland, Lindsay couldn't go with me because she was too far along in her pregnancy to fly.

I went without her, and I fell in love. Switzerland was so beautiful, and I promised I'd take her back there sometime.

But months turned into years, and we always put the trip off.

Just one of the many promises I couldn't keep.

And among all of those broken promises, the one that haunts me the most is the promise of forever.

I glance over at the framed picture on the mantel again, my heart constricting. My wife, my daughter, both trapped in a still moment of time as I continue to live and breathe and feel an unbearable emptiness.

The guilt has been my constant companion ever since. It corrodes my soul, gnaws at me, an incessant reminder of everything I've lost.

Everything I failed to protect.

I down the rest of my whiskey in one gulp, grimacing as it claws its way down my throat. The empty glass clinks against the wooden table as I set it down a little too harshly.

Angie.

She's not Lindsay.

I know this, but she's young and full of excitement about psychiatry.

God, psychiatry.

But it excites her. She's such a stark contrast to my own existence, which feels like it's been in a state of perpetual winter since Lindsay and Julia passed away.

Passed away.

What a fucking euphemism.

I should really be truthful.

Three years earlier...

Dazed.

Confused.

The airbag. It's big and white and all around me.

Someone hit me. Or I hit someone. I'm not sure.

Head hurts. Blood.

My vision swims as I try to untangle myself from the airbag.

My ears.

Ringing.

High-pitched ringing.

Blood. I know the scent. Sharp and metallic. But I'm not in the OR. And the blood I smell is my own.

Blood.

BROKEN DREAM

Panic.

I squeeze my eyes shut and then force them open, hoping my sight will clear.

"Lindsay..." My voice sounds strange to me, distant and muffled. "Julia..."

I try to turn my head, and agony explodes through my skull. But it's not the pain that makes me gasp. It's the thought of my daughter in the back seat.

She's strapped in. She's okay. She's got to be okay.

But why is there no crying? Why?

"Jul—"

I try to crane my neck to see the back seat, but another jolt of pain stops me. Panic and dread seize me when I can't see her.

I fumble with the seat belt, my fingers shaking. Every nerve ending in my body screams in protest. But I can't afford to give in to the pain. Not now.

"Julia...please," I rasp out, choking on the words as I finally manage to unclip the seat belt. The car tilts as I climb into the back seat.

And the pain.

Fuck, the pain!

But I don't care. I need to get Julia—

Julia!

She's not in her car seat.

She's...

"Julia!"

Her small body is wedged on the floor, her stuffed frog next to her.

"No! *No!*"

Tears mix with blood as I reach a trembling hand toward

her, praying for any sign of life. Dread pounds in my chest.

"Julia, please! Oh my God, Julia."

My right hand is numb, so with my left hand I grab her, lay her on the back seat, press my fingers to her carotid to find a pulse.

Blood flows from a cut on her head.

I'm a doctor. I should be able to save her.

I begin CPR. Or try to with only one functioning hand.

The rhythm, so familiar from years of training and practice, becomes a desperate lifeline in the back seat of our totaled car. I press, breathe, press, my heart pounding out a frantic rhythm against my ribs. My body moves mechanically, my mind trying to push away the horror that is unfolding before me.

"Julia...Julia...come on," I plead between each compression. Tears blur my vision, but I can't afford to close my eyes. Not even for a second. "Stay with me."

Time loses all meaning as I continue CPR.

No response, no twitch of tiny fingers or fluttering of eyelids.

A strange calm settles over me as if time has slowed down. I can hear the sirens now—distant but getting closer—and I feel strangely detached from it all.

I don't stop the makeshift CPR until the sirens are on top of me, until firm hands are prying me away from my daughter's lifeless body.

"Sir, we've got it," a voice says, and then a jumble of words I can't comprehend.

My knees buckle as they pull me back, and I crumple onto the cold asphalt, rain still pelting. Everything is spinning and blurring. The flashing lights glow, illuminating the faces of the

BROKEN DREAM

medics working to save my daughter.

It's cold. So cold.

"Julia..." My voice is a broken whisper. I don't even realize I'm sobbing until I taste the salt on my lips. "Lindsay," I croak out, my voice raw from screaming and crying. "Where's Lindsay?"

"Sir? Was there another passenger?"

"Lindsay..."

"Sir, there wasn't anyone else in the car with you."

Nothing matters. Nothing matters anymore.

Lindsay.

She's not here.

Thank God, she's at school.

But Julia...

Julia...

Julia...

The world around me tilts and blurs, as if reality is trying to escape. The steady rhythm of sirens becomes a distant echo, the flashing lights seem muted, and the busy scene of paramedics working on my daughter fades into a nightmarish scene. I'm floating, disconnected from everything and everyone.

"I need... I need to call Lindsay..." My voice is barely a whisper. I struggle to sit up, but my strength seems to have abandoned me. I gasp for air.

A paramedic kneels beside me. She's saying something to me, her words melding together into an indecipherable string of nonsense. She tries to steady me, gives me an oxygen mask, but all I can think about is Lindsay.

All I can think of is how I need to tell her.

In a daze, I fumble for my phone in my pocket, pulling it

out with trembling hands. The screen is cracked. I cackle out a laugh.

It's cracked.

My soul is cracked.

Everything is cracked.

Can't feel my right hand.

I manage to unlock the phone.

Lindsay's contact.

Her smiling face.

God, her smiling face.

I press send and hold my breath.

It rings, rings, rings...

Finally, a click, and then...her voice.

"Hi, it's Lindsay. Sorry I missed your call. Leave a message, and I'll get back to you as soon as possible."

Her voice, so light and cheerful, cuts through the chaotic sounds around me, slicing into my gut with an almost physical pain.

"Li-Lindsay..." My voice trembles on her name, the reality of everything crashing down on me. "Something's happened..." I choke out the words between gasping breaths.

The phone drops from my grip and clatters onto the ground.

Hands grab at me again, pulling me away from the car as they work on Julia. But I can't tear my eyes away from her, from her still form.

"Lindsay... Julia..."

My words are swallowed up as consciousness slips away.

Oblivion.

Blissful oblivion.

CHAPTER NINE

ANGIE

I freeze, a wineglass in each hand.

Ralph?

He's attractive, but I never gave him any signals.

His kiss is soft and sweet, but after today's kiss from Jason...

It'll take a lot more to get my attention.

I set down the wineglasses and push him away.

"What was that?" I demand.

"A kiss," he says, grinning slightly. "You do enjoy kissing, don't you?"

I wipe my mouth with the back of my hand. "I... Well, yeah. But...we're here to study. To help each other. To eat pizza and..."

God, I'm babbling.

"Come on." He furrows his brow. "You know you want it as much as I do."

I cock my head, irritated. "Excuse me?"

He cocks his head, his gaze dark. "I don't think I stuttered."

I drop my gaze to his crotch, where his hardness is evident. Oh, God...

"You like to kiss, Angie. I know you do. I saw you."

I swallow. What the hell is he talking about? The only

person I've kissed since I've been to medical school is—

Oh, shit...

Did he see Jason kiss me?

"What the hell are you talking about?" I demand, willing my voice not to shake.

"Today, after lab. I forgot my iPad, and I went back to the room. I saw you. You and Dr. Lansing."

I don't reply. Just try to keep myself steady.

Ralph raises an eyebrow. "He could lose his job for that."

How do I handle this? Do I admit it? That won't do Jason or me any good at all. I hate lying, but—

"I don't know what you think you saw, but you're mistaken." I pick up one of the bottles of Steel Vineyards Ruby that he brought, uncork it, add the aerator, and pour a glass, hoping the trembling in my hands isn't apparent.

"Really?" He narrows his gaze. "I'm not an idiot. You can't deny what I saw."

I take a sip from my glass, doing my best to steady my shaking hands. "Maybe you should consider getting your eyes checked."

Ralph crosses his arms and lets out a low chuckle. "You're a terrible liar, Angie."

I swallow and set my glass down on the counter with more force than necessary, spilling a few drops of wine. "That's irrelevant, Ralph. We're all here to study, and that's all."

"I wonder what the dean of students would have to say if I told him what I saw?" Ralph says snidely.

"I'm sure he'd ask Dr. Lansing and me what actually happened, and we'd set the record straight." I grit my teeth and look Ralph directly in the eyes. "Nothing happened."

Ralph's snide smile fades, replaced by a scowl. "You're

bluffing."

"You think so?" I challenge.

I grew up with two older brothers and tons of male cousins. You either learn to stand up to them or get walked over. I may be quiet, but I'm no doormat.

Ralph seems taken aback by my defiance, but he doesn't retreat. Instead, he keeps his arms crossed. "You're lying," he says after a pause. "I know what I saw."

"And I know what didn't happen," I retort. "If you want to make baseless accusations, be my guest. But remember, Ralph, the truth always comes out in the end."

He smirks. "I suppose it will."

Just as the tension is about to strangle us both, Tabitha walks into the kitchen, leaving Eli in the living room. She stops in her tracks when she sees our standoff.

"What's going on here?" she asks, frowning at Ralph.

"Nothing," Ralph grumbles.

Tabitha's eyes narrow as she studies Ralph, me, and then Ralph again. "I think it's more than nothing," she says. "You two look like you're about to kick each other's asses."

"Maybe that's because Angie here can't admit the truth," Ralph snaps.

"Ralph..." I begin, trying to keep my voice steady.

Tabitha interrupts me, though, turning her full attention to Ralph. "And what truth would that be?"

Ralph hesitates for a moment, eyeing me. I can almost see his mind struggling with whether or not to spill what he saw.

And he *did* see it.

I was there.

But I'm sticking to my story. I don't want Jason to get into any kind of trouble.

"He thinks he saw something that he misinterpreted," I say.

"And what would that be?" Tabitha asks.

I swallow hard. "It's nothing. Really."

"No, Angie," Ralph counters. "It's not nothing."

Before Tabitha says anything more, Eli walks into the kitchen holding up his hands. "What's going on in here?"

Before Ralph can respond, I cut in. "Let's just drop it." My voice is firm. "Can we just focus on why we're actually here?"

Eli pours himself a glass of wine. "I second that motion. Pizza and textbooks are getting cold."

Tabitha chuckles. "You can toss your books in the oven for a few minutes to warm them up."

Ralph shoots me a final glare before grabbing a slice of pizza from the box on the counter. He heads for the living room without another word.

Tabitha watches him go, furrowing her brows before turning back to me with an unreadable look on her face. She doesn't ask any more questions, though, thank God. Instead, she pours herself a glass of wine.

"Yeah, we're here to study, not to stir up drama," she says quietly.

I try to give her a grateful smile. We join Eli and Ralph in the living room.

Ralph is putting on his coat and gloves, his half-eaten slice of pizza on my coffee table. "Not much in the mood for studying anymore," he says. "See you all in lab tomorrow." He says nothing more before walking out the door.

His exit is followed by an awkward silence, which Eli thankfully breaks.

"What the fuck was that about?"

Tabitha shrugs. "Drama queen."

I force a laugh. "Yeah. Drama queen."

Tabitha presses her lips together. "He seems a little old to be acting that way. Hell, *we're* too old to be acting that way."

Eli scratches the side of his head. "Who knows. Everybody has a story." He gazes out the window. "He was my ride, though."

"So grab an Uber," Tabitha says, shrugging again. "Are we going to study or not?"

"Fine." Eli nods. "What'll it be? Anatomy?" He looks at me. "Psychology?"

I ignore his smirk. Since when does an interest in psychology make you a pariah? Don't they know the importance of mental health?

Of course Eli and Tabitha are both interested in surgery. I have no idea what path Ralph plans to pursue, and after tonight, I sure as hell don't care.

"We cut tomorrow," Tabitha says with a grin.

I hold back a groan.

But apparently the look on my face says it all.

"We dissected fetal pigs last semester," Eli says. "What's your problem, Ang?"

"Pigs aren't human beings," I say. "Plus, I love bacon as much as the next person."

"These human beings are dead." From Tabitha.

"Yeah, but they're—they *were*—people." I sigh. "I don't expect you to understand. I grew up on a beef ranch. My family raises cattle, and I know they go to the slaughterhouse. But it's all done humanely."

"These people died humanely," Eli says. "I doubt any of them were murdered. If they were, they wouldn't be good cadaver material."

"Eli..." Tabitha warns, but I shake my head.

"No, it's fine." I stand from the couch and head toward the kitchen, my appetite completely vanished. "I just think we should show some respect. These were people who had lives, loves, dreams. You make your jokes, but remember that someday it'll be us on those tables."

I'm echoing exactly what Jason said in class today.

I don't feel any better about the whole thing, though.

I leave them in the living room. Too much has happened tonight, and all I want is to be alone. With a sigh, I wash my hands and pour another glass of wine.

The sound of footsteps makes me turn. Tabitha is in the kitchen, leaning against the island.

"You okay?" she asks softly.

I shrug. "Just a lot to take in."

She walks over to me. "You don't have to tell me anything, Angie, but something happened between you and Ralph in here. I'm not sure what, but it's got you on edge."

She's not wrong.

And Jason made all the points today in lab about the bodies being a gift. That we should be respectful. I don't know why I'm repeating them tonight.

I knew when I entered med school that I'd be dissecting human bodies. And I knew it would be difficult for me, but I chose this path anyway.

I force another smile. "I'm good. But I think I'm ready to call it a night if you guys don't mind."

Tabitha nods. "I totally get it. I can drive Eli home."

"Then why'd you tell him to get an Uber?"

She shrugs. "Because I was hoping you and I could talk

BROKEN DREAM

privately, but I see you're not up for that." She gives me a quick hug. "I'll see you tomorrow in lab."

She and Eli grab their coats and leave without any more than a goodbye.

I put the leftover pizza in the refrigerator and let Tillie in. She runs inside, sniffing the spots on the couch where Eli and Tabitha were sitting.

She knows someone new was here.

Just like Tabitha knows something. Or at least has an inkling that something is going on with me.

I like Tabitha, but I hardly know her.

Why did she want to talk to me in private?

If she also witnessed my kiss with Jason, he and I are both in big trouble.

CHAPTER TEN

JASON

Three years earlier...

The room feels too bright, too warm. I want to loosen my collar, maybe just get up and leave. But I can't leave my wife alone here. Not like this.

I glance at Lindsay. She's sitting next to me on the couch, her shoulders hunched, gaze fixed on the floor. She looks so small, so unlike herself. The Lindsay I know is strong, fierce, but now I hardly recognize her.

Hell, I hardly recognize myself.

The therapist, Dr. Morgan, clears her throat softly. She's trying to look sympathetic, but I can see through it. She's just another stranger who thinks she can get inside our heads, rearrange the furniture, and magically fix everything. As if talking about *her* will make this easier.

"So, Lindsay," Dr. Morgan begins, "last week, you mentioned that some days feel harder than others. Can you tell me about one of those days?"

Lindsay shifts, fidgets with her fingers. Then with the sleeves of her sweater. She doesn't answer. I know she won't, and I don't blame her.

"She doesn't need to go over this again," I say, keeping my

BROKEN DREAM

tone controlled even though what I really want to do is scream at Dr. Morgan and throw something. "You know, every session it's the same questions. Same painful details. And we go home just as messed up as when we came in."

Dr. Morgan meets my gaze. "I understand, Jason. Sometimes it can feel like progress isn't happening, especially when emotions are overwhelming. But sharing these feelings can help ease the burden. Sometimes only a little, but it helps."

"I don't see it," I mutter, but I stop myself from saying more. The last thing Lindsay needs is me snapping at the doctor.

Or am I wrong? Because honestly I don't know what the fuck Lindsay needs anymore. I don't know what *I* need either. We've both been stripped of everything. Needs? Hell, where do I start?

Lindsay finally speaks, her voice barely more than a whisper. "I just... I can't stop thinking... It's my fault, Jason. I should've been there." She doesn't look at me. Just says it to the carpet.

My heart clenches. We've been over this. Over and over again. "Lindsay, it's not your fault."

It's not.

It's mine.

I'm the one who lost control of the car.

I'm the one who didn't make sure Julia's car seat was latched correctly.

Me.

It was fucking *me*.

Dr. Morgan nods and leans forward slightly. "Lindsay, it's natural to feel guilt in situations like this, even though we both know you didn't do anything wrong. Losing someone makes us desperate to find answers. And guilt feels like an answer, but it's not."

Lindsay doesn't respond, just keeps staring. But her eyes glisten, and I feel the sting of it too, like salt in a wound.

Lindsay doesn't want to blame me, and sometimes I want to yell at her, to shake her, to make her see the truth of all of it.

It was me.

My fault.

She wasn't even *there*.

"Jason," Dr. Morgan says to me, "I know you feel hopeless when it comes to the therapy process. I know this hasn't been easy for you either."

Hell, no, it hasn't been easy. I want to help my wife. I want to more than I want to live my own life. But I can't fix this. I can't cut into her body and fix what is hurting her. I'm useless now.

I grit my teeth. "I just... I don't see the point of talking. It's not going to bring her back. It just feels like it's making Lindsay worse." I gesture to my wife, who has buried her face in her hands. "She's drowning here, and I don't think rehashing it is helping her breathe any easier."

Lindsay's shoulders go rigid, and I regret the words the second they're out.

But I meant them.

Every single one.

Dr. Morgan stays quiet for a moment. Then, "I understand that talking isn't easy for either of you. And Jason, it's okay to feel like this isn't helping. It's okay to have doubts. But sometimes being here is just about holding space for each other's pain."

I scoff, unable to stop myself. "Holding space," I mutter

under my breath.

Sounds like another therapy buzzword. Doesn't mean anything to me. But then I see the way Lindsay's hand trembles slightly in her lap, her eyes brimming with that familiar hurt, and something shifts. Maybe... Maybe it means something to her.

"Lindsay," Dr. Morgan says, "can you tell Jason one thing he could do that would make you feel supported, even if it's just a small thing?"

Lindsay hesitates and then glances at me for the first time since we walked into this room. "Just... I just need you to listen sometimes, Jason. To sit with me, even if we're not talking. Just so I don't feel alone with it all."

Her voice is so quiet, I almost don't hear her. But those words hit me like a punch to the gut. I'm her husband. All I do is sit with her. God knows I can't work, and she hasn't been back to work either.

I nod slowly, swallowing the anger, the frustration, the helplessness I feel about this whole damned process.

I'm with her all the time, but still she feels alone.

I don't know what else to do.

I try to live with the guilt. I almost feel like it would be easier if Lindsay *would* blame me.

I want to yell at her, tell her to snap out of this and put the blame where it lies. On my shoulders.

But when I yell, all she does is cry.

When I'm nice, all she does is cry.

When I do nothing, all she does is cry.

None of this is helping Lindsay. We come here day after day, and she's not getting any better.

She lost her baby.

But so did I.

And I lost something else.

The ability to do what I love.

The ability to perform surgery.

The nerves in my hand aren't healing, and I'll most likely never cut again.

Every passing day feels like a blur, my heart heavy with grief. Each morning when I open my eyes, there's that moment, just a fraction of a second, when I forget. When everything seems normal. Julia's asleep in her bedroom, and I have back-to-back surgeries scheduled.

But then it crashes into me like a wave, all at once.

I force myself out of bed, into my clothes. The mirror reflects a person I barely recognize—pale, hollow-eyed, with lines on my forehead I don't remember having before.

Lindsay is usually already up when I come down for breakfast. At least she gets out of bed. She doesn't eat much these days. Her coffee turns from hot to chilled as she stares blankly out the window.

We used to share this ritual every morning—sipping our coffee and discussing our plans for the day, joking and laughing. Now our exchanges are limited to hushed good mornings. A heavy silence looms between us, more deafening than any words.

"Did you sleep?" she asks every morning, her voice barely above a whisper.

I shrug. "A little."

That's what I always say, but it's a lie. Sleep has been elusive. I've been haunted by nightmares and memories that twist like knives in my gut.

She nods and turns her attention back to the window.

How can she think I don't listen to her?

A few minutes pass. Dr. Morgan doesn't speak.

"Lindsay," I finally say, my throat dry. "I'll listen. I promise you that I'll listen."

"Okay," she whispers, reaching out to place her hand on mine. It's cold, just like everything else since we lost Julia.

I squeeze her hand. In that moment, I make myself a promise too. That even if all of this feels pointless, even if it feels like we're stuck in this perpetual state of grieving with no end in sight, I won't give up on her.

Because if there's one thing I've learned from all those years in the operating room, it's that sometimes it's not about cutting away the damaged parts or stitching up the wounds. Sometimes, it's about sitting quietly by a patient's side, holding their hand and waiting for them to heal in their own time.

Except how can we heal when my wife won't admit that she blames me?

Present day...

I get to the lab early.

Today these students will cut into a human body—albeit a dead one—for the first time.

God, I remember the thrill, the satisfaction of my first time.

And then the first time I cut into a live body.

It was exhilarating.

And something I'll never again experience.

I look at the lab tables, the bodies covered in cloth. Who were these people? Did they get to live their dreams? Or did

HELEN HARDT

they get them ripped away from them by a cruel twist of fate? As I did?

I jerk when my phone buzzes.

Interesting. It's Dr. Louisa Matthews, my neurologist.

"This is Jason," I say into the phone.

"Jason, Louisa Matthews. Is this a good time?"

"I teach anatomy lab in fifteen minutes," I say. "But I have a little time."

"Good. I'd like you to come in and see me. This afternoon if possible. We have a new visiting neurosurgeon. She thinks she may be able to repair your hand."

I nearly drop the phone but catch it in time before it clatters onto the tile floor of the lab.

"What?" I say, not sure I heard her correctly.

"I know. Don't get your hopes up, but she's been experimenting with a new technique for a nerve transplant."

A wave of hope, tinged with the dread of disappointment, rises inside me. "Louisa, I've been through this before—"

"I know, Jason," she cuts in. "But this is different. Dr. Patel is a pioneer in this field. She has successfully performed this operation already."

"How many times?"

"Well...once. In Switzerland. She's here on an O-1 visa."

"What's that?"

"It's for individuals with extraordinary ability in their field, such as internationally recognized surgeons with significant accomplishments or publications. The hospital is sponsoring her research."

"So she's familiar with my case?"

"Yes. I took the liberty of sharing your file with her. I hope you don't mind."

"Are you kidding me? Of course not."

"Good. It was for a consult, so no HIPAA worries."

"Louisa, I'm not the least bit concerned about any of that."

"I know."

"But what are the chances?" I ask, my voice shaking.

My mind reels with the possibilities. To hold a scalpel again, to feel its cool metal against my skin, to operate on a living body...

"No guarantees, of course," she says. "But Dr. Patel is optimistic after looking through your records. It's not confirmed until we run some tests on you and match nerve types. But there's a fairly good chance this could work."

My mind whirls.

Is it possible?

To have my hand back, to once again perform surgeries...

I feel like I'm waking up from a nightmare.

I look at the covered cadavers sitting on the tables, waiting for the students to learn from them. "What kind of tests? And are we talking a nerve from a live donor or from a cadaver?"

"We'll need to do some extensive nerve conduction studies and MRI scans," Louisa says. "As for the donor... It's a bit of both. The nerve graft is extracted from a cadaver, but it's reanimated using living cells derived from your own body."

I shiver as a chill rushes through me.

I've read about such things. It's cutting edge, for sure. "Reanimated? How does that even work?"

"It's complex," she says. "Dr. Patel will explain it all when you meet her. But in essence, we take your cells, nurture them in a lab, and coax them into becoming nerve cells. These are then integrated with the cadaver's nerve tissue."

I resist the urge to blurt out that it all sounds like

something straight out of science fiction. Again, I stare at the cadavers.

They're learning tools. Tools that were once people.

That's how we learn.

How doctors learn.

A cadaver like one of these might be able to save my career.

"Jason?"

"Yes," I say, my voice breathless. "When can I meet Dr. Patel?"

"Can you come to the hospital this afternoon, around four?" Louisa asks.

I glance at the clock. The students will be here soon. "That should work," I say. "Unless you can see me sooner?"

"Well...I have time now, and Dr. Patel is in the building. But didn't you say you were about to teach a lab?"

"Yeah, but I'll cancel. This is way more important."

"All right, Jason. I'll schedule you in. See you shortly."

The click of the call ending seems to echo in the silence of the lab. The weight of what could happen, what might happen, threatens to pull me under.

With a deep breath, I grab a clipboard from a nearby counter and write *Lab Canceled* at the top of a piece of paper. Then I jot down some textbook pages for them to read about the thoracic area. I draft a quick email to the class letting them know as well.

They'll be disappointed. So many of them can't wait to cut.

But wait they will. Until next Thursday, our next lab.

And I feel not one iota of guilt about making them wait.

If I can regain the function in my right hand... If there's even a chance...

I finish the note and tape it to the door of the lab. Then before I close and lock the door, I gaze back at the cadavers.

"Sorry," I say out loud.

Sorry about what?

That they won't fulfill their duties today? Won't get cut into by eager students?

And some not so eager, as I think of Angie.

Angie...

I may be taking the first step into a return to my old life today.

This is a good thing.

So there's no reason in the world why I should feel a sliver of disappointment at not seeing Angie Simpson in class.

CHAPTER ELEVEN

Angie

Lab Canceled, the sign on the door to the anatomy lab says.

The door is locked, but through the small window, I can see our cadavers sitting on the tables, covered.

A wave of relief flows over me.

I don't have to cut into a dead body today.

I also won't be seeing Jason today, and as relieved as I am about the lab cancellation, part of me is disappointed.

Really disappointed.

I can't get that kiss out of my mind.

It was a good kiss.

A *really* good kiss. The best kiss I've ever had.

"Bummer," a voice says from behind me.

I turn.

Ralph.

Just the person I *don't* want to see.

"I suppose," I say.

"Yeah." He crosses his arms. "You can't see your boyfriend today."

I glare at him. Seriously? We're in medical school, not middle school. And this guy is at least ten years older than I am. Does he still have the brain of a teenager?

"Just shut up already," I say, brushing past him.

BROKEN DREAM

But he catches up to me, walks next to me. "You can deny it all you want, Angie. I know what I saw."

"When was the last time you visited an eye doctor?" I ask. "I think your eyes are playing tricks on you."

"You think I should change my focus from surgery to ophthalmology?" He rolls his eyes.

"This is only our second semester of med school," I say. "I'm sure we'll all change our focuses many times before we get to internship."

He sneers. "Really? I got the idea yesterday in class that you're completely sold on psychiatry. Because of your famous aunt."

I raise a hand in front of his arrogant face. "You don't know *anything* about my aunt. You don't know anything about my family. You don't—"

"I know a lot," he says, interrupting me. "I know you didn't get that uppity townhome in a gated community by working for it. That's for sure."

"So I have a trust fund," I say. "And yeah, it's a big one."

"I'm sure it is. While the rest of us are taking on hundreds of thousands of dollars in debt, you basically get a free medical education. And you're not even going down a path worth taking."

I grit my teeth. "Psychiatry is a worthy pursuit." I stare straight into his eyes. "*You* sure as hell could use a session or two, I'm sure. And why is my life any business of yours anyway? I'm paying my tuition."

"With Mommy and Daddy's money," he says.

I'm so tired of this. I'm so tired of explaining to people that it's not my parents' money. It's *my* money. It's been my money since I was born. That's when the trust funds started, for my brothers and sister and all my cousins.

I don't blame them for not understanding, but I'm sick and tired of it. I was born into riches. Born into the Steel dynasty. I'm done apologizing for it.

"It's *my* money," I say succinctly. "And this conversation is over."

"So what's it worth to you?" he asks.

"What is *what* worth to me?" I say, my voice on edge. Here we go again.

"For me to not go to the dean about you and Jason Lansing making out?"

My heart nearly stops.

Blackmail now? Extortion? It wouldn't be the first time it's happened to our family. But it *is* the first time it's happened to me.

I hold my ground. "Since the kiss you're talking about never happened, it's not worth a damned cent to me."

"What if I said I had evidence?"

I do my best to keep from reacting. "You don't have any evidence. To have evidence of something, it has to have actually happened."

He curls his lips. "I may have just snapped a photo with my phone."

My flesh goes cold. Still, I'm convinced he's bluffing.

"Show me."

He exhales sharply through his nose. "No. I think I'll let you squirm a little."

"Squirm? Why would I squirm? There's no evidence because you don't have any. Because nothing happened."

Besides, even if he does have a photo, I can claim it was manipulated with AI or something. Who's going to believe

BROKEN DREAM

him? Jason and I will both deny it.

"Tell you what," he says to me. "It won't cost you a cent, Angie. All it will cost you is information."

I drop my jaw. "Information about what?"

He grins. "So you *do* have something to hide."

"I have absolutely nothing to hide. And I don't even know what kind of—"

"Hey, guys!" Tabitha scurries up to us, Eli with her.

And I silently thank the universe.

"We just saw the note on the door that lab is canceled," Tabitha says. "Of course I came all the way here before I realized that Jason had sent an email as well." She shrugs. "I guess we've got a free period."

"And I have to wait another week to cut," Eli growls.

Tabitha turns to me, her expression sympathetic. "I guess that makes you happy."

"Or does it?" Ralph says, arching his eyebrows.

Tabitha gives him a curious look. "What's that supposed to mean, Ralph?"

"Why don't you ask lover girl here?" Ralph smirks.

"What the hell?" Tabitha gives Ralph a punch in his arm. "Be nice. Angie's my lab partner."

"Oh, so you're best friends now?" Ralph says.

"Maybe we are," Tabitha says. "What the hell is your problem, anyway? You left our study session last night, and now it looks like you're being a dick."

"Ease up," Eli says. He turns to Ralph. "You having a bad day, man?"

"My day is just fine," Ralph says. "I'm going to go read up for my next class. Ciao." He ambles off.

I'm still breathing quickly, but I force myself to calm

down.

"What the hell was that all about?" Eli asks.

"I don't know," Tabitha says. "He's *your* friend."

"He's my lab partner," Eli says. "I hardly know him."

I stare down the hall, making sure Ralph has safely ducked into the library. "He's just a dick."

Tabitha lays a hand on my shoulder. "What did he do to you, Angie?"

"Nothing. He's a dick. He acted like a dick. That's what dicks do." I draw in a breath. "You want to get a cup of coffee?"

"Actually, I have to do some reading up for my next class as well." She pats my shoulder. "This lab cancellation is actually a godsend. I'm so behind."

Eli widens his eyes. "I'll get a cup with you."

"Sounds good." I purse my lips. "But I don't want the cafeteria coffee. Let's go to Starbucks."

"Crap," Tabitha says. "In that case, I'm coming along. I'm a sucker for a triple mocha."

The three of us leave the building and walk a block to Starbucks.

"I'll have a grande dark roast," I tell the barista, "and whatever the two of them want. It's on me."

"Thanks, Angie!" Tabitha's eyes light up. "Grande mocha with an extra shot, please."

"I'll have an Americano," Eli says. "And a blueberry scone."

"You want that heated up?" the barista asks.

Eli grins. "Obviously."

"Coming right up," the barista says. "What's the name?"

"Tabitha on the mocha, Eli on the Americano," Tabitha replies.

The barista types the names into her console. "Those will be right up."

I scan my card while the barista pours my coffee and hands it to me.

Some of the comfortable seats are open, so Eli takes a chair while Tabitha and I sit down on a fluffy couch. I take the lid off my coffee, and the steam swirls upward.

"You don't take cream or sugar?" Tabitha asks.

"Nope. I'm a purist." I set the coffee down on the table to cool, still watching the steam swirl into the air.

"Are you going to tell us what's going on with Ralph?" Tabitha asks.

"Like I said, it's nothing. He's just being a dick."

I grab my coffee, take a sip.

And fuck.

I burn my tongue.

The same tongue that was swimming in Jason's mouth yesterday—the first day of lab.

Because what Ralph says is true.

We did kiss. We kissed hard.

And I have a feeling that moment may just haunt the next three years of my medical education.

CHAPTER TWELVE

JASON

I sit in Dr. Louisa Matthews's office, my nerves antsy under my skin.

A new technique for a nerve transplant.

Fresh hope.

Nerve conduction studies. MRI scans.

The nerve graft is extracted from a cadaver but reanimated using living cells from my body.

Science fiction.

Or just science?

Whatever it is, I need to hear Louisa and her colleague out.

"Jason!" Louisa swooshes into the room. She's in her sixties but doesn't look a day over forty, with light-blond hair and sparkly blue eyes.

Following her is a beautiful young woman with dark-brown eyes and light-brown skin. She smiles at me.

"Jason, meet Dr. Gita Patel."

Dr. Patel barely looks out of her twenties. Somehow her white coat looks all wrong on her. She should be wearing lingerie on a runway somewhere. But Louisa says she's a pioneer in her field.

I rise. "It's a pleasure to meet you, Dr. Patel."

BROKEN DREAM

"Please," she says, "call me Gita. It's an honor. When Louisa mentioned you to me, I took the liberty of reading some of your papers." She flashes a smile at me. "I'm impressed, Dr. Lansing. And I'm not easily impressed."

"Thank you. And call me Jason."

"Of course."

Gita sits down in the chair next to mine while Louisa takes a seat behind her desk.

"Gita and I have discussed your case at length, Jason," Louisa says. "And I agree with her assessment that you may be a candidate for her revolutionary nerve-transplant procedure."

I glance down at my right hand.

The tremor is so slight that most people don't notice it, but I know it's there. I can feel the unsteadiness. The nerve injury that stole my surgical career from me.

From the accident that stole so much more.

"We'll begin with some new scans," Gita says. "We need to assess the extent of the damage, understand how it has evolved since your last evaluation. Then we have to map out the path for the new nerves."

My heart races. "And if the scans are promising?"

"Then we prepare for the procedure," Louisa says. "The nerve graft will take some time to prepare, given its complexity. It's not just a simple transplant, Jason. We're talking about creating a conduit between your living cells and a harvested graft."

"Yes." Gita nods, her gaze steady. "The sooner we begin, the better."

Louisa leans forward on her desk. "Jason, this isn't without its risks. Gita's technique is groundbreaking, and though she's seen one success, it's still considered experimental. There could be complications."

I look back down at my hand—my unreliable, traitorous hand. The hand that once performed intricate surgeries.

"I understand," I say after a moment. "But what do I have to lose?"

Gita looks at Louisa and nods. Then she turns to me. "Jason, there's a chance this might not work. There's a chance that your condition might even worsen. But there's also a chance that you could regain full functionality of your hand, possibly even enough to operate again."

I glance back down at my hand, now trembling slightly more than before—or maybe it's just my imagination. The scars on my palm are a constant reminder of everything I've lost.

My condition could worsen, she said.

But so what? I'll be no worse off than I am now—unable to perform surgery.

Fuck it.

"I'm in," I say.

"Very well." Gita stands and extends her hand to me. "Jason, we will do everything in our power to bring back your steadiness and your precision. I can't promise miracles, but Louisa and I can promise our absolute commitment."

"And I promise my commitment as well," I say.

"If the transplant takes," Gita says, "there will be months of physical therapy. You'll need to relearn how to use your hand. The nerves will have to grow accustomed to their new home."

I know it won't be easy, but for the chance to reclaim part of what I've lost? It's worth it to me.

So worth it.

BROKEN DREAM

"And if this works..." Louisa begins, her eyes bright. "If this works, Jason, you could open doors for countless other people suffering from nerve damage. You could change medicine."

Silence for a moment.

Then I ask the question.

"When do we start?"

"Today," Gita says. "I want to see your scans as quickly as possible. Finding the right cadaver nerve will take time, so every moment counts."

I look at my hand again, imagining it steady and sure. I nod to them. "Okay. Let's do this."

Louisa rises and extends her hand to me across the desk. "Let's get you back in the operating room, Dr. Lansing."

Gita gives me a reassuring pat on the shoulder as she walks out the door, Louisa following her.

I stand, alone, in Louisa's office. We're friends and colleagues, so I know I can stay as long as I need to. I glance at her degrees on the wall, at all her awards. She's a world-class neurologist, and if she believes in Gita's work, then so do I.

A soft knock on the open door brings me back. Louisa's physician's assistant, James, peeks in. "Ready when you are, Dr. Lansing."

"Thank you," I say, following him.

"We're going to radiology to get your MRI," he says.

"Great." I'm not sure what else to say, so I'm silent as we walk through the maze of hospital corridors until we arrive at the radiology department.

James leaves me in the capable hands of a technician. I change into a hospital gown and then settle into the cold, sterile MRI machine. I stare at the white ceiling tiles and breathe.

In.

Out.

In.

Out.

I was never claustrophobic before the accident.

Now, I hate being closed in.

Breathe.

In.

Out.

In.

Out.

Minutes pass like hours as the hum of the machine whirs around me, echoing the anxious beat of my thoughts. My mind spins with what-ifs and maybes.

Finally, after what seems both like hours and no time at all, the machine quiets and I'm helped up by the technician, who offers a smile. "We'll have these to Dr. Matthews and Dr. Patel shortly."

I nod my appreciation and leave the room. The cool hallways do nothing to calm my heated mind.

I make a pit stop at the small hospital café and buy myself a cup of bitter coffee that I barely taste as I continue back toward Louisa's office.

I knock.

"Come on in," Louisa calls.

As I step back into the office, I find Gita and Louisa, now joined by a third figure I recognize as Dr. Luke Belmont, a respected colleague and an attending neurosurgeon. They're staring at a computer screen, which, mostly likely, has my scans pulled up.

"Jason," Louisa says without looking up. "We've been studying your scans."

Gita takes a deep breath. "These images show the extent of the nerve damage caused by your injury. Come take a look."

I rise and join the others in front of the computer screen. On the black-and-white display, the intricate anatomy of my hand unfolds. The bones stand out sharply, and I can pick out each metacarpal and phalanx perfectly. Tendons arch through the scan like taut cables. But I home my focus in on the nerves. Those are what took away my ability to cut.

"As you can see, near the base of your palm, there's a darkened line of disruption that fractures the continuity of the median nerve," Gita says.

I nod. I've seen scans of my hand before. Swollen and irregular, it looks almost like a river obstructed by debris.

"These bright patches flaring along the nerve's length show us areas of inflammation or scarring," Gita continues. "And we can see your muscles around the nerve look thinner than they should, due to the lack of use since your accident as well as their disconnection from the brain's signals."

My heart falls. I've heard this speech before. And it always ends with "I'm afraid there's nothing we can do, Jason."

"As you can see," Gita says, "the damage is significant."

I nod slowly. "I understand."

Gita holds up a finger, her eyes bright. "But it's also isolated."

I look up. "You mean..."

Louisa nods. "Your injury hasn't spread or worsened since your last scans. This allows us a clear path for Gita's procedure."

"We can work with this, Jason," Gita continues. "We can use the graft to bridge the gap between the healthy nerves and those affected by the injury. It will be challenging, yes, but it's not impossible."

What?

A moment passes before I process Gita's words.

Then, for the first time in three years, a tiny ray of light shines through the darkness clouding my mind. Is there actually hope for a better future? Could this truly be possible?

I want to respond to what Gita and Louisa are saying, but I can't find the right words to express my gratitude.

Belmont chimes in. "The key will be ensuring that the graft takes. If your body rejects it, or if complications arise during the procedure, we'll have to reconsider our options."

I listen. I hear their words.

It might not work. I get it. But the possibility of regaining what I've lost is worth risking the uncertainty that lies ahead.

"I understand," I reply. "I trust you all implicitly."

Louisa smiles. "We're going to do everything we can for you, Jason. We know what this means to you, and we're going to fight for every inch of progress."

"Absolutely," Gita says. "Dr. Belmont will assist me in the OR, and of course Louisa will see to your neurology care as she always has."

"Then let's get started," I say.

"As soon as we find a suitable graft, we'll schedule the surgery," Gita says. "We have a top team researching and searching. It could take a couple of weeks...or it might be tomorrow. We just can't predict it."

"Until then," Belmont adds, "we'll devise a comprehensive physiotherapy plan that you'll begin immediately after surgery. The sooner we stimulate nerve regrowth, the better."

I nod. The waiting game begins again, but this time it's different.

BROKEN DREAM

This time I have cautious optimism.
And this time...
I won't let my own mind defeat me.

CHAPTER THIRTEEN

ANGIE

After coffee with Tabitha and Eli, I decline their invitation to lunch and head back to my place to make a quick sandwich and let Tillie out. Then I return to campus for my afternoon classes.

My last class of the day is Introduction to Psychiatry. It's a required course, but I've heard that most students save it for their third or fourth year. I'm excited to begin. Today is the first day of the class.

The professor is an older man, Dr. Carlos Engel, and when I see him, I'm disappointed. I fear he'll be some dud who simply drones on and on in a monotonous voice.

But I'm delightfully wrong.

"Good afternoon," Dr. Engel says.

His voice is deep and resonant. It reminds me of the sound of the cello at Dave and Maddie's quadruple wedding last fall. Dr. Engel has an accent that I can't quite place—his first name is Spanish, and his last name is German; Engel means angel—but it's smooth and rhythmic.

"Welcome to Introduction to Psychiatry," he continues, his eyes twinkling behind thick-rimmed glasses. "I promise you that this is not going to be what you were expecting."

He dives into a lecture about the human psyche. It's

mesmerizing and vastly different from any psychology class I've attended before.

"You're here because you've chosen—or at least have been nudged—to explore one of the most fascinating, complex, and deeply human branches of medicine." He smiles at us. "Psychiatry doesn't deal in broken bones or malfunctioning organs. It deals in the architecture of the mind, the delicate balance of emotions, and the profound mystery of human behavior."

He turns to the board and writes the words *What makes us human?*

He turns back to the class. "A deceptively simple question. What separates us from the rest of the animal kingdom? Is it our biology—our brains, our neurotransmitters, our DNA? Or is it something more abstract—our relationships, our experiences, the stories we tell ourselves? Psychiatry stands at the intersection of these questions, straddling the tangible and the intangible."

I look around the class. Most of the people were not paying attention at first, but Dr. Engel seems to have all eyes and ears on him now.

"We'll talk about brain chemistry, yes. You'll learn about dopamine, serotonin, and the mechanisms behind disorders like depression and schizophrenia. But you'll also learn to listen—truly listen—to the stories of people in pain. Because psychiatry isn't just about diagnosing and treating. It's about *understanding*. And understanding doesn't come from a lab test or an MRI. It comes from empathy."

That's it. *This* is why I want to go into this branch of medicine. To do what my aunt has been doing for years. To help people in ways that physical medicine can't. People who have been through the worst possible things.

Ralph's opinions be damned. This is just as important as being a surgeon. Maybe even more important.

"As we embark on this journey, you'll encounter things that might challenge your beliefs and make you uncomfortable. You'll meet patients whose struggles are hard to comprehend. You'll study disorders that defy neat categorization. And you'll realize that psychiatry is not about fixing people—it's about helping them find balance and hope in their own unique way."

Dr. Engel picks up a piece of chalk and writes two more words on the board.

Mind and *Heart*.

He turns back to the class, a faint smile on his face.

"These are your tools. Use them wisely."

I look around. No one from my anatomy lab is present. It's a shame. Dr. Engel's words are inspiring.

"We'll dive into a more detailed lecture tomorrow," Dr Engel says. "So I won't keep you much longer today. But I do want to ask one thing." He scans the class. "Are any of you planning to focus on psychiatry?"

I raise my hand.

And it's the only hand in the room.

Unreal.

Dr. Engel meets my gaze and nods. "Good. Excellent," he says. "May I ask your name?"

"Angie Simpson, sir."

"Thank you, Ms. Simpson." He looks back at the class. "I know most of you are here because it's a required course. You might think psychiatry is a lesser science, akin to reading tarot cards or telling fortunes."

I hold back a smile. My cousin Ava loves tarot cards, and

sometimes they've actually helped her look at her problems in a different light.

"But do not doubt that psychiatrists have one of the most challenging jobs in the medical field. We are entrusted with people's minds, their secrets, their fears, their dreams. It is not a responsibility to be taken lightly." But then he chuckles softly. "But don't worry. The field also offers some of the greatest rewards."

I can't help but smile back at him. The other students begin to pack their bags, getting ready to leave, but I stay seated.

As the room empties, Dr. Engel walks to my chair. "Angie," he begins, "why psychiatry?"

I'm touched that he remembers my name. "My aunt is a renowned psychiatrist. I've been following her journey since before I can remember. She's always been there for me, and that's how I got interested."

"And your aunt is...?"

"Dr. Melanie Carmichael Steel," I say.

He raises his eyebrows. "Dr. Steel, yes. A brilliant mind. I've read all her work. Her focus was childhood trauma."

"That's the one. She's amazing. She's been a great mentor to me."

"What else about psychiatry is calling to you?" he asks.

I smile at him. "I believe that the mind is the most complex and fascinating thing about us as humans. I want to understand it better and perhaps help others understand theirs."

He nods. "A noble pursuit. And it starts with an understanding of oneself."

With that, he gathers his notes. With a last encouraging smile, he heads out of the room. I am left alone, feeling both exhilarated and daunted by the journey ahead.

An understanding of oneself.

I understand myself just fine.

Don't I?

Back at my townhome, I can't stop thinking about Dr. Engel's words.

It starts with an understanding of oneself.

I'm a little freaked out.

I know just the person to call.

"Hello, Angie," Aunt Melanie says through my phone.

"Hi, Aunt Mel," I say. "How is Uncle Joe doing?"

Aunt Melanie's husband, my uncle Jonah, is going through experimental treatment for brain cancer.

"He's fatigued, as usual, but his physicians say he's doing better than expected."

"That's good to hear. Tell him I think about him every day."

"He knows that, Angie. It's a rough road, but he has more strength than anyone I know." She sighs, but there's a contentedness to it. "How are you doing at school?"

"Good. I had my first psychiatry class today, and I wanted to talk to you about it."

"How exciting! I know medical school is just beginning for you, and you only have one semester under your belt, but I remember my first psychiatry class. I hadn't actually decided that I wanted to pursue the discipline until I took that class."

"Oh? I can't believe I've never talked to you about this before. I guess I just always assumed psychiatry was your calling."

"Actually, when I went to med school, I was hoping to be a surgeon."

My jaw drops. Aunt Melanie is one of the greatest psychiatrists in the whole country. She's helped so many people, and she's written several books as well. She helped my own family members, and now she's working with my cousin Diana's husband's sister and her daughter, who have been through something horrific.

She's supposed to be retired, but she keeps coming out of retirement when amazing cases come her way. She can't turn her back on a person in need.

"Surgery?" I ask.

"Oh, yes. I was convinced that was what I really wanted to do. Until I had to slice open a cadaver for the first time."

I can't help a gasp. "Oh my God, I feel the same way. We were supposed to do our first cut today in anatomy lab, but the professor canceled the class."

"Oh really? Why?"

"He didn't give a reason. It was probably something personal. You know, things come up."

I haven't even thought about *why* Jason canceled class. I hope everything is okay. There's a little edge of darkness to him, and I can't help but wonder if something is up.

"They do. But is that a little bit of disappointment in your voice?"

I don't know how she does it. No wonder Aunt Melanie is such a great psychiatrist. She can sense even the slightest bit of emotion, even through the phone.

"What do you mean?" I ask, feigning innocence.

"You say you weren't looking forward to cutting your

cadaver, yet you sounded a little bit disappointed that lab was canceled."

"I was relieved, actually."

"Okay, Angie. I won't push you. But I'm glad you enjoyed your psychiatry class."

"Yes. When I first saw the professor, I thought he was going to be old and stodgy, but he was actually brilliant. He gave this amazing introductory lecture. Even the people who have no interest in psychiatry were kind of captivated. And he knows you. His name is Dr. Carlos Engel."

"Oh, yes. Carlos. He's excellent. I didn't realize he was teaching."

"He is. And I'm really looking forward to his class."

"I believe he's written a few books. His specialty is the trauma of loss."

"You mean people who lose something they love?"

"Some*one* they love, Angie. Widows and widowers. Parents who have lost a child. Anyone who's lost someone they love. That's what Carlos excels at."

I pause. "He said something when I spoke to him after class."

"What was that?"

"He said that psychiatry starts with an understanding of oneself."

"He's right, of course."

"I guess I never thought of it that way. I mean, I think I understand myself just fine. But I've never been through any trauma, really. Not like some of the people in our family have."

"True. And be thankful for that."

"I am."

She pauses before continuing. "But that doesn't mean

you know your*self,* Angie. Not as deeply as you need to in order to help others understand *them*selves. It's not just about experiencing trauma. It's about understanding the human psyche. The highs and lows, the joys and sorrows, the fears and hopes. And that starts with understanding yourself."

A silence hangs over us for a moment. Is that what I'm missing? A deeper understanding of myself?

"Do you think I can do it?" I ask finally.

"I believe you can," Aunt Melanie says. "You've always been empathetic, Angie. That's one of the key traits in this field."

"But empathy isn't enough, is it?"

"No, it isn't. Empathy allows you to feel what others are feeling, but understanding requires more than that. You need to analyze those feelings and come up with patterns—patterns that help you understand how human minds work."

"And how do I do that?"

"By studying psychology, of course. By talking to people, by observing them. Read about their experiences, immerse yourself in new situations. See how you react."

"I took a lot of psychology in college for my major. I would have taken even more, but the pre-med course requirements ate up the bulk of my schedule."

"Psychiatry is a different discipline anyway," she replies. "Psychology is the study of human behavior. Psychiatry is the practice of *treating* mental illness. They're two sides of the same coin, but they don't exactly overlap."

I rub the side of my head with my free hand. "So what you're saying is that I have to learn how to treat mental illness as well?"

"That's a given, of course. That's what psychiatry is. But

more than that, you need to be willing to dive deep into your own mind and understand how *you* react to things. Only then can you begin to understand how others might be feeling."

I sigh heavily into the phone. "That sounds complicated."

"It is," Aunt Melanie says with a soft chuckle. "But that's what makes it so fascinating."

"Fascinating..." I echo her words, but my mind is going in circles trying to comprehend the enormity of what lies ahead.

"And remember this," she continues. "A psychiatrist isn't just a doctor who prescribes medicines. We delve into the unconscious, understand the past and present of a person. We seek to change the course of their future. It's a heavy responsibility. We don't just heal. We understand."

"Understand..." I echo.

"And that's only the tip of the iceberg, Angie. You're going to learn so much more. Our job is not just to understand them but to help them understand themselves."

A light bulb shines above me then. "And I can't help them understand themselves without first understanding *my*self."

"Bingo," she says. "It's a lifelong journey, and it's not always pretty. God knows I discovered some things about myself along the way that didn't exactly thrill me."

"How?" I ask. "I guess I always thought of myself as pretty normal."

"Normal is a relative term," she says. "We are all complex beings made up of experiences, emotions, and thoughts that shape us into who we are. And believe me, when you start digging deeper into your psyche, you might uncover aspects about yourself that you never knew existed."

I swallow hard. "How did you do it, Aunt Melanie?" I ask. "How did you dig deep?"

BROKEN DREAM

"It wasn't easy. It took time. It took patience. And it took courage."

"Courage?" I ask, furrowing my brow.

"Yes. Courage to face the truth about myself—the good, the bad, and the ugly."

The line goes quiet for a moment as I let her words sink in.

"Did you ever regret it?" I ask.

"The truth can be painful sometimes," she replies, her voice steady. "Facing it head-on can be daunting. But regret? No, never. Confronting the truth about myself made me a better psychiatrist. It made me a better person."

"I guess I never thought about it like that," I say.

"You're just starting out on this journey. There's so much for you to learn, so much for you to experience."

"But what if I don't like what I discover?" I ask, fear creeping into me.

"You may not," she says. "And that's okay too. Understanding isn't always about liking what we find but acknowledging it and learning how to cope with it."

I take a deep breath. This path I've chosen seems so much more elaborate, more intricate than I imagined. "I guess I have a lot to think about."

"And that's okay," she assures me. "Take your time to digest all this information. Remember, self-discovery is a marathon. A lifelong journey. You're allowed to take a break now and then if you need it."

"Thanks, Aunt Mel. I'm excited. And a little scared."

"Completely normal," she says.

"Dr. Engel made it sound like I needed to understand myself before I could even begin helping others, but I see now that's not what he meant."

"Right. He meant you have to be open to understanding yourself deeply, and that's a process that happens simultaneously with helping others. It's not two separate stages but two intertwined journeys."

"But isn't it possible that I may end up losing myself while trying to understand others?" I ask.

"It's a valid concern," Aunt Melanie says. "But remember that one of the key aspects of being a psychiatrist is the ability to maintain professional boundaries. You're there to guide your patients, not lose yourself in their stories."

"But how do you detach yourself?"

"It's not always easy," she admits. "It requires practice and constant self-reflection. It won't happen overnight, or even over the years of your training. And more importantly, it requires a sense of balance. You have to learn how to be present for your patients without getting emotionally entangled."

"That sounds challenging."

"And it will be, but challenges are what help us grow."

I let it all sink in. Or at least I try to, but Aunt Melanie has dumped a lot of information on me. It'll take a while to let it all marinate.

"Thank you, Aunt Melanie," I say. "You've given me lots of good things to think about."

"Of course, Angie. I'll let you go now. Have to check on your uncle. But feel free to call whenever you need. As long as I'm not with a patient, I'm all yours."

"Thanks. Love you."

"Love you too."

I end the call.

Challenges are what help us grow.

True, for sure. My parents always taught me that. And our

family, while blessed, has had its challenges. My uncle and two of my cousins were victims of horrific sexual abuse as children, and my aunt Ruby is the daughter of a rapist. My own father is the son of a rapist and pedophile as well.

All things I recently learned.

All things that still make me sick.

And all things that helped me decide to pursue psychiatry so I can help people like them, just as Aunt Melanie did.

I continue to ponder while I make a light dinner, until someone knocks on my door.

CHAPTER FOURTEEN

JASON

Angie opens the door. God, she looks beautiful. Her cheeks are rosy, and her dark hair is bouncing in waves around her shoulders.

I'm holding a bottle of red wine. I don't know a lot about wine, and I think someone must've brought it to me. I'm more of a bourbon guy.

The problem is, I don't really have any friends to celebrate with. I have colleagues, of course. But friends?

I kind of let my friendships go after I lost Lindsay and Julia.

All they did was remind me of everything I no longer had.

So I'm coming to see my neighbor.

My neighbor who is also my student.

Who I'm also wildly attracted to and have kissed.

And who's probably no more than twenty-three years old.

But I don't care.

I'm feeling hope for the first time in years, and it feels...

I want to say good, but I'm afraid to.

Louisa and Gita didn't offer me any guarantees. Everything could go up in smoke, and I'll be relegated to teaching for the rest of my life. I could end up losing the use of my hand entirely.

I enjoy teaching. Well, maybe *enjoy* is too strong of a word.

BROKEN DREAM

I haven't hated teaching. I can still hold a scalpel. I can still cut into nonliving flesh, now that I'm teaching anatomy lab. I had to wait for an opening, and this year, I got it. For the last couple of years, I've taught surgery techniques to older students.

My hand is steady as I hold the bottle of wine. I hardly feel the tremor, and it's invisible to the naked eye. But if I tried to make a cut on a living person, I'd make a mistake.

Every millimeter—every fraction of a millimeter—matters.

Everything matters when you're cutting into a human being.

When I was doing my surgical residency, the attendings treated themselves like gods. I thought it was ridiculous. I would never have a God complex, I told myself. Never in a million years.

But when I began to cut...

I realized it wasn't a God complex that they had. It wasn't even arrogance. It was simply confidence. Because without confidence, you can't slice open a human being.

You absolutely can't, unless you're a psychopath.

I've met a few surgeons along the way who might be psychopaths. But the best surgeons—and I was on track to become one of the best—don't consider themselves gods and are certainly not psychopaths.

No.

They're healers. Healers who are confident in their abilities, confident in their steady hands, confident in their knowledge of the human body, and confident in their ability to fix what is wrong in any patient.

God, I miss that.

But for the first time, I feel a sliver of hope.

"Dr. Lansing," she says. "I mean....Jason."

"Hi, Angie. I hope I'm not interrupting you."

A miniature schnauzer runs to the door, yapping its head off.

Angie scoops the small dog into her arms. "No, Tillie," she says.

The dog shuts up.

She looks back at me. "I was just making myself a little bit of dinner." She drops her gaze to the bottle of wine. "Did you... need something?"

"I got some good news today, Angie. I was hoping you might help me celebrate." I hold up the bottle.

She widens her eyes. "I... Sure. Come on in. I'll put Tillie out."

I reach toward Angie and scratch the schnauzer's ears. "Is that this little pup's name?"

She smiles and kisses the dog's head. "Yes. Tillie is my own little hellspawn, but I love her to pieces." She walks into the house, looking over her shoulder. "I'm just making tomato soup and grilled cheese. Would you like some?"

"You know what? Tomato soup and grilled cheese sounds awesome."

"My mom is a gourmet cook," she says. "It's her tomato soup recipe. I didn't make it, though. She sent it to me in one of her care packages. But it's absolutely delicious if you like tomato soup."

"I love tomato soup." I press my lips together. "But honestly I'm not sure I've ever had anything other than Campbell's."

Angie smiles then, and it's a beautiful smile. "Then you will love this, I promise you. Come on in."

BROKEN DREAM

I follow her inside. "So is your mom a chef?"

She frowns. "Yes and no. She's had culinary training, and she's as good as any chef at any restaurant, but no, she doesn't work outside the home."

Right. She's a Steel. She probably doesn't have to work.

But damn it, I am not going to let the fact that Angie Simpson was born with a silver spoon in her mouth—or that she's my student—bring me down tonight.

"Do you like wine?" I ask.

"Oh, love it." She opens her back door and puts the dog down on her back porch. She closes the door and looks back at me. "My uncle and my cousin make some of the best wine in—" She stops abruptly.

"It's all right. I know all about your vineyards. I'm afraid this isn't Steel wine. It's"—I quickly read the label—"a classic red from some vineyard in California."

"I'm sure it's great."

"I don't know anything about wine. I'm not even sure where this bottle came from. Someone must've brought it to me, and I stuck it in a cupboard."

Which means I've had this bottle of wine since...

Since before.

I shake the thought out of my head.

Angie takes the bottle from me and walks into her kitchen. I follow. She grabs a corkscrew out of a drawer and expertly removes the cork. Then she grabs two goblets, places something on top of the wine bottle, and pours the wine through it.

"What's that?" I ask her.

"It's an aerator," she says. "It negates the need for decanting. It breathes the wine for you."

I cock my head. "*Breathes* the wine?"

She nods. "Gives it a little more body. Lets the flavors bloom."

I didn't even know wine should breathe. Tells you how much I know.

Lindsay didn't drink. She was severely allergic to the histamines in red wine, and other than that, she just didn't like what alcohol did to her. So when I wanted to have a bourbon, I would go out with the guys.

The guys don't exist anymore.

"So you want to tell me about your good news?" Angie asks, handing me a glass.

I open my mouth to speak, but then I close it again.

What was I thinking?

Yes, I got some amazing news today. But if I tell Angie what it is, I'll have to tell her the whole story.

I'm not ready to tell her that.

It's not something I like to think about.

Even though sometimes all I do is think about it.

"Earth to Jason?" she says.

"Sorry about that." I frown, grabbing my wineglass. "I just... I suppose you may wonder why I teach."

"Because you like teaching?"

I'm sure she's read my bio on the med school website. I'm a board-certified general surgeon and a fellow. So why wouldn't I be cutting instead of teaching?

"Sure, teaching is okay," I say, "but what I really love is performing surgery."

"So why aren't you doing it?"

"Kind of like the old adage, I guess," I say. "Those who can, do, and those who can't, teach."

BROKEN DREAM

She drops her jaw.

I hold up a hand. "I'm not saying I'm not good enough. Well, I guess I'm not *now*." I take a sip of wine. "But I *was* good, Angie. I was amazing."

I should be embarrassed at tooting my own horn like that, but I'm not. Because I'm not lying. I was on the fast track to being something great. Being an award winner, being a person who came up with new ways to save lives.

"What I mean is, I injured my hand three years ago. My right hand, my dominant hand. Without two steady hands, as you know, a physician can't cut people open."

She gasps. "I'm so sorry. What happened?"

Of course. The question I knew she'd ask. Everyone does.

So I say my rehearsed answer. "I was in an automobile accident."

"Oh no. And there's nothing they can do?"

I gesture to the bottle of wine. "That's why I'm here, actually. Today I got some good news. From two of my colleagues. My neurologist and a bright young neurosurgeon. Dr. Patel—she's the neurosurgeon—has this new technique with nerve grafting, and she thinks I'm a great candidate."

Angie's eyes go wide. "Really? That's wonderful."

"There are no guarantees, of course. But it's the best news I've had in a long time. And I felt like celebrating with someone."

"Why me?" she asks.

Why her indeed?

Because I have no other friends.

Because she's the hottest thing walking.

Because all I can think about is getting her into bed.

Which would get me fired, of course.

"Because you're my neighbor," I say, hating the lie. "I can drink myself into oblivion here and not have to drive home."

God, what a crock. I can drink myself into oblivion anywhere and call an Uber or cab.

Besides the fact that I don't even drink much. Even all those years, going through the loss and the pain, it never occurred to me to take a drink.

"Oh." Her voice holds a trace of sadness.

She thinks I came over here for...

What *did* I come for?

And the answer is a simple one.

Yes, I wanted to celebrate with someone. Even though it could all be for nothing.

But the big reason is simple.

I wanted to see her.

I want to talk to her. Maybe get to know her. Maybe...

God.

She's so different from Lindsay. Dark where Lindsay was blond, quiet where Lindsay was boisterous.

But brilliant, already I can tell. And Lindsay was also brilliant.

She took the MCATs with me for kicks. And she only scored one point below me. She hadn't even taken all the pre-med courses.

But teaching was her calling, and her students loved her. God, those years I was in med school and then my residency were tough on our marriage. But we got through it.

Only to lose everything.

I take another sip of wine.

I don't know anything about wine, but it tastes good.

"It's good," Angie says. "Very fruit forward. Of course

BROKEN DREAM

that's common for table wine."

I raise my eyebrows.

She smiles shyly. "My mom again. She knows a lot about wine, but it's her brother, my uncle Ryan, who knows the most. He's really gifted. A true artist. And my cousin Dale, who now runs Steel Vineyards, is nearly as good. I'd say it ran in the family, except that Dale was adopted." Her cheeks are rosy. "I'm sorry," she says. "I'm babbling. You probably know all about my family."

"No," I say honestly. "I mean, I know *of* them. But it's not like I keep up on all the gossip or anything."

"Just as well." She bites her lip. "I suppose you don't hear about us much here. On the Western Slope, there's always something going on that people are whispering about."

"I'm sorry you have to go through that."

She shrugs. "I'm used to it. Besides, I'm very grateful. Look at the way I get to live. My family is worth a fortune, and I'm a beneficiary of some of it. So how can I be anything but grateful?"

Wow.

She's certainly not a spoiled rich brat. Not that I thought she was. If that were the case, she'd be partying, driving around in an expensive car, and spending her money on frivolous things. She certainly wouldn't be going to medical school. She's *choosing* to put herself through these grueling four years and an even more grueling five or six afterward.

Angie Simpson is about as real a person as I've met in a long time.

"Let me grill the sandwiches really quick," she says. She puts together a second sandwich and then throws them both into what looks like a waffle iron. Then she pours ladles of soup into two bowls and takes them over to the small table in her kitchen.

She wraps her fingers around the fridge door. "Would you like something else to drink? I have water or soda. Or we can just have the wine."

"I think water would be great. Thank you."

I really need to watch myself. I don't drink often, so my tolerance is shit. And if I drink too much, I might just do something that will cost me my job.

Angie nods and fills two cups of water, adds ice, places them on the table, and then returns to the counter, where she opens the waffle iron and uses a spatula to pull out two gooey grilled cheese sandwiches.

"I just use regular old cheddar," she says. "I'm not really into stinky cheese."

I can't help a chuckle. "Cheddar's great. But I kind of think that when it comes to cheese, the stinkier the better."

She wrinkles her nose adorably. "You sound like my mom. I've never met a chef that doesn't love stinky cheese. Or goat cheese, which is the worst."

I laugh. "I love goat cheese."

"Then I'm afraid you're going to have to leave my house," she says, her eyes bright.

I grin. "I guess it would have never worked out between us anyway."

She narrows her eyes. "Because of the cheese? Or because you're my professor?"

I open my mouth, but nothing comes out.

Are we flirting?

It's been so long since I flirted with someone. I'm a little rusty.

BROKEN DREAM

Angie smiles and gestures to a chair. "Have a seat."

I wait for her to sit, and then I take the place across from her. She's even put out cloth napkins.

Impressive.

I place mine across my lap and take another sip of my wine.

"Well," she says, "dig in. But be careful. The cheese is going to be really hot." As she says this, she opens her two slices of bread, and steam drifts out. "Helps a little."

I repeat her movements. Then I take a sip of the water.

I decide to start with the tomato soup.

I bring a spoonful to my lips, blow on it, and then let it float over my tongue.

And wow.

It's like tasting the essence of a sun-warmed tomato. The flavor is rich, velvety smooth, and bright, with that deep sweetness only a perfectly ripe tomato has. The subtle tang is balanced with a hint of roasted garlic and fresh basil that lingers just long enough to make me want another taste.

So I take another taste.

Then another.

And then I speak. "This may be the best thing I've ever put in my mouth."

Her cheeks redden further.

Oh, God...

She's thinking...

And I'm thinking...

I'd love to taste her pussy on my tongue.

Am I ready?

Am I truly ready?

I haven't been with a woman since...

And she's a student, for fuck's sake. A *student*.

Hell, simply being in her home could be grounds for me to be fired.

But she let me in her home.

And I think she might let me in *her*, too.

Angie clears her throat, jerking me out of my thoughts.

"I'll be sure to tell my mom how much you like it."

I nod. "Best tomato soup ever. I don't think I'll ever eat tomato soup out of a can again."

"My mom would love that," she says. "She'll say something like, 'if I got one person off canned soup, I've done my job for the universe.'"

I smile. "Your mom sounds like an interesting person."

She chuckles. "She is. She's the youngest of four, and the other three are brothers, so they were always protective of her. My uncle Ryan is the youngest of the three, and he's seven years older than my mom. My uncle Joe, the oldest, is thirteen years older, and my mom ended up marrying his best friend. So there's a huge age gap between them. Thirteen years."

I tilt my head.

Interesting that she mentioned the age gap.

She and I probably have an age gap of just about that much.

Is she telling me that doesn't matter to her?

Or is she telling me...

I take another sip of wine.

She's telling me absolutely nothing. She's merely making conversation.

"I'm sorry," she says. "I'm babbling again."

"Do you babble when you're nervous?" I ask.

More red cheeks. If this goes on, her cheeks are going to

BROKEN DREAM

be the color of a fire engine before we're done.

The idea arouses me. I wonder if the blush in her cheeks spreads to her breasts.

In fact, I'm pretty hard right now, sitting at her kitchen table, eating her mother's soup.

Thinking about the creaminess of the paradise between her legs.

I can't deny I was attracted to her the first time I saw her. Hell, I kissed her.

But now...

Now that I'm actually feeling hopeful for the first time in so long... I'm feeling...

Feeling for the first time that I would really like to get to know a woman.

This woman in particular.

Why did she have to be my student?

I can't lose my job.

Of course, if the surgery goes as planned, my teaching job won't matter anymore. No one would care if a nonteaching doctor took a medical student for himself. People might roll their eyes, purse their lips. But my job wouldn't be in jeopardy.

"I'm not nervous," she says, looking at her sandwich. She picks it up. "It's probably cool enough now." She takes a dainty bite.

"Good. I don't want you to be nervous." I raise my wineglass. "We're just neighbors, Angie. Tonight we're just neighbors."

She clinks her glass to mine. "Sounds good to me."

I pick up my sandwich and take a bite.

The sandwich is hot, just shy of scorching. The cheddar is sharp and tangy, with that unmistakable bite that fills my mouth in waves of savory goodness. The bread is perfectly crisp, crackling as I sink my teeth in, golden and buttery on the outside, while the inside is soft, almost melting into the cheese.

"This bread is amazing," I say.

"My cousin Ava made it. She owns a bakery in Snow Creek."

I smile. "Is there anything that your family *doesn't* do?"

CHAPTER FIFTEEN

Angie

I nearly choke on my bite of sandwich.

Surely he didn't mean that the way it sounded.

He probably just meant that, you know, my aunt is a renowned psychiatrist, my family is full of billionaire ranchers with their hands in all kinds of other businesses, my uncle and my cousin make award-winning wine, and another cousin bakes delicious bread.

We're a multifaceted bunch.

I have a big family.

But just the way he said it...

Is there anything your family doesn't *do?*

Why am I hearing innuendos that aren't there?

And I know exactly why.

Because I'm horny for teacher.

God, sometimes I disgust myself.

Plus, what if Ralph *did* see something? What if he's already reported it to administration?

Jason could lose his job.

On the other hand, if this surgery he's talking about works, he won't need to teach anymore.

I wonder how old he is.

Do I dare ask?

I take a sip of water to avoid choking on the piece of sandwich.

"I have a large family," I say. "They do a lot."

"What else does your family do?" he asks.

I rack my brain before answering. It's a lot to keep track of. "Well, my cousin Gina is an artist. Her sister is the one who's the baker. My brother Dave works with my uncle Talon in our apple and peach orchards. My other brother Henry helps run our nonprofit foundation. My cousin Donny is a lawyer, and my cousin Diana's an architect. Oh, and three of my cousins are married to bona fide rock stars."

He nods, taking another sip of wine. "You *do* have a big family."

I'm not sure what to say to that, so I take another bite of my sandwich and chew slowly.

I'm still not completely sure why he's here.

He says he wanted to celebrate.

Why with me?

"How old are you?" I blurt out before I have a chance to stop myself.

"Almost thirty-six," he says. "In fact, my birthday is next month."

Thirty-six. I do the math in my head. He's got more than a decade on me. Thirteen years.

When I was born, he was already a teenager. Probably learning how to shave. I bet his jawline was just as magnificent then as it is now.

It's not a small difference. But...it's the same as my parents. And it worked for them.

What am I thinking? I can't be with this man. He's my professor. There have got to be rules forbidding anything from

BROKEN DREAM

happening between us. We may have shared a quick kiss, but that was just us getting caught in the moment.

Wasn't it?

I blink a few times. "Oh. Well, happy birthday, then."

"Yeah. It's weird." He gazes wistfully out the window. "I don't think about birthdays much anymore."

"Why not?"

He doesn't answer right away.

Just when I'm convinced that he's going to change the subject—

He puts his glass down on the table. "I just haven't felt like acknowledging birthdays, I guess."

"Oh."

I'm tempted to ask why, but if he wanted to tell me, he would've put it in the answer to that last question.

"Birthdays are huge in my family," I say. "My mom's cakes are legendary. And then of course Ava—she's the baker—is also great with cakes and breads of any kind. There's always a great big celebration, and everyone in the family comes. Even those who live out of town try to make it in."

"How is that possible?" he asks. "If your family is as big as it seems, you must be celebrating a birthday every month."

I nod. "Sometimes twice a month. And I have the same birthday as my twin, of course, so—"

He raises his eyebrows. "Wait, your twin?"

"Yeah. We're not identical twins, though we do look a lot alike. Sage—that's her name—works for the family business. My dad is the chief financial officer for the umbrella company that oversees all our subsidiaries. He was grooming my brother to take over, but Dave had an epiphany a while back. He didn't want to be cooped up in an office, so he started doing more of the work outdoors. Sage took his place, and she's loving it. Like I said, we look a lot alike even though we're not identical, but we couldn't be more different in our personalities."

"How so?"

"She's really outgoing. The life of the party. And I..." I let out a forced chuckle. "I'm...not."

He lets out a breath, his gaze vacant. "Being the life of the party isn't all it's cracked up to be."

I tilt my head and look at him. At his gorgeous green eyes that seem to have a speck of sadness in them.

Was he the life of the party once?

And now he's not?

I suppose losing the ability to do your life's work has that effect on someone.

"What do you mean by that?" I decide to ask.

He runs his hands through his hair. "I was a partier back in the day, but not every weekend or anything. I think it was because I had to work so hard, you know, to get through med school and then through my internship and residency. When I had the chance to let loose, I took it."

"That makes sense."

"Yeah. It took its toll on—" He stops abruptly.

"Took its toll on what?"

He takes another bite of sandwich, chews, swallows. "On... everything," he finally says. "Working and studying twenty-four seven doesn't leave much time for anything else. So my partying days were few and far between."

"I'm sorry."

He smiles. "No reason to be sorry. I had to work my way through college and med school, and I still had student debt."

"Is it all paid off now?"

BROKEN DREAM

"It is." He looks down. "But I wish it weren't."
"Why would you wish that?"
He takes another sip of wine.
And he doesn't answer.

CHAPTER SIXTEEN

JASON

After Julia was born, we talked to a financial advisor about setting up a college fund for her.

"Why not get her started on a whole-life policy?" our advisor said. "We love to start kids on these. The premiums are cheap, and the cash value builds up. By the time your kid is eighteen, she'll have a nice nest egg. It won't be huge, but if she decides to keep the policy, it will be a big part of her net worth by the time she retires."

Lindsay and I looked at each other.

"Sure, why not?" we said.

So we set it up.

A whole-life insurance policy for Julia, with Lindsay and me as beneficiaries, of course. Once she turned eighteen, she could take over the policy and name her own beneficiary.

The death benefit was one million dollars.

It occurred to me at the time that if anything ever happened to Julia, at least we'd have some money that would help us deal with the loss.

Right.

I'd so much rather have my daughter. I'd give the money back—and everything else I have—in a second to have my little girl.

BROKEN DREAM

I can't answer Angie's question.

I was able to pay off my student debt because of the death of my daughter.

I was able to pay for top-notch therapy to help Lindsay and me get through everything.

Therapy that only made me angry.

Therapy that didn't ultimately help Lindsay.

Therapy that stole everything from me.

So yeah, I wish I were still making those wretched student loan payments.

Because if I were, my daughter would still be alive. She'd be six years old, learning to read. Learning to do simple math. Learning to write sentences.

"Are you okay, Jason?"

Angie's voice jerks me out of my thoughts.

Today's a good day. Today I have hope. That is why I'm here.

For the first time since I lost Lindsay, I'm attracted to a woman.

It's a woman I can never have, of course, but the fact that I'm even looking her way means that I've at least healed a little.

I'll never fully move past Julia and Lindsay—no decent person could—but my life is moving forward whether I want it to or not. There's something nice about the fact that Angie has ignited a spark in me.

"How old are you, Angie?" I ask.

"I'm twenty-three," she replies.

I hold back a scoff.

A thirteen-year age difference. Just like she said her parents had.

Why am I even thinking this? She's my student. I was a

teenager when this girl was born.

But emotions are swirling through me. All kinds of emotions.

Anger, sharp and hot, mixed with an ache so deep it feels endless. Confusion too, like a fog I can't see through and a bitter taste of regret. It's a storm of everything I've held back, and now, in this moment, it's crashing over me all at once. I can barely breathe, barely think.

It's chaos. Everything I thought I'd buried.

Pure chaos.

A wave of grief overwhelms me, but it's different this time. Not quite as isolated.

Lindsay would have wanted me to move on, to find someone else.

I glance at Angie again, her wide eyes still shimmering with such innocent curiosity.

I have an urge to share my story, to open up about my past. To let her see the man behind the doctor, behind the professor, the scars that lie beneath the surface.

But I can't.

Not yet.

I spend my life stuffing it back, and this woman...

This beautiful woman.

This intelligent woman.

This *young* woman.

She wants to go into psychiatry.

If I tell her my story, she's going to want to talk about it. Try to analyze me.

The thought of it makes me sick.

I don't want to be analyzed.

I don't want to talk about my feelings.

Hell, no.

Sure, I came over here to celebrate.

Celebrate the fact that I might be able to perform surgery again in the future.

But then it hits me.

As I stare at her, anger and rage bubble up within me. Anger and rage at the psychiatrist who couldn't help me, who ultimately took everything from me.

How do I make that work with the feelings I'm having for Angie?

On the one hand, I want to yell at her, punish her, because she represents the discipline that was supposed to help me, heal me, but didn't.

And on the other hand—the deep and primal hand that controls my cock, my libido...

I want to grab her.

Kiss her.

Rip her clothes off and fuck her.

Hard, fast, and full of angry passion.

I want two things at once.

To fuck Angie and to punish her. To punish the psychiatrist who failed me.

But also take her, open myself up to a woman in a way I haven't for three long fucking years.

And I shouldn't do any of it.

Hell, she may tell me to leave when I tell her what I want.

She'll be well within her rights, and it would be the best thing for both of us.

I finish my sandwich, swallowing the last bite. I wipe the crumbs off my lips with my napkin and down the last of my wine.

Her glass of wine is still half-full, sandwich half-eaten, but her soup bowl is empty, as is mine.

"Would you like another sandwich?" she asks.

I shake my head, never taking my gaze from hers.

"More wine? Soup?" she asks, her voice softer this time.

I shake my head, again, never taking my eyes from hers.

Her eyes are deep pools of mystery, unreadable and endless. They pull me in. Just staring into them feels like falling, like slipping into a place where nothing is certain, and everything is possible.

Fuck.

What a metaphor for my life right now.

Where nothing is certain...

But for the first time in a long time...where *everything* is possible.

"No thank you," I say.

She nods, rises, grabs my plate and soup bowl, and takes them to the counter.

I follow her, stand behind her, only inches separating us.

My dick is hard and pulsating inside my jeans.

"Angie," I say, my voice gruff.

She turns with a light gasp, faces me.

"Yes?" she says, her voice cracking.

I don't reply.

I simply crush my mouth to hers.

CHAPTER SEVENTEEN

ANGIE

His mouth is on mine before I can react. His kiss is intense, desperate, and starving. It's a hunger I feel myself, throbbing in every cell of my body. Yet it scares me. Not in a creepy, aggressive way, but in an overwhelming passion that threatens to consume me.

I gasp into his mouth. My knees weaken, but he steadies me with his arms around my waist, pulling me closer to him.

He tastes like wine and sadness and a hidden fire that he's only just letting out. It's intoxicating. And terrifying.

I clutch on to his shirt, the fabric crumpling beneath my grip. A strange fluttering blooms in my stomach, fueled by his sudden intensity and the taste of his lips against mine.

I recognize his kiss, but this time it's different.

It's not only sadness I sense but anger.

Rage even.

But beneath all of that, I sense something tender. Something faint and almost fragile.

Longing. Need. Hope.

He deepens the kiss, and I throw inhibition to the wind. It's not as if Ralph can see us now. My heart beats wildly as I kiss him back. His tongue is both harsh and smooth. He tastes of tomatoes and wine, of lust and savagery. Of...Jason.

He presses our bodies together. A low groan escapes him, vibrating through me and making me quake.

But then he breaks the kiss, his breath ragged. He pulls away slightly. His green gaze is intense, almost pained. Emotions flicker across his face, all unreadable.

He swallows hard, a muscle in his jaw ticking. Then without a word, he turns away abruptly and strides toward the door.

Without thinking, I follow him. Grab his arm. Jerk him back toward me. "Don't go, Jason. Please."

"You don't know what you're asking for," he says.

I widen my eyes. "I'm not asking for anything. You can't leave." I run my fingers up and down his arm. "Something's bothering you. Let me help."

"Help?" He laughs. "You psychiatrists are all the same."

I tilt my head. "I'm a first-year medical student, Jason. I'm far from a psychiatrist. I just want to help you."

His green eyes darken. "There's only one thing you can do to help me right now, Angie, and it's not talking."

I bite my lower lip, swallowing. "Then let me. I want to help you in any way I can."

His lips are on mine once more, his tongue devouring me, until he breaks the kiss again with a smack. "Be sure," he says, his voice rough. "Be fucking sure, because once we start this, we're not stopping."

"I—"

"I don't care that you're my student. I don't care that I'm your teacher. I don't care about any of it. So *be fucking sure.*"

I'm not sure. Not even slightly.

Except that I am.

I want this.

I want him.

And damn the consequences.

"Kiss me," I say. "Kiss me, Jason, and let me show you how sure I am."

His eyes flicker with something like relief before he pulls me against him, his hands rugged and rough. His lips collide with mine, a storm of passion and unspoken promises. He touches my cheeks, my shoulders, my arms. My heart drums out erratic beats that thump all the way through me.

He pulls slightly away and stares at me with those intense eyes clouded with desire yet still carrying a hint of vulnerability.

And I see him.

I see Jason.

He's strong yet broken. Guarded yet yearning for something more.

Does he see *me*?

Does he see that I'm not untried but still pretty innocent? That I'm imperfect too?

"Are you scared?" he whispers, his breath hot against my ear.

"A little," I say in truth. "But not enough to stop."

A ghost of a smile flits across his face before being replaced by a look of raw desire. "Then don't."

In the dim lighting of the kitchen, I see him again. All of him. The beauty and the pain, the strength and the vulnerability. His eyes speak volumes—stories of hurt, betrayal, solitude, yearning—and it draws me in like a moth to flame.

I want to help him. Give him what he needs in this moment. And if it's not talking? I'm good with that.

He pulls me closer and wraps his arms around me. His lips descend onto mine once again. The kiss is demanding and intense—a kiss that stirs up feelings inside me that I never knew existed.

He moves from my mouth to my ear. "I need you," he whispers.

And I realize with a jolt of surprise—and maybe a bit of fear—that I need him too.

He pulls back, his gaze locked with mine, those piercing eyes looking for some sign of resistance, some hint that I want him to stop. But there's none. Because right now, in this moment, all I want is him.

"Right here, right now," he grits out before he pulls my shirt over my head and discards it on the kitchen floor.

He drops his gaze to my breasts before he pops open the front fastener of my bra.

He sucks in a breath. "Fucking gorgeous." Then he drops his head and takes a nipple between his teeth, biting it harder than I expect.

I let out a sharp yelp but move to tangle my fingers in his hair as pleasure and pain collide, swirling around in my chest. I arch my back, and he groans against me, the vibrations sending shock waves through me.

He slides his free hand down my stomach before sneaking under the waistband of my jeans. His touch is flaming hot against my skin. Even through the fabric of my panties, I feel the searing heat of his fingers.

"Jason," I gasp, clutching on to his shoulders for support as he teases me through the fabric, sending sparks of electric pleasure through me.

He pulls away from my breast with a smug grin. I can't help a whimper at the loss.

His grin only widens at my frustration, and he presses a

BROKEN DREAM

quick kiss to my lips before dropping to his knees.

He unbuttons and unzips my jeans and pulls them down along with my panties, leaving me exposed and vulnerable. He looks at me with an intensity that makes me shiver in anticipation. Then he leans in, wrapping his arms around my thighs to pull me closer.

He slides his lips over my abdomen, trailing a path from my navel downward. With every touch, every flick of his tongue, he sends pleasure coursing through me.

"Jason," I gasp again.

Without giving me any warning, he delves deeper with his tongue, sliding it through the folds of my pussy. The sensation is so intense, I can't help but cry out. My legs buckle beneath me, but he holds me up, his grip on my thighs tightening as he continues to eat me.

The pleasure builds up inside me until it becomes unbearable. "Jason," I plead as I buck against him.

But he doesn't let up, only quickens his pace.

And I'm spiraling...

Spiraling out of control. Ecstasy crashes over me in waves, and I cry out his name as my body convulses under the assault of pleasure.

The orgasm pulses through me like a freight train.

It goes on and on and on and on...

Jason is relentless with his tongue, and when he slides a finger into me, I shatter once more. Even harder this time.

My God, I've had climaxes before, but this...

This...

The waves shred me, leave me in a puddle on the kitchen floor.

And he still licks, licks, licks...

As the last tremors of my release fade away, he rises. His eyes are smoky and intense as he gazes at me, a satisfied smile playing on his lips.

"God, Angie," he says hoarsely. "You're incredible."

Before I can respond, he's kissing me again, his hands roaming my body as if he can't get enough.

I taste myself on his tongue. A tang of musk mixed with tomato soup and wine.

Without breaking our kiss, Jason unbuttons his shirt and discards it on the floor next to mine. His chest is sculpted, a work of art adorned with a smattering of dark hair that trails down to his lower abdomen. I explore him, tracing the hills and valleys of his muscles. He shivers against my touch, a low moan escaping his lips.

He steps back, grabs a condom out of his pocket, and then unfastens his belt and pushes down his jeans and briefs in one swift motion. He stands before me, naked, his body an irresistible blend of raw masculinity and vulnerability.

And his cock...

A gorgeous masterpiece of velvet over steel.

"Jason," I breathe. I trace the line of hair from his chest to his pubic hair. I close my eyes, feeling the rough texture under my fingertips.

I hear the rip of the condom wrapper, and then I feel him guiding me back against the kitchen counter, its cold marble surface pressing into my bare skin. His body is a warm contrast as he pulls me close to him again, claiming my lips.

We touch each other's bodies, exploring every curve and crevice. His touch is urgent, desperate.

It mirrors my own.

He lifts me with ease and sets me onto the cold kitchen

BROKEN DREAM

counter. I wrap my legs around his waist, pulling him closer as he positions himself between them.

No hesitation or second thoughts now.

This is the point of no return.

And I'm more than ready.

CHAPTER EIGHTEEN

JASON

The primal need I feel for Angie is something I've never experienced before. It's raw and powerful, a force of nature that sweeps me up and threatens to overwhelm me entirely. It's terrifying yet exhilarating, a heady mix of fear and desire.

Her eyes are wide as she watches me. She's beautiful, utterly breathtaking in her trust. The sight of her nudges at the beast inside me.

The beast...

Fuck, it's been so long.

She tasted like heaven, and the way she came for me...

So responsive. Like no other.

I guide myself to her pussy, teasing her with the tip. Her thighs tighten around my waist in response, a small whimper escaping from her parted lips.

Then I thrust into her.

The sensation is electrifying.

She gasps at my size but then moans as I begin to move. She responds, meeting every thrust with an eager push of her hips.

"Jason," she moans, digging her fingers into my shoulders.

I pepper her neck with kisses as I thrust deeper and faster. Each plunge sends a wave of pleasure rippling through me.

BROKEN DREAM

God, it's been so long.

So fucking long.

She sucks me in so perfectly, as if she was made only for me.

She wraps her legs tighter around my waist, pulling me deeper into her. I can feel her muscles tighten around me as she nears another climax.

I don't stop moving even as she writhes beneath me, her body shaking with pleasure. Her release only spurs me on, and I continue to thrust into her, seeking my own climax.

"Angie," I grunt out, the heat building in the pit of my stomach.

"Jason." She pulls me down, crashing her lips onto mine and muddling our moans together.

That's all it takes for me to tip over the edge. With a deep shudder, I spill into her, my body going rigid as waves of pleasure crash over me. The world blurs around the edges, all sounds fading into a distant hum.

I'm coming.

Coming inside a woman.

A beautiful woman.

But a woman who's not my wife.

Slowly, reality begins to seep back in.

I pull out.

She's still smiling with a look of pure and hazy contentment on her beautiful face.

Oh my God.

What have I done?

We're in her kitchen.

I didn't even take her into the bedroom.

I look down at my dick, still wrapped in the condom.

It was inside another woman.

Lindsay was my first. I didn't have sex until I was in college. Late bloomer, I guess. I've never been inside another woman before.

And I chose Angie. A student. A twenty-three-year-old student.

The desire. The heat between us.

It was new, erotic, forbidden, and so intoxicating that I lost control. Is this how it feels to be with someone else after years of monogamy and then celibacy? To take another woman into my arms, to taste her skin, join our bodies in the best fuck of all time?

A pang of guilt stabs me.

Angie cups my cheek and scrapes her fingers against my stubble. "Jason," she murmurs softly. Her voice is heavy with satisfaction. And with...affection?

I swallow hard, determined to mask my vulnerability. I pull away from her slowly, making sure she's all right before adjusting myself and discarding the condom.

Reality has a nasty way of crashing in. I've crossed a line that should not have been crossed. She's my student, she's younger than I am, and she expects me to guide her through her education.

Not through this.

But what's done is done.

I can't turn back time and undo what just happened between us. In some twisted way, I don't want to, either. As wrong as it may have been, being with Angie felt right—so right that it scares me.

I quickly dress, finding my clothes strewn around in the kitchen.

I need to say something to her...but what?

My heart hammers as I finally muster up the courage to look at her. She meets my gaze, her eyes still shining with warmth, her cheeks flushed a rosy pink.

She's beautiful, no doubt about it.

"Angie," I say. "This... This was..."

Was what?

A mistake? I'm not sure if I can label it as such when every nerve ending in my body is still humming with the pleasure of our encounter.

How can I find the right words?

She shushes me, placing a finger on my lips. "Don't," she murmurs. "Don't spoil it with words."

What she says has merit. How amazing would it be to just revel in the gratification?

But we can't ignore this either.

"No," I say. "We need to talk about this."

She sighs, slides off the counter, and walks over to me, her naked form illuminated by the harsh kitchen lighting.

Fuck.

Gorgeous.

Perfection.

She wraps her arms around my waist and buries her face in my chest, the warmth of her breath seeping through the thin fabric of my shirt.

"Can we not talk about it tonight?" she whispers, her voice heavy with an emotion I can't quite place. "Just for tonight, can we pretend that there's nothing wrong with this? That we're not teacher and student, but just...us?"

I pull her closer and tangle my fingers in her silky hair. "All right."

But just for tonight.

Still naked, she opens the door to a panting Tillie. Then she leads me out of the kitchen and to her bedroom. It's decorated in a soft feminine style. On the wall are black-and-white posters of the Eiffel Tower in Paris, the Ponte Vecchio in Florence, and Big Ben in London. My stomach twists as I realize that these probably hung in her dorm room in undergrad. At least she's bought frames for them.

I turn my attention from the posters to her bed, which is covered in light-yellow plush pillows and blankets. The sight of it, beckoning me over, almost makes me forget about the lines I just crossed.

Almost.

She slides into the bed first, her movements as graceful as a swan. Her eyes never leave mine as I strip off my shirt and toss it on a nearby chair.

"Jason." She pats the empty spot beside her on the bed.

I walk over and sink onto the mattress, the soft fabric molding to my body as I remove the rest of the clothes I just put back on. Angie moves closer to me, tugging at me until I'm lying down next to her. She rests her head on my bare chest and snuggles into my side. I instinctively wrap my arm around her and pull her closer.

As I lie there next to her, breathing in the sweet scent of her hair, I can't help but feel solace in her presence—her soft sighs and the faint rhythm of her heartbeat against my chest.

I don't know how long we lie there, entwined in each other's arms, but I know I could stay like this forever.

"Jason?" Angie's soft voice breaks through the silence. "Thank you."

Thank you?

For what?

For complicating our lives? For crossing a line that should never have been crossed?

But then I look at her face and see the sincerity shining clear in her eyes.

This isn't about propriety or the rules we've broken tonight. It's about us—two people who found solace, comfort, and an unexpected connection.

"I don't regret anything," she continues, her voice a whisper against my skin.

I want to echo her sentiments, tell her that I too harbor no regrets.

But something gnaws at me.

A fear.

A fear that I now yearn for Angie's touch over Lindsay's.

I feel like I've cheated on Lindsay.

But Lindsay is gone.

Dead and buried.

Unable to be helped by the practice that is Angie's passion.

Fuck it all.

I finally desire another woman.

But she's a student.

A future psychiatrist, of all fucking things.

Angie doesn't seem to be concerned that I don't answer, so I just hold her for the next hour, allow her to drift off into a peaceful slumber.

Once I'm sure she's in a deep sleep, I untangle myself from her beautiful body and dress quietly. Tillie sits next to the bed, staring at me.

"Shh," I say to the pup.

She doesn't bark. She's probably glad enough to be rid of

me.
   I leave and return to my own place.
   Where guilt and nightmares plague me.

CHAPTER NINETEEN

ANGIE

I wake up with a smile on my face.

My body feels satiated and wonderful.

Jason...

I move toward the center of the bed...

Disappointment overwhelms me.

He's gone.

And he's been gone for a while. The bed and covers aren't warm at all.

It's Saturday. No classes. So the only reason he would have left without saying goodbye is if...

No. There could be other reasons. He has a life outside of med school. Maybe he's going for a consultation with the doctor who's going to try to repair the nerves in his hand.

Or maybe he has to grade papers. Work on his curriculum.

Speaking of which, I have a lot of studying to do myself.

I can't waste the day away mourning the fact that Jason left me.

He wanted to talk about what happened last night, no doubt to tell me it was a mistake.

I asked him not to spoil it with words.

So he didn't. He let me lead him into my room, and he slid into bed with me, held me.

Then he left.

He left without saying goodbye.

I have to hand it to him—he didn't use words.

Saturday means no teaching for him as well, and now that I think of it, probably no appointments with his doctors either.

Which means he's most likely at home.

I could get up, shower, dress, and go pound on his door.

It's tempting. So tempting.

But though I have no regrets, I know he does. I'm a student, and he no doubt feels like he crossed a line.

I sigh.

If only I could stay in bed all day and relive the passion between us.

It wasn't sweet. It wasn't gentle.

No.

It was raw and feral and animalistic.

And it was perfect.

I've never had sex like that. First of all, it's always been in a bedroom, and second of all, it's never had that rawness, that realness to it.

I never even imagined it could be like that. Never imagined an orgasm could be so intense and long-lasting.

And I want more of it.

But Jason left.

I have to face the fact that this isn't what he wants.

I can't blame him. He shouldn't be sleeping with a student. He and I both know that.

So I lie in bed. I'll give myself half an hour to relive the passion. To feel it again as I slide my hand between my legs.

The orgasm hits me, spreads through the veins in my body, out my fingers and toes and then plummets back to my pussy.

BROKEN DREAM

And it feels good.

But not as good as it felt last night with Jason.

His head between my legs, his tongue tantalizing me...

Nothing will come close to that.

Then how he filled me, his big hard dick inside me as he used my body for his own pleasure.

Oh, to be used that way again.

I check the digital clock on my nightside table. My half hour is up.

Tillie starts to whine at me. How do dogs always seem to know what time it is?

I slide out of bed and lean down to scratch her ears. I quickly put her out to do her business and then traipse to my bathroom and turn on the shower. As I stand under it, washing the earthy and masculine smell of Jason from my body, a profound sense of loss hits me.

I power through anyway.

Once I'm clean and dressed, my hair falling in damp waves around my shoulders, I brew a pot of coffee, scramble a few eggs, and then sit down in my living room with my iPad and textbooks.

I force myself to concentrate on the study of medicine. I can't allow my mind to keep drifting back to Jason and our tryst in my kitchen.

But my God... It's difficult.

The words on the textbooks blur on the page, and the diagrams become blurs as well.

I rise, pace around my coffee table, head back to the kitchen to refill my coffee.

That's it.

I have to confront him. We have to talk about this. I have

HELEN HARDT

to know if it's something more than a onetime thing.

I slide my feet into my boots, throw on my down jacket and muffler, and walk to my door, ready to go to Jason's.

I open the door—

"Oh!" Tabitha stands there holding two cups from Starbucks. "Surprise!"

"Hey, what are you doing here?"

"Bringing you coffee." She walks in without being invited.

"Okay."

She wrinkles her forehead at me. "But you have your coat on. Were you on your way out?"

"Yeah, I was, but I'd rather have coffee with you." I force a smile.

She grins. "Great, because I want to talk to you about something."

Crap.

Has Ralph talked to her? Does she know about Jason's and my kiss?

"You look all flushed," she says, touching my cheek. "Are you feeling okay?"

"I'm fine."

Then she touches my forehead. "I don't know, Angie. You might have a slight fever."

I can't help a soft chuckle. It's a medical student thing. After one semester, most medical students are convinced they can diagnose anything.

"I don't have a fever, Tabitha. I'm fine."

"If you say so." She hands me a cup of the coffee she brought. "Black, no cream and sugar. I remember."

I take it and click the paper cup to hers. "Cheers."

She laughs and takes a sip of the—most likely triple

BROKEN DREAM

mocha—in her cup.

Yeah, it is. She has a slight whipped-cream moustache that she licks off.

I gesture her over to the counter, where she takes a seat. "You hungry? I made some scrambled eggs earlier. I can make some more. Or I have some croissants. My cousin on the Western Slope made them. They're the best you'll ever eat."

"Don't mind if I do," Tabitha says.

I walk to the fridge, but she's right on my heels. Damn. She really does want to talk to me about something.

I grab a couple of Ava's croissants out of the fridge, heat them for a few seconds in the microwave, and then grab some of my mom's spiced peach jam.

"Here you go." I put a croissant on a plate and hand it to her. "Have a seat." I bring the jam over to the table and offer it to her. "My mom makes this stuff from our Western Slope peaches. It's the bomb."

Tabitha spreads some over her croissant and takes a bite. "Oh my God," she says. "I think I just had a tiny orgasm."

I laugh.

I'm beginning to really like Tabitha. She reminds me of Sage, my sister. So outgoing and always up for a good time.

"Glad you like it. I'll let my mom know that her jam is orgasmic."

She closes her eyes. "Not just the jam, but the croissant. You come from a talented family."

She's not wrong. I've always felt like I'm the one who has no talent. I'm not outgoing, not an artist like Gina, I can't cook like my mom, bake like Ava, make wine like Dale and Uncle Ryan.

But what I *can* do is care. Have empathy. Which is why I

decided to follow Aunt Melanie into psychiatry.

"So..." Tabitha begins.

Shit. Here it comes. She's going to mention—

"What do you think of Ralph?" she asks.

I raise my eyebrows. Ralph? Okay. Not what I was expecting. She's the one who said he was being a dick yesterday. Unless he told her what he saw...

"Honestly?" I ask.

She swallows a bite of croissant. "Well, yeah. I wouldn't be asking you otherwise."

Do I tell her the truth? That he came on to me in my kitchen and tried to kiss me? That when I rebuffed his advances, he threatened to go to the dean about the kiss I shared with Jason? Which would not only end his teaching career but would also make me a pariah among my peers?

Better to leave all that out.

I scratch my nose. "We talked about this, didn't we? I think he's kind of a dick."

She wrinkles her forehead. "He did have that weird moment when we were all here for pizza. But... I don't know. Something about him... I kind of like him, and... He's hot." She bites her lip. "Guess I've got a bit of a thing for older men."

You and me both, sister.

That's what I want to say. But I don't know if I trust Tabitha enough to let her know about my ongoing romance— or whatever it is—with Jason.

So I just shrug. "He's good-looking, yeah. I don't know if I'd go so far as hot."

She giggles. "Well, I stalked you online, of course. I saw your two brothers—one blond, one with brown hair. They put the heat in hot. Is everyone in your family good-looking?"

BROKEN DREAM

My cheeks warm. "I don't know about that." A lie, of course. My entire family is great-looking. Besides the fact that we're rich, that's the second thing people know about us.

"Lucky." She narrows her eyes coyly. "Are your brothers available?"

"Dave is newly married." I scratch my chin. "Henry's not seeing anyone, though. But he's a lot older."

She waggles her eyebrows. "Like I said, I like older." Her bright eyes deflate slightly. "But jeez, Angie, something about Ralph..."

I really don't need her getting close to Ralph. One, because he's a dick and Tabitha deserves better. And two, because if they get close, he might spill the beans about Jason and me.

So I'm going to push her gently in another direction.

"Why not Eli? He's got his eye on you. You'd have to be blind not to see it."

She purses her lips. "He's sort of cute, in a Jeff Goldblum kind of way." She rolls her eyes. "But he and I are just study buddies. Besides, he's so devoted to school and surgery. I imagine he's not going to date for the next ten years."

"I don't know," I say. "I think you could convince him to give dating a try."

She scoffs. "He's like my brother, but Ralph... I was hoping you'd say he's not a dick after all."

I sigh. Do I out him? And if Tabitha is really interested in Ralph, I should probably tell her that he came on to me.

But I don't want to hurt her.

She and I aren't besties. Maybe we could be, but we haven't known each other long enough or spent enough time together.

Tabitha is like my sister. She'll go up and talk to anyone.

Pretend they've known each other forever.

I'm not like that.

But if I want Tabitha to be my friend, to trust me as a friend, I owe her the truth.

I grab her hand. "If I tell you something, will you promise you won't hold it against me?"

She raises an eyebrow. "Why would I do that?"

I sigh. "The other night when we were studying here, Ralph...came on to me in the kitchen."

She doesn't reply. In fact, I can't read her expression at all.

"Uh-oh." She bites her lip. "So I guess you two..."

"No, of course not. I just told you he's a dick."

She widens her eyes. "Oh my God, he didn't force you, did he?"

"No, he stopped when I told him to."

She rolls her eyes. "So he's not a rapist. Great."

I frown. "But he did threaten me. Sort of."

She leans in, her voice hushed. "My God, what do you mean?"

How much can I tell her? Do I open up to her about Jason? Do I trust her enough to do that?

Damn. I really don't know what to do.

I press my lips together. "He just said...he'd expose something he knew about me."

She drops her jaw, her eyes gleaming. "Oh my God. What?"

"It's...nothing I'm real comfortable talking about. I'm sorry about that, but I hope you understand."

She pats me on the hand. "Angie, we're friends, aren't we?"

Again, just like Sage. Everyone's a friend.

But I'm not like that.

I'm about to answer her—how, I'm not sure—when my doorbell rings.

Never has *saved by the bell* meant more to me.

CHAPTER TWENTY

JASON

Lindsay.
    Julia.
    Angie.
    All ghosts in my nightmare.
    Love.
    Loss.
    I toss and turn as I wake, the echoes of their names still whispering in my ears. The room is filled with darkness and the chill of night, and I'm haunted by memories I'd rather forget. With a heavy sigh, I sit up in bed.
    Lindsay.
    Her laugh was like the tinkling of wind chimes on a breezy afternoon. The way her eyes sparkled when she looked at me, as if I held all the secrets of the universe. Each memory feels like a shard of glass, sharp and painful.
    Julia.
    My baby, her laugh so contagious. So young and innocent.
    Their absence is a tangible presence in this hollow room, filling up every forgotten corner. I can almost hear Lindsay's laughter intertwined with Julia's childish giggles.
    My heart yearns for them, my soul cries out for their touch. But all I get is silence.

BROKEN DREAM

Then...Angie.

So quietly vibrant, a beacon of light in my bleak world.

Sleep is a distant wish once I banish the nightmare.

Lindsay.

Her touch used to bring comfort on sleepless nights.

Julia.

Watching her sleep was a sight that could mend any broken heart. Her little snores and dreaming twitches were so full of life and peace.

Guilt.

Remorse.

Regret.

Anger.

Rage.

They're all there, taking me back to the void where I spent most of the past three years.

Until her.

Until Angie.

I let out a huff.

This is all ridiculous.

I untangle myself from my blanket and get out of bed, not bothering to shower. I splash some cold water on my face and riffle my fingers through my hair.

I have a day's worth of beard growth. Scruffy. Messy. I don't care.

I throw on a pair of jeans, sweatshirt, moccasin slippers.

Then I grab my leather jacket and walk the three doors to Angie's place, where I ring the doorbell.

A moment later, she opens the door.

She looks like an angel. Her dark hair is damp from a shower. She's wearing leggings and a large sweatshirt that says

146

HELEN HARDT

Steel Vineyards on it. Her feet are bare, toes painted red.

Why didn't I notice that last night?

Red toenails.

Lindsay never would've worn red. She thought it was too garish.

Angie seems too quiet to be a red-toenails girl, yet here she is.

She widens her eyes upon seeing me. "Jason. Good morning."

I walk past her into her home but then stop short.

Another one of my students is here. Tabitha. The same one who showed up the day I realized I lived three doors down from Angie.

Fuck. She's caught me here twice now. She's going to be suspicious.

I take a few steps back. "Oh. I'm sorry. I didn't realize you had company."

"Dr. Lansing," Tabitha says. "It's good to see you again."

"Jason, please." I give her an awkward wave. "Hi, Tabitha."

Tabitha stares at me. No doubt because I look like I tumbled right out of bed. Which, of course, I did.

I can see the gears shifting behind her eyes. She's wondering why I'm here. Why I always seem to show up at my student's house.

And the obvious conclusion she's going to come to is exactly what happened.

"We're...um...having coffee." Tabitha gestures to the two paper cups on the coffee table. "I only brought two, but I'm sure Angie can make a pot."

"No, that's not necessary. I just came over to..." I search for the words in my mind.

147

None come.

"To say hello," I finally finish, aware of how hollow the words sound.

Angie, bless her, doesn't question my intrusion and instead offers a gentle smile.

"Hello then, Jason," she says, her voice soft.

My heart lurches at the sound of my name on her lips.

Tabitha looks between us, the curiosity in her eyes magnifying. I ignore the look and focus on Angie.

Her eyes meet mine, and for a moment we get lost in each other's gaze. I find myself drowning in the depth, and it's both terrifying and comforting.

Angie breaks the silence first. "You are welcome to have coffee with us if you'd like, Jason."

It's a simple statement, but it holds so much more under its surface. It's an act of reaching out in friendship, the same as she's doing with Tabitha.

At least that's what I tell myself.

"Sure," I hear myself saying before I can stop myself.

Coffee with two students is fine.

It's Saturday, and Angie is my neighbor.

Tabitha looks at me, her head cocked, but Angie shoots her a reassuring smile and walks to her kitchen.

I stay standing, saying nothing, until Tabitha excuses herself and goes into the kitchen with Angie. A few minutes later, the smell of freshly brewed coffee fills the townhome. I inhale the warm and comforting aroma. It takes me back to those mornings with Lindsay when we used to sit on our small balcony with two mugs of coffee and watch the world wake up while Julia was still asleep in her crib.

"Jason, do you take cream and sugar?" Angie calls from

the kitchen.

"No," I reply, shaking myself out of my thoughts. "Just black."

A moment later she and Tabitha emerge. Angie hands me a steaming mug and gestures toward the living area. I take a seat on a recliner, while Angie and Tabitha sit across from me on the leather couch.

Tabitha's expression is curious. I'm sure she's wondering what I'm doing here. Why would I come over on a Saturday morning just to say hi to one of my students?

She's not wrong to question it.

"Anatomy," I say out of the blue.

Both women look at me, Angie with a hint of amusement flickering in her eyes, Tabitha with confusion.

"We're studying anatomy," I say. "You're both my students, and we're bound to bump into each other from time to time since we're neighbors."

What the hell did I just say?

"Yeah, of course," Angie says.

"What does that have to do with anatomy?" Tabitha asks.

I raise my eyebrows. "Doesn't everything a person does have to do with anatomy?"

I'm talking in circles. She's going to think I'm high or something.

"I... I mean..." Tabitha takes a sip of coffee. "Never mind. I missed having lab yesterday. I hope everything is okay with you."

"Why wouldn't it be?" I ask.

"You canceled lab and all," she says.

Right. I did. For my appointment with Louisa and Gita.

Good news. Hopeful news. Which I celebrated by fucking

my student.

"Yes, everything is fine," I say. "Something came up. An unforeseen appointment. But we'll be back in lab next Thursday to begin cutting."

"I wish we could have lab every day." Tabitha grabs a spoon and absentmindedly stirs her coffee. "Not just Thursdays and Fridays."

I'm not sure what to say to that. That's when the lab is scheduled, Thursday and Friday mornings.

Angie, on the other hand, is looking a little green around the gills. "We'll be cutting on Thursday?" she asks.

"Yes. I'm sorry we couldn't start yesterday as planned."

Tabitha is beaming. "I can't wait."

"And you, Angie?" I ask.

She blinks for a few seconds before responding. "I'm looking forward to *learning*." She bows her head.

I know how she feels about cutting into cadavers. She's made that very clear.

"No matter what kind of medicine you decide to practice, you'll still be a medical doctor," I say, "which means you need to learn anatomy in lab."

"I know, I know," Angie says. "I'll be fine. I promise."

I have no doubt she'll be fine. Most of them are really looking forward to this, like Tabitha.

I finish my coffee quickly. Then I stand. "I should let you get back to your studies. Thank you for the coffee, Angie."

"Of course. You're welcome. Anytime." She bites her lower lip. "Anything for...a neighbor."

I nod as my cock responds to the glistening full lip she's nibbling.

Then I leave.

I still need to talk to her.

Figure out what the hell this is between us.

And make sure it never happens again.

CHAPTER TWENTY-ONE

ANGIE

Of course Tabitha pounces as soon as Jason leaves.

"What on earth was *that* about?" she gasps.

I attempt to shrug nonchalantly. "He lives a couple of doors down in another townhome. He was just...checking up on me. I think he lives alone. Probably gets bored."

She cocks her head, her lips pressed together. "I wish *I* had hot professor neighbors."

"What do you mean by that?" I say a little more harshly than I mean to.

Her eyebrows rise a bit. "I just mean, if you have questions about anything. He's right here. Able to answer them."

I swallow. "I'll save my questions for class."

"But don't you find it strange that he just showed up at your place to say hi this morning?"

No, I didn't find it strange at all, considering we fucked like bunnies last night. In fact, I very much want to talk to him. But I can't let Tabitha know any of this.

Part of me really wants to confide in her. Tell her what went on, how Jason made me feel. How he came to me to celebrate something good that happened to him.

But I don't know Tabitha well enough. What if she's a big gossip? Or worse, what if she has a dark side and uses this information as leverage to get me to do what she wants?

I already have Ralph to deal with.

"No," I say in response to her question. "He's just being neighborly and all."

She furrows her eyebrows. "He looked like he'd just gotten right out of bed." She sighs. "Man, is he ever good-looking."

"Yeah, he is," I say.

I can't lie to her. We all have eyes.

"Well, I won't keep you." She downs the rest of her cup of coffee. "I really just came over to bring you the coffee and ask you about Ralph. You certainly made your feelings known about him."

I bite my lip. "Yeah, but that doesn't mean you can't like him."

She sighs. "He's just so gorgeous. I can't believe he tried to blackmail you about something."

The question is apparent in her voice. She wants me to confide in her.

If I knew I could trust her, I would. But we just don't know each other well enough. So I simply say, "It's not the first time. When you come from money and all..."

Not exactly true. It is the first time for me. But not for other members of my family.

"Can I tell you something?" Tabitha asks me.

Oh, great. She's thinking if she confides in me about something, then I'll confide in her.

I'm a vault, of course. I keep secrets all the time for Sage, Gina, and Brianna. They all come to me when they need to talk but can't risk anyone finding out.

I'm the keeper of secrets in our little foursome.

The awesome foursome. That nickname kind of makes

BROKEN DREAM

me want to gag now.

"Sure, if you want to," I say to Tabitha.

She takes a deep breath and then nods, as if she's squaring up her thoughts. "It's about Ralph," she begins, and I can't help but feel my stomach tighten at the mention of his name. "We met last semester at orientation, and we..." She draws in a breath. "We had a one-nighter. Neither one of us mentioned it again. And he *was* a dick yesterday. But I can't help that I'm feeling things."

I keep my face neutral, not wanting her to see the surprise that's definitely written there.

"You're not saying anything," she says, sounding slightly worried. "Do you think it's weird?"

"No," I quickly say, shaking my head. "No, it's not weird. We've all had one-nighters. And you like who you like. It's not like you can control who you're attracted to."

"But he tried to blackmail you." She wrings her hands in her lap.

"He did." I shrug slightly. "But that's between me and him. You shouldn't let it affect your feelings." A pang of pity for her shoots through me. I can't imagine how she must be feeling right now, being caught between her feelings for Ralph and the fact that he tried to blackmail her friend. "You can always talk to me," I assure her.

"You can talk to me too," she says.

I smile.

Nope. Still not giving it up. Not until I'm sure I can trust her.

"I guess I'll get over Ralph," she says. "I mean, it was just sex. We didn't have any classes together last semester, so I hardly saw him, but now, with lab... And he and Eli are lab partners and all."

"Listen," I say. "You can do a lot better than Ralph. Sure, he's decent-looking, but think about Eli. He's really cute in a nerdy kind of way."

"Nah," she says. "That'll never happen."

"If you say so. But Ralph..."

She holds up a hand. "I get it. You think he's a dick, and you have a valid reason for thinking it." She pauses a moment. "You can talk to me, you know."

Gads.

She really wants me to spill it.

I sigh.

"He saw me...kissing someone," I say.

She wrinkles her forehead. "So what? He wants to blackmail you over that?"

"It was..."

"Go on..." she urges.

"It was someone who's...in a relationship with someone else," I say, scrambling. "He threatened to tell the other woman."

"Oh my God, who was it?" A devilish grin curls across her lips. "And what were you doing kissing somebody else's boyfriend?"

I clear my throat, struggling to find more words. "I don't want to add fuel to the fire, so I won't say who it was. But Tabitha, you have to believe me. I didn't know he was in a relationship."

She drops her jaw. "Was it Jonathan Baxter? He's so hot, and I think he just started dating someone."

Jonathan Baxter? I don't even know who the hell that is.

"No. It was someone else."

"You know you can trust me."

I shake my head. "I can't say any more. Please understand."

She scoffs. "I thought we were friends."

Friends? We hardly said two words to each other before we became lab partners.

"You remind me a lot of my sister," I say, smiling.

She cocks her head. "I hope that's a good thing."

"Yeah, it's a good thing. We're twins. Not identical, but we look a lot alike. But she's way more outgoing than I am. Always wants to pounce on the latest gossip. Becomes besties with people within about five minutes. You're just like her, Tab."

"See?" She pokes me in the shoulder. "We're friends. You're using a nickname."

"I can't possibly be the first person to call you Tab."

"No, but most people—my family—call me Tabby. Which I hate. My dad calls me Tibs, which I would hate from anyone else, but from my dad I don't mind."

"Well, I'm happy to call you Tab. But you need to give me a few more days. I'm not like Sage."

"Sage?"

"Yeah, that's my sister."

She nods. "That's a really pretty name."

"Yeah. She was named after a friend of my grandmother's who died when she was young. My mother really liked the name."

"Who were you named after?"

"My mother. Her first name is Angela, but she goes by her middle name, Marjorie."

"Sage and Angela are both beautiful names." She wrinkles her nose. "So much better than Tabitha."

"Tabitha's a great name."

"Yeah, if you like being named after a character in an old TV sitcom."

I raise my eyebrows. "You were seriously named after an old TV show?"

"Yeah. From an old sitcom called *Bewitched*. My sister's name is Samantha."

"Oh, that's a gorgeous name."

"Yes. Much better than Tabitha." She shrugs. "But I'm used to it. You want some more coffee?"

"No, I'm good. But I can get you a cup."

"No." She sighs. "I should get going. I have so much studying to do."

"You can study here if you want. We can help each other."

She smiles. "I'd like that. If we spend more time together, maybe you'll start to trust me."

"It's not that—"

She gestures me to quiet. "It's okay, Angie. It takes you time to make friends. I get it. Once you get to know me, you're going to love me."

I laugh then. "You know what? I think you're right."

CHAPTER TWENTY-TWO

JASON

I don't go back to see Angie again.

Even though I know we need to talk, I can't bring myself to do it. To have the conversation that has to be.

I continue checking in with Louisa every now and then to see if they found a suitable nerve for my graft.

Finally, Thursday rolls around.

Anatomy lab.

I'll see Angie.

And we'll cut into the cadavers for the first time.

I get to class early and wait for the students to arrive.

I stand at the front of the room, the faint smell of formaldehyde heavy in the air, and look at the covered bodies on the lab tables.

The students begin to file in and gather around their cadavers. They pull on their gloves.

Angie doesn't look at me.

She doesn't look at her cadaver, either, though Tabitha has a huge smile on her face and is clearly eager to begin.

"All right," I begin, keeping my voice steady. "Before we start, I want to remind you again that these donors made a choice to be here, to give you the opportunity to learn. Treat them with the respect they deserve. Every incision you make today is not just about anatomy. It's about honoring that choice."

I walk to the table next to Angie's. "Your first task is to uncover the thoracic and abdominal region like we did last week. Only the area we'll be working on today. The rest stays covered. You'll find that keeping the rest of the body draped helps preserve the tissue and keeps you focused. It's also a way to honor the modesty of the patient you're working on."

Most of the students nod, and some murmur in agreement.

"Peel back the sheet slowly, folding it over itself as you did before." I demonstrate on the cadaver where I'm standing, lifting the drape gently and folding it toward the cadaver's feet.

The skin beneath is pale and slightly discolored.

"Good. Now, you'll notice the midline here." I trace my gloved finger along the linea alba, the faint ridge that runs down the abdomen. "This is your guide. It's a natural anatomical landmark, free of major blood vessels, which makes it the ideal place for your first incision."

I pause and look around the room to make sure every student is paying attention.

"This first cut is about precision, not depth. You're not trying to get all the way through in one go. Start with a shallow incision and then gradually deepen it layer by layer. Think of this as peeling an onion. Skin, fascia, muscle—each layer needs your care."

I pick up a scalpel from the tray. "Hold your scalpel like this." I demonstrate a firm but controlled grip. "And when you're ready, make your incision from the base of the sternum here"—I point—"to just above the pubic bone. Use smooth, even pressure, and let the blade do the work."

I hand the scalpel to a student at the table and step back.

159

BROKEN DREAM

"Take your time. There's no rush. Remember, this is your first step into understanding the human body—not just in theory, but in reality. And that's what being here is all about."

I move around the room slowly, the sound of gloves snapping and metal clinking filling the air as students pick up their scalpels. Some are already diving in, too eager, while others hesitate, their hands hovering over the cadaver.

"Linda," I say, stopping at a table. She's gripping her scalpel like it's a knife in a bad action movie, her knuckles surely white underneath her gloves. "Relax your grip. You're not hacking at it. You're guiding the blade. Loosen up, like this." I demonstrate with a practiced motion.

Linda nods and adjusts her grip. Her partner, Jonathan, looks more comfortable.

Moving on, I hear Tabitha murmuring to Angie at their table in the front. "I just don't want to mess this up," she says, her voice barely above a whisper.

"You won't," Angie replies, her tone calm, reassuring.

Tabitha's hands are already steady, her scalpel poised. My chest tightens as I approach their table, the pull of Angie's presence something I wish I could ignore. I force my focus to Tabitha instead.

"Tabitha," I say, keeping my voice light but firm. "It's not about speed. Just take it one layer at a time. Look at how the skin stretches slightly before the blade cuts. That's your cue to use even pressure."

She nods, her movements jerky but improving as she follows my guidance. Angie doesn't look up, but I feel her awareness of me, like a current passing between us. I grip the edge of the table to ground myself and clear my throat.

"Good work," I say briskly, stepping back and turning my

HELEN HARDT

attention to the next group.

Elijah and Ralph are next. Elijah is already slicing, his confidence almost startling.

"Elijah, you're a natural." I nod as he makes smooth, even cuts.

He beams, but Ralph looks less certain.

"Ralph, it's okay to press a little more," I say, standing beside him. "The tissue won't tear if you're controlled. Let the blade do the work, not your hand."

"I'm *trying,*" he says a little sharply.

I raise an eyebrow. "Everything all right there, Ralph?"

He glares at me for just a moment. But then his eyes soften as he realizes who he's talking to. "Sorry, Dr. Lansing. Just a little overexcited, I guess."

I pat him gently on the shoulder. "We all react differently on the first day. Not a problem, Ralph. Just keep yourself focused."

He nods, his eyes narrowed at me. "I will, Dr. Lansing."

"Call me Jason, please."

"Right. Jason." He exhales sharply, nodding as he finally pushes down with just enough force to make a clean incision.

"There you go. Perfect," I say. "Keep going like that."

As I move back toward the center of the room, I glance at Angie again. She's leaning over the cadaver, her hair tucked neatly under her surgical cap. She's not cutting. So far she's letting Tabitha do everything.

If it were any other student, I'd put a stop to it, tell them they both need to share the burden equally.

But I can't. Not today. The idea of standing there, close enough to catch the faintest trace of whatever perfume lingers on Angie's skin, feels dangerous. Unprofessional. I continue

BROKEN DREAM

walking, keeping my distance, focusing on the others.

Next time, I'll make sure Angie cuts.

Next time.

"Linda, how's it going now?" I ask, circling back.

"Better," she mutters, her voice tight with concentration.

"Good. That's what I like to hear."

As I circle back to Tabitha and Angie's table, I linger despite myself. Tabitha is focused, her brow furrowed as she carefully deepens her incision, the tension in her shoulders giving away how hard she's concentrating. But it's Angie who catches my attention—or, more specifically, her stillness. Her gloved hands hover above the cadaver, the scalpel poised but unmoving, as though the blade weighs a hundred pounds.

"Tabitha," I say, my voice steady, "you're doing well. Just follow the natural line. Smooth, even strokes."

Tabitha nods, offering a quiet, "Thank you."

Angie still hasn't said a word, her body stiff, her face pale. She's staring down at the incision, not with curiosity or focus, but with something else—something closer to dread.

This time I have to say something.

I force myself to keep my tone neutral, professional. "Angie, is everything all right?"

She nods quickly, but it's unconvincing. "Yes, I'm fine," she says, her voice so quiet it's almost a whisper.

I know she's lying.

The room is alive with the sound of scalpels slicing through preserved flesh, whispered conversations, and the occasional clink of instruments being set down. But at this table, there's a heaviness, a tension that feels like it's drawing my attention no matter how much I want to ignore it.

"Tabitha," I say, keeping my voice steady, "you're doing

great. Time for a break."

She widens her eyes but then puts down her scalpel, clearly okay with stepping away for a minute.

I step around the table, moving to Angie's side. I shouldn't. I should let her figure it out on her own or pair her up with someone else later. But something in me—something I don't want to name—won't let me walk away.

"Angie," I murmur. "Talk to me. What's going on?"

Her shoulders tighten, and for a moment, I think she won't answer. But then she exhales, her breath shaky. "I don't know if I can do this," she says, her words rushing out in a quiet, desperate tumble. "I thought I could, but... I just... I don't want to cut into someone."

I nod slowly. "I know this is hard, especially if you intend for your focus to be psychiatry. But this part of your training isn't just about learning anatomy. It's about understanding the body as a whole, even if your work someday focuses on the mind. You don't have to like it, but it's important."

She swallows hard, her gaze fixed on the untouched scalpel in her hand. "I understand that," she says, barely above a whisper. "But it feels...wrong. Like I'm disrespecting them."

Her words hit me in a way I wasn't expecting. "You're not disrespecting them, Angie. This person chose to donate their body to help you learn. To help you become the kind of doctor who saves lives. What you're doing here honors that choice."

It's nothing I haven't said before. She knows that as well as I do. I don't expect my words to change her attitude now if they haven't already.

She doesn't respond right away, her jaw tight as she stares down at the cadaver. I want to tell her she can step back, let Tabitha take the lead—but that won't help her. She needs to

BROKEN DREAM

find her own way through this.

"Start small," I say gently. "One shallow cut. You don't have to rush or go deep. Just get a feel for it. You might surprise yourself."

She glances up at me again, and there's a flicker of trust in her eyes now. She nods, her movements hesitant, but she sets the blade against the cadaver's pale skin. Her hand trembles slightly as she presses down, the scalpel gliding over the surface. It's a small cut, almost tentative, but it's a start.

"There you go," I say quietly. "That's all it takes. One step at a time."

I step back to give her space. Tabitha shoots me a quick look as she returns, confused but not questioning. Angie keeps her focus on her work, her lips pressed into a thin line, but her hand steadies with each pass of the blade.

I exhale, moving to the next table, but my thoughts linger. Angie is stronger than she thinks. I just hope I can keep my focus where it belongs—on teaching her, not on the way she makes my chest tighten every time I'm near.

But all I can think about is how I felt inside her, how I want to feel it again.

CHAPTER TWENTY-THREE

Angie

The scalpel feels heavier than it should, like it's mocking me.

Tabitha is doing fine, her focus locked on the pale line of her incision, her movements confident and precise. I should be grateful she's not pressuring me to take over, but her calm competence only makes me feel worse. My chest tightens as I stare at the cadaver, and I can't bring myself to make another cut.

Across the room, Jason is with another group, his voice steady as he gives instructions. I can't hear exactly what he's saying, but his tone carries that same calm authority, that quiet encouragement that somehow makes you feel like you can't fail as long as he's there. I steal a glance at him, watching the way he leans slightly toward one of the students, his hands moving confidently as he demonstrates the proper grip on a scalpel. He makes it look so easy, so natural.

I wonder what he's thinking. If he's disappointed in me.

I shake my head, trying to shove the thoughts away. This isn't about him—it can't be about him. I'm here to learn, to focus, but my brain doesn't seem to care. Every time I hear his voice, every time he moves into my line of sight, my stomach twists into a knot. It's not just that he's good at what he does, though he is. It's the way he carries himself, the way he seems to command the room without trying. The way his green eyes flicker with an intensity that makes me feel seen, even when I'm trying my hardest to disappear.

"Angie," Tabitha says softly, jolting me out of my thoughts. She's still focused on the cadaver, her voice quiet but steady. "Do you want to take the next layer?"

My throat tightens. "Uh...no, you go ahead." I pretend to adjust my gloves.

Tabitha doesn't push. Why would she? If I choose not to cut, she gets to do it more, and she *wants* to do it.

She nods and continues working, and I hate myself for feeling both relieved and ashamed. I glance toward Jason again—he's with Jennifer and Tobias now, correcting Tobias's grip on the scalpel. He's patient, focused. A perfect teacher, and as I watch him, I can imagine what a perfect and precise surgeon he was before his hand injury.

"Angie," Tabitha cuts through my thoughts. "Are you okay?"

I nod quickly, too quickly. "Yeah, I'm fine."

But I know I'm not fine. Not even close.

I glance at Jason again, my pulse quickening. He's helping Jennifer and Tobias, leaning over the table to guide Tobias's hand with a calm, steady presence. His voice is low, clear, and even though he's too far away for me to hear what he's saying, I can almost feel the warmth of it curling in the pit of my stomach.

It's been a week. Just seven days, and I still can't stop thinking about him. About the way he showed up at my door unannounced, a bottle of wine in one hand and that hesitant grin on his face. He said he wanted to celebrate—some good news from a specialist about a possible surgery that might fix the nerve damage in his hand.

I poured the wine, trying to act casual, but I felt the tension simmering between us. The next minute we were fucking in my kitchen.

"Angie," he'd murmured, his voice low and rough, his forehead resting against mine. "This can't happen..."

But it already had.

And neither of us stopped it.

Now, standing in the bright and sterile lab, the memory of that night feels like a secret I'm carrying around, too heavy and too precious all at once. I shouldn't be thinking about him like this, especially not here, not while I'm supposed to be focused on my first dissection. But every time I hear his voice or catch a glimpse of him out of the corner of my eye, the memory crashes over me again—his hands in my hair, the way he pulled me close, the quiet way he said my name like it meant something more.

"Angie." Tabitha's voice jolts me back to the present. She's watching me, her brow furrowed. "Are you sure you're okay? You haven't made another cut yet."

I nod, gripping the scalpel tighter. "Yeah, I'm fine," I mumble.

Tabitha glances toward Jason. "Do you want me to ask him to come help us?"

"No!" I say too sharply, too fast.

Tabitha's eyebrows shoot up.

I scramble to recover. "I mean, no, it's fine. I can figure it out."

The last thing I need is Jason standing next to me, close enough to catch his scent, close enough for him to see the flush rising in my cheeks, the way my hands won't stop shaking. I'm already unraveling, and having him near would only make it worse.

Across the room, he looks up briefly. For a split second, our gazes meet, and my breath catches. His expression doesn't change—calm, professional—but there's something in his eyes, something flickering behind that composed exterior, that makes me wonder if he's thinking about it too.

I drop my gaze back to the cadaver, my cheeks burning. My hand trembles as I position the scalpel.

It's been a week, and I thought I could push it aside, bury it beneath work and focus and sheer willpower. But Jason is here, and so am I. And no matter how much I try to pretend nothing happened, I can't stop remembering how it felt to cross that line—and how much I want to do it again.

I force the thought out of my mind and make a cut.

"Good," Tabitha says softly, her voice steady and encouraging. "You've got it. Just follow the line."

I nod, not trusting myself to speak, and focus on deepening the incision, layer by layer. My hands are steadier now, but my thoughts are anything but. Jason's presence is still like a current in the room, tugging at me even when I'm not looking at him. I can feel him moving from table to table, his voice calm, his attention focused on everyone else.

Everyone but me.

Which is exactly how it should be. Exactly how I *need* it to be.

But when I glance up, just for a moment, my resolve wavers. He's at the far end of the room now, his hand resting lightly on the edge of a table as he speaks to Eli and Ralph. He looks so composed, so in control, like nothing could ever shake him. Like the Jason who was in my townhome, his hands gripping my waist, his mouth on mine, was a different man entirely.

I drop my gaze again, my pulse quickening. I focus on the cadaver, on the precise line I'm carving into its surface. This is what matters. This is why I'm here. Not Jason. Not the memory of his hands, his voice, his kiss.

Forget that this used to be a living human. It's merely a shell now. A tool of science.

"Angie," Tabitha says. "That's great. Just keep going. You're doing fine."

I nod again, muttering a quiet "Thanks."

But as I finish the cut, I feel the weight of someone's gaze. My stomach twists, and I know before I look that it's him.

Jason is watching me from across the room, his expression unreadable, but his eyes—his eyes tell a different story. They linger on me for just a second too long before he turns back to his students, resuming his explanation as though nothing happened. As though the look wasn't loaded with the same tension I've been trying to bury all week.

I exhale and grip the scalpel tighter as I move to the next layer of tissue.

I can't afford to think about Jason. Not here, not now. But no matter how hard I try, I can't ignore the way my body reacts to his presence, the way my heart races every time I catch him looking at me.

This is dangerous, and I know it.

But even as I force myself to make the next cut, I can't help but wonder how much longer we can keep pretending nothing happened before the tension between us becomes impossible to hide.

CHAPTER TWENTY-FOUR

JASON

I've been staying away from Angie and Tabitha's table as much as I can. I don't want to seem like I'm hovering.

Plus, I can't show any favoritism.

Just being in the same room with Angie is difficult. All I want to do is touch her, run my fingers over her flesh, feel her heart beating next to mine.

She's probably angry with me for leaving late in the night. And rightfully so.

But too much is going on in my life right now. I have a chance to become a surgeon again. To take back some of what life has taken from me.

While I'll never get Lindsay or Julia back, perhaps I can at least get my livelihood. I was a talented surgeon—quickly becoming one of the best in the field.

And then—

It all came crashing down.

For so long I didn't care. I never wanted to wield the scalpel again. Because the accident cost me two things I valued more than my ability to cut into human flesh.

The grief never goes away. The loss is always with me.

But it does begin to hurt less.

I didn't believe anyone at the time. I certainly never

believed that idiot psychiatrist who promised me she could help Lindsay.

Day by day, I've learned to cope, to exist.

To exist in a world without Julia and Lindsay.

To exist in a world where I can no longer perform surgery.

Of course, that was all it was. Existing.

But now I have hope.

But I have something else as well.

Something I'm not keen to give up.

I've met a woman. A woman who speaks to me in ways I never imagined I could hear again.

A woman who is different from Lindsay.

But a woman who almost makes me believe I can feel again.

Because already I'm feeling things. Feelings I've never felt before.

It frightens me. Especially since she's a student.

And that is why I left her in the middle of the night. I shouldn't have been there in the first place, but...

I'm finding it harder and harder to make excuses for my behavior.

Because quite frankly, I'm not sorry it happened. And while I've been focused on the surgery and the hope that it's given me, just as much of my focus has been on Angie Simpson.

It's forbidden.

Taboo.

And I've given that some thought. Is that why I'm so attracted to her? Because it's so wrong?

But I've been teaching for two years. Four semesters. I've taught many beautiful women, but not one of them has affected me like Angie Simpson has.

BROKEN DREAM

We finish up lab, and as I give the instructions, I deliberately look away from Angie.

The students did well today. Most of them were excited to start cutting—all of them except for Angie.

But she did it.

She faced her fears, and she made the cut with as much precision as I've seen any first-year medical student make.

She has the gift. She may not want to be a surgeon, but she could be.

The other two students in the class who seem to be the most gifted are her lab partner, Tabitha, and Elijah Garrett.

But they all did well.

"Excellent work," I say as I dismiss the class. "Same time tomorrow, and we'll continue this exercise."

Then they applaud.

I'm not sure what they're applauding. Certainly not my lecture. They've heard me lecture before. They must be applauding the fact that they cut today for the first time.

But Angie's not clapping.

She's looking down at her cadaver as she covers it. And I see her mouth the words *thank you*.

She's something else.

I made it clear in our first lecture what a gift this was, how we should be grateful for these amazing people who gave us the ultimate gift of their bodies to study and learn from.

She took it to heart.

This is a woman who probably thanks the animal before she eats a steak.

In fact I wouldn't doubt it, since she comes from a family of beef ranchers.

She's something else, Angie Simpson.

Emotions coil through me—emotions I haven't felt in so long. Emotions I didn't think I was capable of feeling any longer.

And some of it...

Some of it's *not* familiar.

And because it's not—because I'm feeling something that I don't think I ever felt for my wife—guilt overwhelms me.

How can I feel something for another woman that I never felt for Lindsay? I always thought Lindsay and I were soulmates. Perhaps we were. Perhaps you don't have just one soulmate.

I'm not in love with Angie Simpson. I barely know her.

But I feel a pull. A magnetic attraction that yanks at my chest, twisting my heart in perplexing directions. I feel a connection, an undercurrent of shared understanding that seems to bind us like an invisible thread.

It's different from what I had with Lindsay. Our love was comfortable, solid as the ground beneath our feet. Perhaps it lacked the raw intensity I'm grappling with now, but it had a quiet strength, a resilience that lasted through good times and bad. Until it got too bad for either of us to handle.

With Angie, everything is new and disturbingly intense. There's an odd familiarity about her that has nothing to do with memories or past experiences. It feels more like a deep-rooted knowledge, as if some part of me recognizes her from other lives lived long ago. And since I don't believe in that stuff, it's all the more frightening.

Guilt gnaws at me, making every breath a struggle. Is it fair? Is it right to have such feelings for someone else when my love for Lindsay still lingers?

But then again, isn't love supposed to be selfless?

BROKEN DREAM

Isn't love supposed to be a celebration of another's existence, rather than an obligation driven by guilt? Perhaps it's not my attraction to Angie that belittles my feelings for Lindsay, but the guilt itself. It's the guilt that makes me question, that breeds self-doubt and regret.

I haven't told Angie about Lindsay. About Julia.

Every time I look at Angie, I see a different life, one filled with possibilities and happiness. A life where my heart doesn't feel like it's made of lead, where guilt doesn't gnaw incessantly at every moment of joy.

But for that life to exist, do I have to erase Lindsay and Julia from my past?

None of that matters anyway.

Angie is my student.

I need to stop this before it goes so far that neither of us can take it back.

I head out to lunch when my phone buzzes. It's Louisa.

"Hi there," I say into the phone.

"Hey, Jason," she says. "We've run into a little snafu with the surgery."

My heart falls.

Of course. Why should this surprise me at all? It was always too good to be true.

"Fuck. Are you kidding me?"

"I wish I were." She clears her throat. "Gita and I went in front of the hospital medical board yesterday evening. They convened a special session to discuss your surgery. Gita's presentation was flawless, and we both figured this was just a formality."

"But..." I prompt.

She sighs. "They have doubts about allowing the surgery

because of the potential complications. The nerve graft in your hand is a complicated experimental procedure, and they worry about the potential for permanent damage if it doesn't go as planned. They want you to understand all the risks before proceeding."

I lean against the wall, closing my eyes. This surgery was supposed to be my second chance, a new beginning away from all the guilt and pain.

"I do understand," I reply, willing myself to stay calm. "I'm willing to take the risk."

"Jason, it's not that simple," she replies. "They want you to meet with the board before making a final decision. They want you to understand clearly what could happen and make sure you can cope with every possible outcome."

The news crashes into me like a tidal wave. My mind is a whirl of thoughts and fears. More delays, more uncertainty, more waiting. I'm a surgeon, for fuck's sake. I understand complications. I understand what could happen. I'm not a damned moron.

The board just wants to be free of any liability if something goes wrong. And they're going to do everything they can to convince me not to undertake this challenge.

"And..." she says.

"And what?"

She pauses. "They're concerned about your...mental health. What you've been through with the loss of your wife and child and your ability to perform surgery. They're concerned that without a proper support system, you might not be able to handle the potential stress and complications, should any arise. It's not just about the physical risk, Jason. It's about your emotional well-being too."

BROKEN DREAM

A bitter laugh escapes me. "They think I'm unstable?"

"It's more about your ability to cope under such stressful circumstances. Surgery can take a toll on anyone, Jason, even those who haven't experienced the kind of trauma you have."

I push away from the wall, anger surging through me. My personal life is my own damned business. How dare they pry into it like this? They wouldn't do it if I were a normal patient. They just happen to have this extra information on me. Information I wouldn't dare let them know if I were going into the hospital as a normal patient.

"I have a support system," I argue weakly.

It's not entirely untrue. There *are* people who care about me, but since Lindsay's death, I've pushed them away.

But if I really needed them, I could reach out.

"Gita and I tried," Louisa says, "but the board is adamant."

"Fine," I say, my voice clipped. "When is this meeting?"

"We'll schedule it as soon as possible," she says.

I end the call abruptly without saying goodbye.

Yeah, that was rude as hell. This isn't Louisa's fault.

But I know what's coming. If I want this surgery in this hospital, they're going to make me go to therapy.

Fucking therapy.

Therapy cost me my wife.

And God damn it, it won't cost me my hand as well.

CHAPTER TWENTY-FIVE

ANGIE

When I reach anatomy lab on Friday, the sign is there again.

Anatomy Lab Canceled

I'm relieved.
And also disappointed.
I don't have to cut again, but I also won't see Jason.

"Are you kidding me?" Eli walks up and bangs his hand on the door. "He's canceling *again*?"

"I know, right?" I answer, trying to sound upset. I *am* upset, but not for the right reasons. "We're never going to learn at this rate."

Eli runs a hand through his black hair. "This is unprofessional."

I shrug, though really I want to agree with him. But I don't want to seem too eager or too invested. Plus, Jason probably has another appointment about his surgery.

Eli looks at me, one eyebrow raised. "Something wrong, Angie?"

"No," I lie quickly. "Just tired, I guess."

He nods and doesn't press me further. We stand there awkwardly for a moment before he smacks the door one more time and then walks away, leaving me alone in the hallway.

BROKEN DREAM

I lean against the door, staring at the sign as if it might change if I look hard enough. But it remains stubbornly the same.

Anatomy Lab Canceled

Another day without Jason. Another day without the excitement that his presence brings, without the sparks that fly whenever our eyes meet. The hallways seem gray and lifeless.

Is he avoiding me?

I can't blame him, of course. I'm his student, and what happened with us...

But no. He's not avoiding me. He wouldn't punish his other students like that.

"You're still here?" A voice startles me from my thoughts. It's Tabitha.

I shrug. "I guess I was hoping the sign would change."

She gives me a sympathetic smile that doesn't quite reach her eyes. "It won't," she says, setting her books on the floor and then leaning against the wall beside me. "But that's surprising, coming from you."

"I made a perfect cut yesterday," I say.

"You did." She smirks. "After much prodding. You sure you want to stick with psychiatry?"

"I'm sure."

"Well, we've got over three years of med school before we have to decide on our internship rotations." She gently punches my shoulder. "You may change your mind yet."

"Maybe," I say, though I already know I won't. The study of the mind has always fascinated me. It's a puzzle to solve, a mystery to unravel. And it doesn't involve any cutting.

Not physically, at least.

Tabitha nudges me with her shoulder. "You never know.

You might just find yourself falling in love with some other field. Maybe even surgery."

I give her a small laugh. "Yeah, maybe if they invent bloodless surgery."

Tabitha laughs along with me and picks up her books from the floor. "I'd better head to the library. I'm going to grab some snacks first and then get some studying done."

As Tabitha fades down the hall, I reach for my own bag and start to turn away when a familiar figure catches my eye. Jason. He rounds the corner, looking harried. His eyes meet mine, but he quickly looks away.

He's close enough now that I can hear his labored breathing, see the troubled tenseness in his jaw. Something is wrong.

"Jason?" I call out.

He stops in his tracks but doesn't turn to face me.

"Are you okay?"

For a moment, I'm not sure he's going to respond. Until finally—

He turns. "I'm fine."

"Really?" I ask. "Because you canceled class. And you kind of look like shit."

He winces at my bluntness but doesn't argue. Instead, he leans against the wall, his breath still ragged.

"You canceled lab," I repeat, "so why are you here?"

"I have a meeting, and I forgot my notes in the lab yesterday." He unlocks the door to the classroom.

I follow him in without being invited.

The cadavers sit, covered, at our lab tables. The scent of formaldehyde greets us, familiar and nauseating all at once. Jason moves toward his desk at the front of the room, riffling

BROKEN DREAM

through scattered papers.

"You look awful, Jason," I say again as I walk up to his desk. "And you're not acting like yourself."

He stops and looks at me then, really looks at me. His eyes are bloodshot and tired. "What do you want from me, Angie?"

"I don't know." I sigh heavily and glance around the room. The stillness of it echoes my own confusion.

Jason turns back to his papers without responding. His shoulders are slumped. A silence grows between us, thick with words unspoken and feelings unexpressed.

"You should go," he says as he picks up a few papers.

A sudden surge of anger hits me. "Well, if you're going to be like that," I snap, "then maybe I will."

It's an empty threat, and we both know it. But I also know that this isn't the place or the time to push him. Jason needs something, but right now, he's not willing to accept any help.

I turn and—

He yanks me back, my body slamming against his chest.

The faint smell of liquor emanates from his breath.

"Are you drunk?" I demand.

He scowls. "Of course not."

"Then what do I smell?"

He looks down. "The remnants of my bender last night."

Bender? He told me he doesn't drink much. Or did he say that? Hell, I don't remember. I was too enamored with him being at my home, wine in tow, looking like a dark god with piercing green eyes.

"Why?" I ask.

"None of your damned business."

Then his mouth comes down on mine.

It's a ruthless kiss, a desperate one, full of pent-up

180

frustration and hurt. He pulls me closer, tangling his hand in my ponytail. He rips out the band, and my hair falls down my back. I can taste the bitterness of alcohol on his tongue.

His lips move against mine with an urgency that leaves me breathless. I push against him, trying to create some semblance of distance, but he's relentless. He tightens his grip and pulls me closer until there's no space left between us.

I should resist him. I should push him away. But I don't. Instead, I kiss him back and clutch at his shirt.

When we finally break apart, we're both panting. He doesn't let go of me. Instead, he rests his forehead against mine, his breath drifting over my lips.

"I'm sorry." He steps backward.

There's a wild desperation in his eyes that frightens me. He looks lost, tortured even. And I realize then just how little I actually know about this man.

Then—

"You know what? Fuck that. I'm not sorry. Not the least fucking bit sorry."

CHAPTER TWENTY-SIX

JASON

I kiss her again, hard and needy, knowing full well I'm probably bruising her beautiful lips.

And I don't care.

I don't care that this is wrong. That she's my student. That the guilt is eating me alive.

Our lips are smashed together, our teeth clashing, our tongues tangling.

I can't get enough of her. I don't ever *want* to get enough of her.

My mind whirls, but I tamp down the thoughts—the knowledge that this is wrong, that I should walk away.

God only knows I have enough of my own baggage.

Why drag an innocent woman into it?

Except that she's awakened feelings in me I thought were long dead and buried.

I deepen the kiss, devouring her, until she grips my shoulders, pushing me away from her. The kiss breaks with a loud smack.

"Jason…"

"What? You want to tell me you didn't want that, Angie? Because I know damned well you did." I rake my gaze over her body. "Your nipples are hard. I can see them through your shirt." I inhale. "And you're wet. I can smell you. Like an animal stalking his mate. I smell you, Angie. I smell how much you want this. How much you want *me*."

She gulps audibly. Her lips are trembling—swollen from my kiss and trembling.

"Jason..." she ekes out.

"God, the way you say my name..." I'm as hard as I've ever been. I'm uncomfortable in these damned clothes.

She drops her gaze to my crotch.

"That's right," I say. "See that? See what you do to me? I want you just as much as you want me. I don't fucking care that it's wrong. I don't care. I'm not sorry. You understand that, Angie? I'm not fucking sorry."

She gulps again. "Jason... I'm...not sorry either."

I grab her then, crush our mouths together once more.

We're in the lab.

The anatomy lab.

The cadavers watch us, judging us, their bodies splayed out like grisly spectators, and although covered, their lifeless eyes still seem to hold an eerie presence as witnesses to our passion.

The air is thick with odd smells and unspoken desires. The quiet hum of the refrigerator units is drowned by the frantic pounding of our hearts.

"Jason," Angie gasps, digging her fingers into my back as I trail hungry kisses down her neck.

Her voice echoes in the room, bouncing off the cold tiled walls.

My breathing grows ragged at her touch, my senses heightened to a frustrating level. I don't care about the consequences anymore. My need for Angie overpowers every

BROKEN DREAM

shred of guilt and fear.

I press her body against one of the empty tables, feeling her legs wrap around my waist, pulling me closer.

"Stop," she breathes, her voice barely above a whisper.

But she doesn't want to stop what we're doing. It's not a plea.

It's a command—one filled with the same relentless need that has our hearts racing and our bodies trembling. She wants control. She wants me as much as I want her.

I let her take it. I let her push me back until my spine meets the cold steel of the table behind me. The chill sends shivers racing down my spine, but it does nothing to quench the burning heat coursing through my veins.

With one swift move, she pins me against the surface and captures my lips in a passionate kiss. She unbuttons my shirt, her touch leaving a trail of fire on my skin that only fuels the need coursing through me.

Her own shirt falls to the floor. When—how—did she take it off?

I cup her gorgeous breasts through the lace of her bra as we continue to devour each other, the taste of her skin intoxicating. She leans into my touch, a soft moan escaping her. But then she pauses, her breath hitching as she looks toward the door.

"Jason," she whispers, pulling away slightly. Her eyes are wide with fear, her body rigid. "What if someone walks in?"

I reach out and gently cup her face with my hand, brush my thumb over the softness of her cheek. "Let them," I breathe, my voice rough with desire.

And then I'm kissing her again, pulling her close until there's not a single inch of space left between us. She threads her fingers through my hair, our bodies moving in sync as if we've done this a thousand times before.

The entire world could be walking by, and I wouldn't care. All I can think about is Angie—her taste, her touch, her gasps and moans that send a primal thrill coursing through me.

I feel her heart pounding against my chest, beating in sync with mine as we grind against each other. I explore the curves of her body, mapping out a path of desire and lust that leaves us both gasping for breath.

She slides her hands down my back, pulling me closer as she arches against me. The feel of her bare skin...

God, I want her.

I need her.

I crave her.

I'm ready. So ready.

Until she pulls away slightly, looking up at me with those mesmerizing dark eyes of hers that are filled with an intoxicating mix of fear and desire.

"Jason," she says. "The door."

God, she's right. What am I thinking? Anyone could walk in. I move toward the door, push the deadbolt into place.

And then I return to Angie.

"I want you," I tell her. "That's no secret. It's wrong and I don't care. I've told you that. So my question to you, Angie, is... what do *you* want?" I caress her cheek, brushing a few strands of hair out of her face. "Do you want this fuck? Because I'm ready to fuck you again. Right here in the anatomy lab."

CHAPTER TWENTY-SEVEN

ANGIE

I'm ready to tell him yes.

Yes, I want this fuck more than I've ever wanted anything.

When Aunt Melanie's image pops into my mind.

At the most inopportune moment. Talk about a libido killer.

She's my mentor. What would she say? What would she think about what I'm doing right now?

It's a breach of ethics, she would tell me.

Probably more so for Jason than for me, but still, he's my teacher, and I should know better.

Push him away, I tell myself.

Tell him you don't want this.

But the words don't make it to my mouth.

Because the truth of the matter is that I *do* want this.

I've never felt anything like this before. This desire, this passion, this unwavering want.

"I want this fuck," I say, my voice cracking. "I've never wanted anything this much."

And he kisses me again.

His lips press against mine, firm and demanding. His hands—those skilled surgeon's hands—roam over my body with a thirst that matches my own. But there's something else in his touch, something beyond pure lust. An intensity, a need that goes deeper than I've ever known. I respond to him, arching toward him.

"Jason," I whisper against his lips.

This is so forbidden, and that's part of what makes it so sexy. Against all the rules, all the ethics that we were supposed to uphold, we're giving in to each other right here in the anatomy lab.

The cold steel of the dissection table beneath me is a stark contrast against his warm body pressing into me. He removes the rest of my clothing and then his own, and soon our bodies are bare against each other.

He buries his face into the crook of my neck, his breath hot against my skin. He tightens his grip as if he's holding on to me for dear life. And maybe he is. Maybe we both are.

His kisses move lower, trailing down my throat to the valley between my breasts. There's an urgency to his touch, a desperate need to feel every inch of me.

"Yes," I breathe out, sinking into his hair, pulling him closer, wanting to feel more of him, all of him.

My phone buzzes from somewhere underneath our discarded clothes. We both freeze momentarily, but then he shakes his head and continues his exploration. The world outside this lab doesn't matter anymore.

He traces a searing path down my belly and lower still. I gasp as he finds the spot that makes my breath hitch, and he smirks against my skin.

"I knew you wanted this," he whispers.

That was never in question, and we both know it.

His touch sends shivers through me. I lose myself in him, forgetting everything else. The world is reduced to Jason and me, the anatomy lab, and our shared desperation.

The metallic scent of the lab mingles with our heated breaths, and the faint smell of disinfectant only adds to the illicit thrill of it all.

All thoughts of rules, ethics, and consequences are forgotten as we surrender ourselves to this heated moment. The world outside the lab, with its rules and constraints, fades into oblivion. It's just Jason and me, lost in a whirlwind of desire.

His movements become more urgent. He thrusts two fingers inside me, and I nearly shatter as he massages my G-spot.

I meet him, move for move, our bodies colliding.

"Fuck," he growls. "I love to penetrate you. You have the tightest little pussy, Angie. So wet and perfect."

All I can do is sigh against him. With his other hand, he tweaks my nipple. His hard cock brushes against me.

I grasp it.

He groans.

And I love it. I love what I do to him. What I can do to this magnificent man.

He drives his finger into me harder, until I cry out.

Can anyone hear us outside the lab?

I cry out again, and I don't care.

"Fuck," he grunts, withdrawing his fingers.

Before I can whimper in protest, he slides a condom onto his cock and thrusts into me.

The cold steel table below me is soon forgotten as I get lost in his touch, his warmth seeping into me and igniting a fire with each deep thrust.

His lips find mine again, swallowing my gasps and cries,

turning them into a shared secret between us. There's only his mouth on mine—a hot, desperate kiss that says more than any words—and his dick inside me—a primal fuck that brands me like the cattle on our ranch.

At least that's what it feels like.

I'm his. At least in this moment, I'm purely his.

I wrap my legs tighter around him, driving him deeper. His breath hitches, his movements become erratic, and as he thrusts, each nudge against my clit drives me further, further, further...until—

"Oh my God, Jason!" The orgasm hits me with the force of a thousand hurricanes.

He buries his face in the crook of my neck and breathes heavily as I soar to the moon and then back, plummeting into my body as everything culminates in my pussy pulsing around his cock.

"That's it, baby. Come for me. Come for me, Angie. Only for me."

"Only for you," I echo.

Then, with one final thrust, a low growl escapes his lips, and he shudders against me.

Another wave of pleasure crashes through me at the same time, making me cry out. It's overwhelming, a sense of completion unlike anything I've ever experienced before. For a moment, we stay like that, holding on to each other as we ride out the aftershocks.

Slowly, reality seeps back in.

The coldness of the lab table. The acrid smell of formaldehyde.

But there's something else too—the scent of us, of our shared moment. It's musky, earthy, and the most delicious

BROKEN DREAM

fragrance I've ever smelled.

The sweet and seductive smell of our secret.

Without saying a word, Jason reaches for my hand and threads his fingers through mine. In a strange way, holding his hand is more intimate than what just happened. A quiet understanding passes between us as we stand there, naked.

My phone rings once more, breaking through the heavy silence. The reminder of the world beyond the lab walls is intrusive. But I can't bring myself to break away from him, to reach for it and face whatever message awaits me.

He turns toward me. His green eyes are unreadable under the fluorescent lights. He squeezes my hand lightly and then moves away from me and gathers his clothes.

"I should probably check that," I say quietly, nodding toward the sound of my phone.

He says nothing while I find my phone inside the pocket of my discarded jeans.

Oh, God.

It's Aunt Melanie.

Two missed calls, and a text.

> **Surprise! I'm coming to Boulder.**
> **Flight gets in at four. Dinner tonight,**
> **my treat!**

CHAPTER TWENTY-EIGHT

JASON

Angie's eyes go wide as she chews on her swollen lower lip.

"Everything okay?" I ask.

She nods. "Yeah, fine. It's just my aunt."

"The psychiatrist?"

"Yeah. She's coming to town."

"Why?"

"I don't know. But apparently she's flying in, and she'll be here this afternoon. She's invited me to dinner."

"Free dinner is always good," I say.

But I want to smack myself. Angie doesn't have to worry about paying for food or anything. She's a trust-fund baby.

I'll do well to remember that.

She begins to dress, so I do the same.

I want to say something to her. I want to tell her that this meant something to me. But honestly, I don't know what to say.

The fact that it's all so wrong still lies heavy on my mind.

And the feelings that are creeping up on me—things that I haven't felt in so long, maybe never felt—have me disoriented.

"See you later, Angie," I mumble, forcing a smile onto my face.

She returns it, but her eyes are distant. She's already preoccupied with thoughts of her visiting aunt.

BROKEN DREAM

She leaves the lab first, while I stay behind for another fifteen minutes to keep up appearances. I look around. The cadavers no longer seem to be judging me.

No.

I'm only judging myself.

And the fact is that Angie being a student isn't the thing that's weighing the most on my mind.

No.

What's weighing most on my mind is that I'm feeling something new. Something more intense than I've ever felt.

And Lindsay didn't cross my mind once.

As I leave the lab, I feel a cold wave of loneliness. I shake my head, swallowing down the lump in my throat. It's not like Angie and I are dating or anything.

Do I want that?

There was a time when I was certain I'd never be with a woman again. I'd live out my life in solitude.

But now? If Angie weren't my student, I believe I'd want to pursue this. Find out if we're compatible in ways other than physically.

I trudge down the hall, my steps heavy and slow. Laughter and chatter from students fill the hallways as I make my way to my office.

The brass plaque stares at me.

Dr. Jason Lansing, Professor of Anatomy

It may as well say Dr. Jason Lansing, once an up-and-coming general surgeon.

Dr. Jason Lansing, who may not get the surgery he needs because he's a fucked-up mess.

HELEN HARDT

Dr. Jason Lansing...who may be falling in love with a student.

I unlock the door to my office, walk in, and fall into the first chair across from my desk.

The walls seem to pulse. My undergrad degree, my medical degree. They all seem to laugh at me in a dark way as they close in on me.

I clutch the armrests of my chair, my knuckles whitening. The walls of my office are closing in on me now, the multitude of degrees and honors that once signaled a promising career now taking on an ominous, mocking tone.

Dr. Jason Lansing, a man who had everything, only to lose it all.

Dr. Jason Lansing, a brilliant mind wasted on a broken body.

Nausea travels up my throat as I stare at the surgical diplomas lining the walls. They symbolize everything I'm supposed to be. Everything I should be.

Dr. Jason Lansing, hopelessly, pathetically in love with a student.

No.

Won't go there.

Can't go there.

I'm not in love with Angie Simpson.

Love isn't sex. Love isn't easing loneliness.

I drag my gaze away from the damning degrees and let out a bitter chuckle. The future. A concept that once held promise and potential now holds nothing but uncertainty. The ghost of my past clings around me, haunting every corner of my office with chilling whispers of what might have been.

BROKEN DREAM

Three years earlier...

This is the worst day of my life.

Except it's not.

I've had so many worst days that I've lost count.

Losing Julia.

Finding out I'll never operate again.

And today...

My wife lies in the bathtub upstairs in our master bathroom.

Blood all over her.

Her wrists slit.

And I feel...

I feel nothing.

Numbness. Pure numbness.

Oh, the pain will come later. I'm well aware of that.

I've been through this before.

I walk over to the desk, the mahogany surface covered with bills and letters yet to be opened. Among the clutter is a solitary envelope—stark white, crisp, untouched. I pick it up, flipping it over to reveal two words on the other side.

To Jason...

She left a note.

I sit down in the leather chair behind the desk, the envelope trembling in my hands. Do I really want to know what's inside? The last words of a woman who saw no way out but to take her own life?

Inhale, exhale. It's just another worst day.

I open the envelope and pull out Lindsay's final goodbye.

I don't read it.

I can't read it.

I simply sit, holding the paper, tempted to burn it.

But I don't. I put it back in the envelope and stuff it in my pocket.

While my wife lies lifeless in our bathroom, blood congealing around her.

I sit in denial.

My breath hitches as a single tear rolls down my cheek, landing with a soft pat on the white paper. I gaze at it blankly, watching as the moisture soaks into the paper.

A sob rips through my throat, raw and jagged. The sound echoes around the room, bouncing off the walls and slicing through the heavy silence. It's an alien sound, one that doesn't belong in this office filled with accolades and prestige.

The letter lies forgotten on the desk as I lean back in my seat, staring blankly at the ceiling. The pain, long delayed, breaks free from its confines and washes over me in a relentless tide. It's crushing, suffocating. I can hardly breathe.

I rise from the chair, the letter fluttering down to the hardwood floor. I pace, back and forth, my own footsteps echoing in time with the ticking of the clock.

Every tick, every tock, a reminder.

A reminder of the numbness that grips me, a deafening silence that fills my ears and clouds my mind. A reminder of Lindsay. Of her laughter, her smile...her lifeless body in our bathroom.

"Damn it!" I rake my fingers through my hair.

I've lost everything now.

BROKEN DREAM

I'm no longer a promising surgeon.

No longer a devoted father.

No longer a loving husband.

Just Dr. Jason Lansing, a broken man with a broken dream.

And a broken heart.

CHAPTER TWENTY-NINE

ANGIE

Of course I'm meeting Aunt Mel at Flagstaff House, the most lavish restaurant in Boulder.

I've been here before, but not for a while, since most of my med school friends—if you can even call them friends—can't afford this place and probably wouldn't take kindly to me offering to pay.

I didn't make any good friends during my first semester. Just kept to myself mostly, and though I was lonely every once in a while, mostly I was just alone.

My entire life was spent as one of the awesome foursome. We were inseparable in high school and in college, where we all pledged the same sorority.

Brianna is now married. Seriously married, and to a rock star, Jesse Pike.

Sage is at home working with our dad, and Gina is pursuing her master's degree in visual arts.

It's always been the four of us.

So it was odd being alone, beginning this new chapter of my life.

But it was also refreshing, in a terrifying, exhilarating kind of way. The four of us had always been a unit, moving as one, acting as one. Being alone gave me the chance to be something other than one of the foursome. It gave me the chance to just be me.

I walk into Flagstaff House and immediately feel out of place, even though I'm familiar with it. Med school has made me accustomed to late-night takeout and ramen noodles rather than lobster bisque and filet mignon.

The host leads me to our table where Aunt Mel is already seated, sipping on her martini and looking out over Boulder. Her silvery blond hair is pulled back in a stylish bun, and her green eyes sparkle. Dressed in a tailored blazer and slim black pants, she's the epitome of mature beauty.

"Angie!" She rises to give me a hug. "You look gorgeous, as usual."

I take a seat at the window and look out over the lights of Boulder framed by the deep shadows of the surrounding wilderness.

Boulder is the best of both worlds.

The city juxtaposed against the calm, undisturbed wildness just beyond. I let out a deep sigh, feeling the tension in my shoulders ease a bit. Aunt Mel gives me an understanding smile from across the table.

Our server heads over. "Can I get you something to drink?" he asks me.

I glance at Aunt Mel's martini. It's Uncle Joe's favorite, which he turned Aunt Mel on to when they first met over twenty-five years ago.

I shrug dismissively. "Sure. It's Friday, and I can always catch an Uber if I need to. A glass of Malbec, please."

I gaze at Aunt Mel. Her eyes are troubled, as they have been since Uncle Joe's cancer diagnosis nearly a year ago.

I don't talk to Aunt Mel or my cousins Bradley and Brock

about it unless they bring it up, but I hear from my mom and dad that the experimental treatment is going well, which is the best news ever. But Uncle Joe still has a long way to go.

It's strange that Aunt Mel is here when her husband is ill. I don't want to ask.

She takes another sip of her martini. "I suppose you're wondering why I'm here."

I smile slightly. "I think you just read my mind."

"Uncle Joe is good." She sighs. "I mean, as good as can be expected. He's weak. He hasn't been doing much. Attending the wedding a few months ago was about as much as he could take."

She's talking about the quadruple wedding where her son Brock, my cousin, along with my brother Dave and my cousins Brianna and Donny all got married.

"And the prognosis?" I ask.

"Still undetermined," she says with a sigh. "We just have to wait and see."

I nod.

I hate talking about this. Uncle Joe is Jonah Steel, the oldest of his siblings and the de facto head of our family.

Watching him go through this has us all freaked out.

But he and Aunt Melanie were adamant that we all go on with our lives. I started med school as planned, and the wedding went off without a hitch.

The waiter returns with my wine. "Can I get you another, ma'am?" he asks Aunt Mel.

Aunt Mel's martini glass is still half full.

"I don't think so," she says. "I have a big meeting tomorrow."

He nods and leaves.

BROKEN DREAM

"Tomorrow?" I ask. "Tomorrow is Saturday."

"Yeah. Uncle Joe insisted I come. He said it's important that I still do my job for people who need me."

"What job do you have here?"

She takes another sip of her martini. "I recently resigned my position on the board of the university hospital, as you may know."

"Yeah, you resigned all of your positions that you were still holding so you could be there for Uncle Joe as he goes through treatment."

"Yes, but the hospital board gave me a call a couple of days ago, asking that I do a psychiatric evaluation for a potential patient who's about to undergo an experimental surgery."

"Oh, I see. What kind of surgery?"

She frowns. "I can't really talk about it. HIPAA and all."

"Oh, yeah. Of course I understand."

"All I can say is that the potential patient has a history of trauma, and the board is concerned about whether he may be able to handle the experimental surgery, especially if something were to go wrong."

"I see. I'm sorry you had to come all the way here."

She gives me a melancholy smile. "Joe is in a good spot. He's between treatments and is feeling pretty good. Plus, it was a chance to see you. To take my favorite niece to dinner and find out how everything's going."

I laugh. "I know you call all of us your favorites."

"True." She chuckles. "I don't play favorites. None of your aunts and uncles do. But I do feel particularly close to you, Angie. Neither of my children followed in my footsteps, so it's wonderful that you are."

I nod. "I'm convinced now more than ever that I want to

go into psychiatry. Anatomy lab has me freaked."

"Yeah, like I said, I didn't like it much either. But it *is* very important."

I bite my lip. "I made my first cut yesterday."

"Congratulations!" She raises her martini glass. "Was it as bad as you thought it would be?"

I clink my glass against hers. "No, not really. I have a great lab partner who wants to go into surgery, so she's really into it and helps me get into the vibe. I'm happy to let her take the lead. And, of course, the person I cut is dead."

"Well, if you go into psychiatry, you'll probably never have to cut a live person."

I widen my eyes. "Probably?"

She shrugs. "I mean, never say never. But it's good to have skills, just in case you're in an emergency and they're needed."

"Have you ever been in an emergency like that?" I ask. "Where you had to cut?"

"A couple of times, actually," she says. "One time when I was in my last year of my residency, we were short-staffed at the hospital because of an outbreak of the flu. So I had to insert a chest tube into a man who came into the emergency room."

"And it went okay?"

Her eyes brighten. "It went perfectly. Because I had been trained to do it. Psychiatrists are still medical doctors, Angie."

I resist an eye roll. "Aunt Mel, I know that."

She reaches her hand across the table, squeezing mine. "So we need to be able to handle basic medical emergencies. Another time I was on a flight. I was coming back from New York to Colorado. This was before I met Uncle Joe and got married. A woman on the flight passed out and wasn't breathing, so I had to do an emergency crike."

BROKEN DREAM

"Crike? You mean a cricothyrotomy?" I ask, my eyes widening.

"That's right." Aunt Mel nods and sips her martini. "It was just like a movie. A flight attendant came on the PA saying, 'Ladies and gentlemen, is there a doctor on board?' I looked around, seeing if someone more qualified might volunteer. No one did. So I stood, knowing I had to do the best I could. The FAA-mandated medical kit had basic airway tools, IV fluids, and a defibrillator, but no scalpels or cannulas. I had to improvise. I used a pen to make the incision and a straw to keep the airway open."

I shudder. "That sounds terrifying."

"It was," she admits. "And it taught me an important lesson. You never know when your training may come into play. That's why it's crucial to learn as much as you can and take every experience seriously."

I take a sip of wine before asking Aunt Melanie the obvious question.

"Did she...survive?"

Aunt Mel smiles at me, her eyes twinkling. "Yes, Angie. She did."

I let out a sigh of relief as the waiter comes by to take our dinner orders. "We have two specials tonight," he begins, "a filet mignon with a red wine reduction and a seared scallops dish with a mango salsa."

Aunt Mel chooses the filet mignon, while I opt for the seared scallops. As the waiter leaves, Aunt Mel leans back in her chair, staring out the window for a moment.

"The woman on the plane... She wrote me a letter afterward. She thanked me for saving her life. It was one of the most moving things I've ever read."

I blink back tears. "That's incredible, Aunt Mel."

"Sometimes it's not just about prescribing medications or listening to patients. Sometimes being a psychiatrist is literally about saving someone's life."

I look down at my bread plate. Her words resonate deeply and reaffirm my decision to go into psychiatry. The path may not be an easy one, but it holds meaning. It holds purpose.

"You never told me those stories before."

"You never asked," she says. "We've talked about the therapy portion of psychiatry mostly, and about how pharmaceuticals can help those who struggle with mental illness, but we've never really touched on the medical emergency aspect. But it's there, and it can be vital."

The waiter returns with our salads—mine a house salad with balsamic vinaigrette and Aunt Mel's a Caesar—and I pick up my fork.

"Did you ever doubt your decision to go into psychiatry?" I ask.

She takes a moment before answering, wiping her mouth with a napkin. "Of course," she admits. "No path worth pursuing is without its bumps and moments of uncertainty. And some of the stories are heartbreaking, especially in my specialty of childhood trauma."

"I can imagine."

And indeed I can. Aunt Mel was doctor to one of my uncles and two of my cousins, who had all been through horrific childhood abuse.

"But each time I doubted myself," she continues, "I would remember why I chose this specialty in the first place—to help those in need. That would always bring me back. I remember every single patient I've helped, Angie."

BROKEN DREAM

I widen my eyes. "Every single one?"

"Yes. As a psychiatrist, I get the privilege of spending more than just a few minutes with my patients. A surgeon will meet a patient once, study his scans, do the surgery and a follow-up, and then it's over in most cases. But as psychiatrists, we have the opportunity to go on a journey with our patients. We witness their lowest points, their times of triumph, their tears and their smiles. That's what makes it rewarding."

"And that's what makes it hard too, I suppose," I say.

She nods, taking another sip of her martini. "There is no reward without risk. Psychiatry is not a field for those who want an easy way out. You'll see things that will break your heart. You'll have patients that, despite your best efforts, do not get better."

"Did you ever feel... I mean...did it ever get too heavy? The emotional burden?"

Aunt Mel sighs. "There were days when I felt the weight of the world on my shoulders. Seeing so much pain and suffering. Feeling like I had failed when a patient didn't improve. It can be very heavy."

I bite on my lip.

"But it's not all darkness," she adds quickly. "There are moments of light too. When you see a patient who was once on the edge of giving up standing tall and smiling again. When you witness the strength of the human spirit in its rawest form. Those are the moments that make it all worth it."

"I always wondered," I begin, playing with the stem of my wineglass. "How do you separate your work from your personal life? How do you manage to switch it off at the end of the day?"

She chuckles lightly. "Oh, Angie, if only there *was* a

switch! The truth is that you don't really switch off. Especially not in the beginning. The stories of your patients—their pain and their struggles—tend to follow you home. They sneak into your dreams, cloud your thoughts. But it's part of the process."

I raise an eyebrow. "The process?"

She nods. "The process of understanding that you're not just a witness to your patients' lives but an active participant. You can effect change, but you can't control everything. Some things are beyond our reach."

"So how do you handle that? How do you deal with knowing that there are things you just can't fix?"

Aunt Mel pauses, swirling the tiny bit of liquid left in her martini glass. "You learn to accept it," she says finally. "Acceptance is a big part of being a psychiatrist. Accepting that not every story has a happy ending, accepting that some wounds run deeper than others and might take longer to heal, accepting that sometimes all you can do is be there for someone, even when it feels like you're not doing enough." She finishes her drink and gazes out the window a moment. "In a way, it's like learning to dance in the rain. You can't stop the storm, so you learn to move with it, to find your rhythm amid the chaos."

Find your rhythm among the chaos.

The words settle inside me.

And for some reason, they remind me of Jason.

CHAPTER THIRTY

JASON

This is so fucked up.

It's Saturday, and the hospital has convened a special board meeting to deal with me. With my surgery. Because they don't think I'm mentally fit to handle it.

What a fucking crock.

I dress in a pair of navy slacks and a crisp white shirt. No tie, because ties make me want to strangle someone. Kind of fitting for today's proceeding.

The boardroom is on the sixth floor, as far removed from life-and-death situations as possible. It's all pristine glass and sleek chrome adorned with uninteresting paintings that look like giant blurs of something no one wants to see. Abstracts. Modern art. It's all crap. The hospital probably paid some pompous artist millions for them—money that could have gone toward saving lives.

I wish I were anywhere but here.

But if I want my surgery, I'm going to have to prove to these self-important asses that I'm mentally and emotionally capable of handling it.

Why wouldn't I be?

Only my entire life was stolen from me three years ago.

And these people want to steal my only opportunity for

getting part of it back.

I recognize the chief of surgery, Dr. Peter Bailey, and the CEO and president of the hospital, Dr. Roger Stanich. I recognize the faces of the two other board members present, but I can't recall their names. I guess they didn't need to convene the entire board for this.

It's only my life, after all.

Also seated at the table are my doctors, Louisa Matthews and Gita Patel, alongside my former psychiatrist, Dr. Vanessa Morgan.

Why the hell is *she* here? She's responsible for my wife's death.

One more woman is seated next to Dr. Morgan, and she looks slightly familiar to me. She's older, with graying blond hair, a slightly wrinkled but still beautiful face, and striking green eyes even brighter than my own.

"Welcome, Dr. Lansing." Dr. Bailey stands and gestures. "Please have a seat."

"We don't need to stand on ceremony, Pete," I say dryly, taking the seat at the foot of the table.

Peter sits opposite me at the head, with Dr. Stanich and the other board members to his right, and my doctors plus the familiar-looking woman to his left.

"Let me make introductions just as a formality," Peter says. "Dr. Stanich, our CEO and president, and board members Dr. Lisa Frohike and Mr. James Pigg, president of Long Pharmaceuticals here in Boulder. On my left, of course, are Drs. Matthews and Patel, Dr. Vanessa Morgan, and our former board member who we've asked to join us, Dr. Melanie Steel."

I catch myself before my jaw drops.

No wonder she looks familiar.

BROKEN DREAM

Not only is Dr. Steel one of the most preeminent psychiatrists in Colorado—hell, in the whole country—she's also Angie Simpson's aunt.

What the hell is she doing here?

Angie said yesterday she was in town...

Did Angie somehow put her aunt up to this?

No, she couldn't have.

"Good morning," I say. "It's nice to see all of you."

Did that sound sincere?

Probably not.

Peter clears his throat. "As you know, Dr. Lansing, we're here to make a decision about whether to allow Dr. Patel to perform the experimental nerve graft on your right hand at this facility."

I nod. "I've already consented to the procedure, and Drs. Matthews and Patel have been forthcoming about all the risks."

"One of which is the possibility of you losing all function in your right hand," Peter says.

I grit my teeth but manage a fake smile. "I read the informed consent, Peter."

"We know you have," Dr. Stanich interrupts, leaning back in his chair, "but the board feels it necessary to ensure, given your past medical history, that you fully understand the potential consequences."

I meet his gaze, remaining steady. I will not let their words undermine me. They're not concerned about my past medical history. They're concerned about the losses I've endured. Why not just say it?

I draw in a breath. "I'm not asking for any guarantees. Just the chance to regain what was taken from me."

Dr. Frohike leans forward, tapping her pen against the

notepad in front of her. "That's precisely why we're here, Dr. Lansing," she says calmly. "We need to ascertain whether you are prepared mentally and emotionally for this change, given your history."

I can't help scoffing. "I lost the use of my hand in an automobile accident that took the life of my daughter. Then my wife took her own life a few months later. And you"—I point to Dr. Morgan—"said you could help her. That you could help *me*. Why is this quack even here?"

"With all due respect, Dr. Lansing," Dr. Morgan says, "you and your wife didn't complete—"

"Leave it, Vanessa," Dr. Stanich says. "We've all seen the records."

Of course they have. Because privacy doesn't exist here. HIPAA means nothing. This is all a "consult." Board business.

Psychiatry is quackery.

How I want to say the words.

But that won't help my cause.

"It won't change anything," I say sharply. "And neither will all this. Can we just get to the point, please?"

Peter nods. "All right, Dr. Lansing. The board has thoroughly analyzed your medical and psychological records. We have concerns about the potential impact of the surgery on your mental health, particularly given the trauma you've experienced from the loss of your family."

"My mental health is none of your concern anymore," I retort. "The trauma I've experienced doesn't invalidate my right to regain what I lost, Doctor. And I don't see how it relates to this."

Dr. Morgan opens her mouth but then closes it after a gesture from Dr. Steel.

BROKEN DREAM

"Dr. Lansing," Dr. Steel says, "I don't know you. I'd like to, if you're open to it. The board has asked me to assess your mental health with regard to the trauma you've experienced and how it might relate to this experimental surgery should it fail."

"I see no reason to talk to yet another therapist," I say.

"I understand," Dr. Steel replies, her voice even and nonconfrontational. "This isn't about therapy, though. It's about understanding your capacity to handle the potential outcomes of this operation."

"You think I can't?" I shoot back, my patience wearing thin.

"I have no opinion on the matter," she says gently. "I don't know you. The board simply wants to ensure that you're adequately prepared for all scenarios, good or bad."

"Your concerns are noted," I reply tersely. "But let me make myself perfectly clear. I am willing to take any risks associated with this surgery if it means regaining some semblance of my old life. So can we move along?"

The room goes quiet as everyone exchanges glances.

Dr. Stanich finally breaks the silence.

"Very well," he says, leaning back in his chair and folding his hands over his stomach. "You have two choices, Dr. Lansing. You can meet with Dr. Steel, and if she believes you are mentally fit to handle the surgery, the hospital will allow Dr. Patel and her team to perform it here."

"What's my other choice?"

"Find another hospital," he says.

My jaw tightens. The audacity of him—of *them*—to tell me that I have to jump through their hoops or find another hospital, like it's as simple as changing clothes. This is the best

HELEN HARDT

facility in Colorado, a top hospital in the country with state-of-the-art equipment. I trained here, practiced here.

"Is that a threat, Roger?" I ask, my voice low.

"It's not a threat," Dr. Stanich says calmly. "It's your choice."

"Your free will, Dr. Lansing," Dr. Frohike adds.

"Dr. Lansing," Dr. Stanich says. "This isn't about punishing you. It's about making sure that we're acting in your best interest."

I scoff at his words. My best interest. As if any of them could truly understand what that is.

"One shrink couldn't help me." I glare at Dr. Morgan. "What makes you think another one can?"

Dr. Steel folds her hands on the table before her, those bright-green eyes of hers meeting mine. "There are no guarantees, Dr. Lansing," she says, her voice calm. "And I am not here to 'help' you in the general sense of the word. I'm here to make an assessment, nothing more."

"Your opinion could block my surgery," I say, crossing my arms.

"Only if I believe it's not in your best interest," she replies.

My best interest—that seems to be today's catchphrase.

I look at each face around the table, one by one. They're not individuals to me. They're a tribunal passing judgment.

"I'll tell you what's in my best interest." I stand abruptly, the chair scraping loudly against the floor. "*My* best interest is reclaiming my life, my career—whatever remains of it."

"And what if you can't?" Dr. Steel's words slice through the tension in the room, her tone still even. "What if, despite your surgeon's best efforts, the surgery fails? Can you handle that?"

"Are you implying that I'm too weak to handle failure?" I snap back.

"No," she answers calmly. "I'm asking if you're prepared for it."

"Preparation has nothing to do with it," I scoff. "None of us is ever truly prepared for anything."

"Perhaps," she concedes. "But that doesn't mean we shouldn't try. And that's all we're asking of you, Dr. Lansing. To try."

I ball my hands into fists. The arrogance of these people, thinking they can tell me what's best for me.

"I don't need to try." I scowl. "I am ready. Completely and utterly ready."

Dr. Steel leans back in her chair, studying me with her thoughtful green eyes. "Are you ready to live with the possible consequences, though? If it fails, if it causes more harm? Can you handle that?"

I grit my teeth and hold her gaze. "I'm not afraid of the consequences."

A silence descends upon the room, heavy and thick.

Peter clears his throat, breaking the tension. "Dr. Lansing, we understand how desperate you are for a second chance, but desperation can cloud judgment."

I shoot him a nasty look. "Are you implying that my judgment is impaired?"

"No one's implying anything," Dr. Frohike interjects. "These are just precautions we have to take to ensure everyone's safety."

"Everyone's *safety*," I echo mockingly, "or the hospital's reputation?"

"That is not fair, Jason," Peter retorts, a harsh edge to

his voice. "This is not about our reputation. This is about you, your health, and your well-being."

"Is it?" I shoot back, my blood boiling at their condescension. "Or is it just another way to cover your backs? Just in case the 'world-renowned surgeon' fails?"

"Dr. Lansing," Dr. Steel says, her tone still annoyingly diplomatic, "nobody here doubts the strength of your resolve or your right to pursue this procedure. And we certainly don't doubt Dr. Patel's skills. We are merely trying to ensure that you take the step with an understanding of all possible outcomes."

"You think I haven't thought about the possibilities?" I snap back.

"I'm sure you have," she replies calmly. "But have you truly prepared yourself for them? Even the worst ones?"

I take a deep breath, forcing myself to still the whirlpool of emotions threatening to spill over. "I've lived with the worst outcomes already," I say, my voice barely a whisper. "I lost my family, my career is in shambles, and every day is a constant reminder of what I used to be." I meet Dr. Morgan's gaze with daggers in my eyes. "*You* were supposed to help my wife. And she killed herself. She's dead because of you. And I won't leave my fate in another psychiatrist's hands."

I walk out of the room, rage boiling inside me.

And I know exactly where I need to go.

CHAPTER THIRTY-ONE

ANGIE

I'm immersing myself in my psychiatry textbook when—

I jerk.

Someone is pounding on my door. Tillie starts yapping.

I rise, leaving my book on the couch, and walk to the door. When I look through the peephole, my heart lurches.

Jason.

He's wearing his leather jacket, his hair is mussed, and he has a crazed look in his eyes.

His gorgeous green eyes that I can't resist.

I put Tillie out quickly and then open the door. "Jason? Why are you pounding—"

He grabs me, crushes his lips to mine.

He tastes of desperation and fear. I try to pull back, but his grip is firm, like a vise around my waist. When he finally pulls away, his breathing is as labored as mine.

"Jason," I whisper against his lips. "What's wrong?"

"I need you," is all he says before devouring me with another punishing kiss.

And I let him.

I have no idea what this thing is between us. He's my teacher. I'm his student. He's thirteen years older than I am.

And I don't care about any of that.

In this moment, if it cost me my fortune, I'd continue kissing him.

He rips his mouth from mine and inhales sharply. "Bed. Now."

Without hesitation, I take his hand and lead him to my bedroom. The door closes behind us with a soft click, sealing us off from the rest of the world.

Before I have a chance to speak, he presses me against the wall, his body heavy against mine. His eyes are wild, unreadable. It's a look that both terrifies and excites me. He buries his face into my neck, his breath hot on my skin. His hands tremble slightly as he explores my body, and for the first time since we started this dangerous game of ours, I see vulnerability in him.

"Jason," I say, my voice trembling with uncertainty. "Talk to me."

"No talking," he growls against my skin before pulling away abruptly.

He undresses quickly and stands before me, his cock hard and ready.

"Take off your clothes," he commands, "before I rip them off you."

I obey without a second thought, my mind clouded with desire. My hands tremble as I pull my sweatshirt over my head and let it fall to the floor. He devours me with his eyes as I unclasp my bra. My breasts fall gently against my chest.

"Keep going," he growls. "God, you're fucking beautiful."

I shiver as I kick off my slippers and then slide my leggings and panties over my hips.

When I'm fully naked, he closes the distance between us.

He's holding me against the wall again, his hard length

pressing against me. His kisses are desperate now, a fierce duel of tongues and teeth that leaves us both breathless.

He pushes me onto the bed with force, never taking his wild eyes off me. He moves over me. His body is warm and heavy, his scent intoxicating. He captures my mouth in another heated kiss, but then he pulls away and gazes down at me with a passion that takes my breath away.

"Say it, Angie," he breathes, his voice husky and charged with an intensity that mirrors the look in his eyes. "Tell me you want this. Tell me you want my hard cock inside your tight little pussy."

"I want this," I whisper back without missing a beat.

And I do. God, I do.

His eyes glow with something I don't recognize as he enters me with one swift, hard thrust. A gasp escapes my lips as pleasure and pain mingle together. He fills me completely, stretching me around him, marking me as his.

With each thrust, he takes us both closer to the edge of oblivion. I dig my nails into his muscular back, savoring the feel of his flesh beneath my fingertips.

"Look at me, Angie," he commands in a voice laced with raw desire. "Watch me fuck you."

I open my eyes to see his face contorted in pleasure. His eyes are like molten pools of emerald where an array of emotions swim—desire, hunger, fear, and something that looks suspiciously like love.

Or is that me?

Am I the one feeling love?

Our bodies are slick with sweat as we move together. He hits deeper with each thrust, reaching spots inside me I never knew existed. He slides one hand down my body and teases my clit.

I gasp as currents ripple through me. "Jason," I whimper, clinging on to him.

He's relentless, savage even. He quickens his pace, and the room fills with the sound of our labored breaths and the rustle of the sheets. The coil inside me tightens more and more until it snaps abruptly.

My orgasm sweeps over me like a tidal wave, wrenching a cry from my throat. My body convulses beneath him as wave after wave of pleasure crashes through me. Jason follows soon after, his own release ripping a guttural growl from his throat.

He collapses on top of me.

He's heavy, but I relish the feel of his weight on me.

We lie there, panting and exhausted, our bodies still intertwined. I feel his heart pounding against my chest—a steady drumming that matches the rhythm of my own.

For what feels like forever, we just exist. The silence is deafening in its intensity, broken only by the sound of our ragged breaths.

I don't know how long it lasts—minutes? Hours? All I know is that time seems to stand still. We are two bodies pressed together in my bedroom, the outside world forgotten.

Slowly, the reality of what just transpired begins to seep in. I've slept with my teacher. Again.

What would my mother say?

Worse, what would Aunt Melanie say?

I know better.

A wave of guilt washes over me, but it quickly subsides, replaced by a sense of contentment that I've never known before. His arm is draped over me, possessive and comforting at the same time.

BROKEN DREAM

"Angie," he eventually murmurs against my skin.

"What?"

He rolls over in bed. "I have to go."

CHAPTER THIRTY-TWO

JASON

For a moment, Angie looks at me like she's going to say something but then seems to think better of it.

I move from the bed and dress as quickly as I can.

I've used her.

I've used her to sate my own desires, to escape from the troubles plaguing me.

I force myself not to look at her as I button my navy slacks. I know what I'll see—confusion, hurt, maybe even a glimmer of understanding. But I can't face it. Not right now. I'm not sure what's more frightening—the fact that she might understand... or that she might not.

She remains silent as I button my shirt and put on my jacket. My chest aches with a dull throb of guilt and regret that intensifies with every passing second. But beneath the guilt, I feel relief. Relief that the fire burning inside me has been extinguished. At least for now.

"I'm sorry," I whisper, though I'm not sure why.

For using her? For leaving?

Or perhaps for everything?

No response. Did she even hear me?

Maybe not.

But the silence doesn't fool me. I feel her gaze on my back.

BROKEN DREAM

It's heavy, questioning. It's tangible, almost physical, like a hand reaching out to stop me. But I've built walls around me for a reason. Walls that are meant to keep everyone out.

Without another word, I make my way toward her bedroom door, my heart pounding. I pause, hand on the doorknob.

From behind me, I hear her soft whisper. "Jason."

I don't turn around. I can't.

"Would you like me to let your dog in?" I say, facing the door.

She pauses. "No. I can let her in. Thanks, though."

Good enough for me. I leave her bedroom. Leave her home.

Leave her life.

I walk the few yards to my own townhome and enter, pull my phone out of my pocket, and call Peter.

"It's Jason," I say to his voicemail. "I'll agree to the mental health assessment. I'll do whatever I have to. I need this surgery, Pete. I need to cut again."

Later, after I've had a pizza for dinner—along with a couple glasses of bourbon—my phone buzzes.

It's Pete.

"Hey," I say into the phone.

"I got your message. Dr. Steel can see you tomorrow."

I wince at the name. "Does it have to be Dr. Steel?"

"She's the best, and she came a long way to help us out. Her husband is quite ill, but she still made the time."

Her husband? That's Angie's uncle, Jonah Steel. "What's

220

HELEN HARDT

wrong with her husband?"

"Cancer. Glioblastoma."

Fuck. That's harsh. Usually a death sentence. "I'm sorry to hear that."

"Apparently he's responding well to experimental treatment. They're cautiously optimistic."

Experimental treatment? Oh, yeah? Did *his* hospital make him jump through mental-health hoops to get his experimental treatment? Fuck.

How do I tell him I may have a conflict with his choice of psychiatrist? That I happen to be fucking her niece, who is also my student?

Yeah.

Can't very well say that.

"Do you have an issue with Dr. Steel?" Pete asks.

And again, I can't really tell him.

"No," I say.

"Then eleven a.m. tomorrow. Will that work for you?"

"On a Sunday?"

He clears his throat. "She doesn't want to be away for any longer than she has to be. So yeah, tomorrow, if you can make it."

I sigh. "Eleven, you said?"

"Yes," he says. "You can use my office."

"I'll be there."

"Jason?"

"What?"

"You sound a little off. Have you been drinking?"

"Is the Pope Catholic?"

He sighs into the phone. "Look, we all know what you've been through, Jace. We all—"

221

BROKEN DREAM

"Stop it. Just stop it." My voice cracks slightly, but I steady it. "Until you lose a spouse and child and your ability to perform in your chosen career, don't tell me you know what I've been through."

He pauses a moment.

Then, "Fair enough."

"Good. So we understand each other, then."

"Jason, if you've been drinking, you need—"

"I'm not a fucking drunk, Peter. This isn't a problem. I ordered a pizza and had some bourbon. It's been a rough fucking day. Hell, it's been a rough fucking three years. I'm entitled to have a drink if I want to."

Then again, "Fair enough."

"Tell Dr. Steel I'll be there at eleven. How long will it take?"

"As long as she needs to make her assessment."

"Fine." I take a deep breath and sigh it out before continuing. "But I've been through therapy before, Pete. One hour didn't do a damn thing. Hell, hours and hours didn't do a damn thing. It certainly didn't help my wife. I can't believe you even had Dr. Morgan at that meeting today."

"She was..." he begins but then seems to think better of it. "It was probably a mistake to have her at the meeting."

"Damned right it was."

"Jason, please. We all know—"

"There you go again," I cut him off. "Saying you know. You don't know shit, Pete. Your wife is alive. Your kids are alive. You can still practice medicine in your chosen field. So shut. The. Fuck. Up."

"I'm going to assume that that's the alcohol talking," he says. "I'm still your chief of surgery."

"I'm no longer a surgeon, Pete. So you're not my chief of anything."

I end the call with a click.

And I wish that instead of a cell phone I had an old-fashioned phone that I could fucking slam down.

Three years earlier...

I've been sitting in Dr. Morgan's office for half an hour, and I haven't said anything. She hasn't tried to prompt me.

Lindsay's memorial was this past weekend, but still I came to my session.

With this doctor who couldn't help my wife.

With this doctor who I know can't help me.

Yet she's going to bill me for the hour that I sit here and say nothing.

"This is crap," I finally say.

"Yes, it is."

I roll my eyes.

"Is that it, Jason?" Dr. Morgan's voice is quiet, patient. It's the kind of voice that makes you feel guilty for yelling, even when you want to yell.

"It's not just *it*," I snap back. "It's everything. It's this room, this situation, my life. All of it."

Dr. Morgan scribbles something in her notepad. It's a distant scratching sound, like mice in the walls. For a moment I imagine that she's just doodling, maybe drawing zeros and ones or houses and trees. But I know she's writing about me.

"I know this is a difficult time for you," she begins.

I cut her off. "Difficult?" I laugh harshly. "That doesn't

BROKEN DREAM

even *begin* to cover it."

She nods, her expression unreadable behind her glasses. "Perhaps you'd like to talk about Lindsay?"

The mention of her name causes a lump to lodge firmly in my throat. I can taste the saltiness of impending tears threatening to spill down my cheeks. I never did read her letter. I showed it to the cops and then shoved it back into its envelope.

I swallow hard, narrowing my eyes at Dr. Morgan. "Perhaps I'd like to drown in the ocean," I retort. "Feels about the same."

Silence spills between us again, heavier this time. Dr. Morgan doesn't respond immediately, doesn't try to fill the void with empty reassurances or clinical observations. Instead, she inclines her head slightly and just waits.

It's like being under a microscope, tiny particles of my grief magnified and scrutinized.

"I'm not here for your amusement, Doctor," I spit out.

"And I'm not here to amuse you, Jason," she responds evenly.

I scoff again. "Like I said. Crap. That's what this is."

"What?"

"All of this." I gesture. "Psychiatry. All you do is throw my own words back at me. So you're not here to amuse me. This is what I'm paying God knows how many dollars an hour for? What a crock."

"You're angry, Jason," Dr. Morgan states.

I laugh, the sound bitter and empty. "Did it take you four years of med school and five years of residency to figure that one out? Because I could've told you that for free."

She doesn't rise to my bait. Just watches me with those

224

unwavering eyes. There's no judgment, just...understanding? No, not quite. Empathy, maybe? I don't want her empathy.

"Anger is a part of grief," she says.

I grip the armrests of my chair, my knuckles turning white. "Yeah, well, maybe I don't want to grieve. Maybe I want to be angry."

"And that's okay," she replies calmly. "You're allowed to be angry, Jason."

I snap my arm out, pointing a cold finger directly at her. "*You* were supposed to help her. To help Lindsay deal with the loss of her daughter. Our *daughter*. You said you could help. And now she's gone. By her own hand. And it's your fucking fault!"

Dr. Morgan's expression finally changes. It's not shock or surprise or even defense that crosses her face, but a kind of quiet sorrow. She doesn't look away from me, still meeting my gaze with her own. Her pen is suspended over her notebook.

"Jason..." she begins, her voice soft, measured even, as I hurl blame at her.

"No," I interrupt harshly. "Don't *Jason* me." My heart is pounding, a drumbeat of guilt mixed with grief and anger. Anger at Lindsay for leaving me alone in this mess, anger at myself for not being able to stop her, and anger at Dr. Morgan for failing us. "I didn't come here to be placated. I came here to tell you that you failed. You failed Lindsay, and you failed me."

"Psychiatry isn't a—"

I scoff. "Psychiatry is quackery. Psychiatry failed Lindsay. It failed me. And I'm done here."

CHAPTER THIRTY-THREE

ANGIE

Guilt consumes me as I sit next to Aunt Melanie over breakfast at a local Boulder diner. I want to talk to her about Jason, about what I've done, but I can't.

First, she'd be so disappointed in me that I got involved with a professor. And second, and more importantly, she's got her own problems with Uncle Joe's illness. I can't give her more of a burden to bear.

Still, as I pick at my scrambled eggs, I can't help but feel her knowing gaze on me. Aunt Melanie has always had an uncanny ability to see through my facades, and right now I feel as transparent as glass.

"Angie," she starts, her voice gentle. "You've been quiet this morning. More than usual. Is something bothering you?"

"Not really," I mumble, pushing down any trace of emotion that threatens to seep into my voice. "Just...thinking about school stuff."

Was I more talkative at our dinner Friday evening? Hell if I know. That was before my most recent encounter with Jason. The one where he left in silence after the deed was done.

"Medical school is no picnic," she says. "Believe me, I know."

But does she?

Aunt Mel went to medical school nearly forty years ago. She's just trying to help.

"I know, Aunt Mel." I look at my feet. "It's just harder than I thought, is all."

She pats my hand. Her touch is warm and comforting, a stark contrast to the cold, hard knot of guilt sitting heavy in my stomach.

"Angie," she says softly, holding my gaze with an understanding that makes me want to crumble. "You don't have to do this alone. You can talk to me about anything. You know that, right?"

I blink back the tears threatening to spill from the corners of my eyes and give her hand a weak squeeze. The temptation to spill everything is almost too much. To tell her about Jason, about how I feel like I'm drowning in my secret.

But I don't.

I can't.

Not only am I embarrassed by my lack of willpower when it comes to Jason, but I can't add to her troubles. She has enough going on with Uncle Joe.

Instead, I swallow hard against the lump forming in my throat and manage a shaky smile. "I know, Aunt Mel. Thank you."

She doesn't push further. "All right, sweetheart. But remember, it's okay to ask for help sometimes."

The rest of our breakfast passes in silence, punctuated only by the occasional clinking of silverware against plates. I'm grateful for her understanding, the way she doesn't push for more than I'm willing to give. Still, the guilt doesn't leave.

Once we finish eating and the check is paid, Aunt Mel stands and pulls on her coat. "I have a meeting I have to get to,

BROKEN DREAM

and then I'm off to the airport to fly home."

I nod and glance out at the snow falling gently outside the window, the weather mirroring my mood.

"Be careful. The snow and all."

She smirks. "It's just a few flurries. You know we see a lot worse on the Western Slope."

I rise and give her a hug. "Take care, Aunt Mel," I whisper into her coat, clinging on to her just a little longer than necessary.

She wraps her arms around me, her hug steady and comforting. Like an anchor in the storm that's been my life lately.

"You too, Angie," she murmurs into my hair before pulling back. "Remember what I said. You're not alone."

I nod as I watch her walk out of the diner, leaving me alone at the breakfast bar. I stare at the glass dome covering scones and muffins. As much as I appreciate Aunt Mel's words, they resonate hollowly within me. Because despite what she says, I do feel alone.

Alone with my guilt. Alone with my secret.

And with the fact that I think I might be falling in love with Dr. Jason Lansing.

My professor.

"Hey."

A voice interrupts my thoughts.

I turn to see Ralph.

I hold back a groan.

I'm really not in the mood for more of his threats.

"What do you want?" I demand.

CHAPTER THIRTY-FOUR

JASON

I sit outside Peter's office, waiting for the renowned Dr. Melanie Steel to arrive.

She's a well-respected psychiatrist. I have to think of her that way. I have to separate her from what I think of the field of psychiatry.

Otherwise, I'm not sure I'll be able to contain my anger at the world.

I also have to separate her from Angie.

A few moments later, she arrives, her cheeks red from the chill of the outside air. Her silvery blond hair is pulled up in a loose bun, and her green eyes sparkle.

"Dr. Lansing," she says. "I apologize for being a little bit late. I was having breakfast with my niece, and she seemed a little troubled, so I wanted to give her as much time as I could."

Dr. Steel has many nieces, but she can only be talking about Angie. I assume the rest of them live out west.

"Peter gave me his keys." She unlocks the door to Peter's office swiftly. "Come on in. Please take a seat and make yourself comfortable."

Dr. Steel's voice is gentle, soothing. It's a stark contrast to the icy weather outside and, in a way, the turbulence inside me. She's comforting, a quality that I suppose is essential to her profession. If I believed in her profession, that is. I still think it's all BS.

I follow her into the office. I've been in Pete's office many times, but still I gaze at the shelves lined with hardback books, his medical degrees and awards on the walls. The office is huge. He's the chief of surgery, of course. A plush sofa sits in one corner while two armchairs flank a mahogany coffee table in the center of the room. Next to the window is Peter's desk, neat as a pin.

"It's Sunday, so the staff aren't here," Dr. Steel says. "I apologize that I can't offer you any coffee."

"I'm good," I say.

"Okay." She smiles. "Have a seat." She gestures to the chairs facing the desk and takes Peter's chair behind the desk. "As you know, we're here for me to assess your mental health with regard to the experimental nerve graft to restore full function to your right hand."

I simply nod.

"It's important that you're honest with me, Dr. Lansing."

"Of course."

"The reason the board is concerned is because of the trauma you've been through. The accident that took your daughter's life and resulted in the injury to your hand, and your wife's subsequent suicide."

I try not to wince. "That all happened nearly three years ago," I say.

"Yes, I understand that," Dr. Steel replies, her voice steady and empathetic. "But as you know, the ripples of such traumatic events can linger for a long time. It is crucial to make sure you are emotionally stable before undergoing such an experimental procedure."

HELEN HARDT

I nod again, clenching my good hand into a fist. This woman in front of me isn't wrong, but underlining each tragedy is like reliving them all over again. I try to force myself to relax.

I'm unsuccessful.

"Dr. Lansing," she says. "I think it would be beneficial to further discuss these past traumatic experiences. To understand your coping mechanisms."

"I've coped," I insist. "It's not like I had any choice in the matter."

She studies me with a soft yet probing gaze. "Coping and healing are two different things, Dr. Lansing," she says gently. "You're a well-respected surgeon, and I admire your resilience. But sometimes, even the strongest among us need assistance with mending the parts of ourselves that aren't visible to the naked eye."

I glance at the framed pictures on Peter's desk, his family's cheery faces mocking my internal turmoil. His wife. His children.

Those things I no longer have.

I swallow hard and nod.

"Let's start from the beginning." She leans back in Peter's chair. "The accident with your daughter, Julia. Can you tell me about that day?"

I close my eyes for a moment, letting the memory wash over me. It's like wounds being reopened. Here we go.

Again.

"Dr. Lansing..."

"I had a big surgery scheduled—a Whipple with a high-risk patient—and Lindsay had parent-teacher conferences. I was supposed to take Julia to her grandmother's for the day instead of to daycare. It was raining. Raining really hard."

BROKEN DREAM

She nods, keeping her expression impassive.

That's what shrinks do. They force you to talk about things while they have no feelings themselves.

But if I want this surgery at this hospital, I have to jump through the fucking hoops.

"A car was coming through a red light and T-boned me." My heart starts to accelerate. "I tried to stop. Tried to..."

The words get stuck in my throat.

"It's okay. Go as slowly as you need to go."

I close my eyes again and take a deep breath. "My airbag deployed, and I screamed for Julia. But she... She was forced out of her car seat and..."

Forced out because I had neglected to make sure she was secure.

No. I buckled her in. I remember.

The click. I heard the click.

Or did I?

Dr. Steel nods. "Go on."

I open my eyes. "Why? Why do I have to relive this? Therapy didn't work for me. It didn't work for Lindsay. I'm sure you've seen Dr. Morgan's records."

"You know I can't look at Dr. Morgan's records without your consent."

"But you're consulting."

"It's not the same thing. I'm consulting at the request of the hospital board. Not at Dr. Morgan's request. You're no longer her patient."

"Right," I mutter. "So is this what it comes down to? Rehashing my grief as a form of penance? Some sort of toll I have to pay to fix my hand?"

Dr. Steel holds my gaze. "The process is not meant to be

punitive, Dr. Lansing. You know that. It's about understanding your emotional state and ensuring that you are in the best place for a positive outcome, whether the surgery is successful or not."

"I'm not the same man who was in therapy three years ago," I say. "I've learned to live with my grief. I've accepted that life is cruelly unpredictable."

She nods. "Trauma has a way of changing us. How we come out on the other side can often speak more about us than the traumas themselves."

I exhale slowly, absorbing her words. She has a point, but it still irks me. It feels like my worth, my competency, is being determined by how well I've healed, how well I've adapted to the unexpected blows life has dealt me.

"All right," I say finally. "What do you need to know?"

"I'd like to understand how you've coped. Particularly on the more difficult days."

I contemplate her words, mulling over the ways grief has become a part of my everyday life. "Some days are harder than others," I admit.

Though the last few days have been less difficult.

Because of Angie.

But I can't say that.

But damn... That day after the meeting with Louisa and Gita, when I felt hope.

I was almost happy that day.

Until the powers that be decided I might not be mentally fit for the surgery.

Dr. Steel simply nods, patiently waiting for me to continue.

"I sleep less on those days," I say. "I tend to throw myself into work or research. I find it easier to cope when my mind is occupied."

"And when you're not working?"

"It varies," I respond honestly. "Sometimes it's just...quiet reflection."

Or more accurately lately...fucking her niece.

But nope. Can't say that.

"And what about your support system, Dr. Lansing?" she asks. "Family, friends?"

Right.

No family to speak of.

And any friendships Lindsay and I had have dried up. My own fault. I just didn't want to deal with the questions, the pitying looks.

"I have colleagues," I reply.

She presses her lips together. "Colleagues can be a form of support too, but it's not quite the same as having a close friendship. Do you have anyone you trust, someone you can confide in when things get tough?"

The question hangs heavily between us, an unwanted reminder of the isolation I've found myself in these past years.

Except...now I have Angie. Sort of. But a couple of good fucks isn't a support system.

Shit. For a second I actually understand why the board is insisting on this.

Then it fades.

"Dr. Lansing?" Dr. Steel prompts.

"No," I admit, a bitter taste in my mouth. "There isn't anyone."

She is silent a moment, her pen tapping lightly against the notepad in her lap. "What about hobbies? Anything that brings you joy or at least some form of distraction?"

"I run. Go to the gym."

"Alone?"

"Yeah. I used to run with Lindsay."

Dr. Steel lifts her gaze from the notepad and gives me an attentive nod.

"We'd go for runs in the park every Sunday," I explain, staring past her at the bookshelves. My voice is distant, as if it belongs to someone else. "It helped us unwind. I've tried to keep up the habit. It's one of the few things that still makes sense."

"And do you think it has helped? This routine?"

I shrug. "To some degree, I suppose. There's comfort in the physical exertion, in the constancy. It's like, if I can keep going one more mile, then I can keep going through everything else."

"You've built a routine around your resilience," she says, scribbling something down on her notepad. "That speaks volumes to your strength, Dr. Lansing."

Strength. I huff out a laugh. "Then I'm strong enough for this surgery, wouldn't you say? Regardless of the outcome?"

She sighs. "If I said yes at this point, I'd be doing you a disservice, as well as a disservice to the hospital board who asked me to do this evaluation."

I furrow my brow, unable to hold back the frustration that bubbles to the surface. "You think I'm not fit for the surgery," I state, more as an accusation than a question.

Dr. Steel looks at me, her gaze unreadable. "I think," she says slowly, "that there are still some unresolved issues you need to deal with. These are not disqualifications, Dr. Lansing, but they are obstacles."

"Obstacles," I repeat, my voice thick with sarcasm. "Is

that what we're calling it?"

"Call it whatever you like," she says calmly. "But the fact remains that emotional well-being is just as crucial as physical capability when it comes to an experimental surgery that may give you back something crucial that you've lost. Or it may not. It may make things worse. And that, Dr. Lansing, is my concern. If the surgery works, I feel certain that you'll be fine. If it doesn't..."

Her words are left hanging in the air, echoing with unspoken implications.

I'm silent, unable to respond immediately. It's a scenario that I've considered many times, but hearing it from her adds a new layer of weight to it.

"If it doesn't," I finally echo, forcing a neutral tone. "You're worried about my reaction."

Or more precisely, she's worried I may do what Lindsay resorted to. I may take my own life.

She nods. "That's right, Dr. Lansing. It's my job to ensure the hospital that you can handle whatever outcome you'll face. Especially since you don't seem to have an adequate support system."

Anger boils up inside me, and for the first time in our monotonous conversation, I feel my control slip. "So what do you propose, Dr. Steel?" I snap. "Another round of therapy? More digging into my past?"

"I'm not proposing anything yet," she says, seemingly unfazed by my outburst. "I am, however, suggesting we continue this conversation."

CHAPTER THIRTY-FIVE

ANGIE

"Do you mind?" Ralph gestures to the stool next to me, the one Aunt Mel vacated.

"Knock yourself out," I say. "I'm just leaving."

"Stay. Please."

He's got to be kidding. "Thanks. But no." I rise.

He grabs my arm.

I yank it away. "Don't fucking touch me," I say through clenched teeth.

He rolls his eyes. "For God's sake, Angie, we're in a public place. What kind of man do you think I am?"

I sit back down so I can lower my voice and be sure that he hears every word.

"You've already shown me who you are. You threatened to blackmail me with a story that isn't true." The lie is bitter on my tongue.

He looks at me, cocks his head, narrows his eyes. "You know, I wouldn't expect you to be such a good little liar, yet here we are."

His words hang heavy in the air, a foul stench that makes me want to vomit. "You think you know me, Ralph?"

He smirks. "I know enough."

"You know nothing." The words escape my mouth before

BROKEN DREAM

I can stop them. There's no point in playing nice anymore. Not with this man.

"Is that so?" He leans back on his stool, his eyes never leaving mine. "Enlighten me, then."

I inhale deeply, the smoky scent of bacon somehow making me stronger. "I'm not going to let you blackmail me," I say, meeting his gaze head-on. "I'm not going to let you ruin my life or Dr. Lansing's over a lie."

He chuckles. "You've got guts, Angie. But your little miss innocent act is lost on me. I saw what I saw, and the two of you were in a clench so tight that it could choke a snake."

"If you saw someone kissing Dr. Lansing—and I'm not convinced you did—it wasn't me."

He crosses his arms. "Believe what you want. But the truth is a stubborn beast. It refuses to stay buried."

"*Your* truth," I reply, forcing the words out between gritted teeth. "Your twisted version of reality. It's not a weapon you can use against me, Ralph."

He leans in closer, his breath reeking of alcohol and stale coffee. "We'll see about that," he whispers, his voice slithering into my ear.

I shiver but hold my ground.

"I'm not afraid of you," I say quietly.

"I know you're not. You can pay me off in the next minute if I demand it. And if I do go to the dean, nothing will happen to you. Not to the sweet little heiress. Dr. Lansing is another story, though. He'll lose his job, and wouldn't that be a shame after all he's been through?"

I tilt my head. "What are you talking about?"

"Save your little innocent routine. After that clench you were in, do you expect me to believe you didn't stalk his socials and find out everything you could about him?"

I gesture to the waitress. "Could I get another cup of coffee, please?"

She flashes me a smile. "Coming right up."

"And a Denver omelet for me," Ralph says, "with hash browns and bacon. Put it on her tab."

I glare at him.

He shrugs. "You can afford it. Right?"

I suppose if I want to protect Jason, breakfast is a small price to pay.

"Sure," I say, "it's on me."

"That's more like it." Ralph grins and settles back onto his stool. He takes a sip of his coffee, the smugness in his expression making my skin crawl.

The waitress returns with my coffee, and I thank her as I wrap my hands around the warm mug. The scent of fresh coffee fills the air, and for a moment, I let it distract me from the man sitting next to me.

"What do you want, Ralph?" I ask eventually, breaking the silence that has settled between us.

His grin widens at my question, and he shrugs. "I'm looking for information," he says nonchalantly.

I narrow my eyes at him. "And blackmailing people is the way to go about it? Haven't you heard of the internet?"

He laughs again, that horrible, low rumbling sound that reverberates in my ears. "The information I'm looking for isn't the kind you'd find there."

I grit my teeth and take a long, slow sip of my coffee, forcing myself to stay calm. "You're making a mistake," I say quietly.

His smile fades slightly. "Is that a threat?"

BROKEN DREAM

"No," I reply, matching his tone. "It's a fact. You're making a mistake if you think I'm going to let you destroy people's lives for your own enjoyment."

"Oh, I don't intend to destroy anyone's life," he retorts. "Just shake things up a little."

I set down my coffee cup with more force than necessary. "You have no right—"

He cuts me off with a dismissive wave of his hand. "Save your moral outrage, Angie. We both know this situation isn't about rights."

"Then what is it about?" I grind out, struggling to keep my temper in check.

Ralph's eyes glint with a predatory anticipation. "Power," he says, his voice low and menacing. "And control. And people getting what's coming to them."

A shiver of fear and revulsion runs down my spine, but I refuse to let him see it. "I won't play your games, Ralph," I say quietly.

He chuckles, looking thoroughly amused. "Angie, you're already playing."

The waitress returns then, setting down Ralph's breakfast with a cheerful smile. It's an abrupt return to reality that momentarily stuns me into silence.

"Enjoy your meal," she tells Ralph before shooting me an empathetic look.

"Thanks," Ralph replies, his attention already on the food in front of him.

"Well," I say after a moment's pause, my voice steady despite the turmoil within me. "I hope you enjoy your breakfast." With that, I push back my stool and stand.

"Where do you think you're going?" His voice is casual,

but there's a hard edge to it.

I toss some bills onto the counter for his meal, ignoring his question.

"I'm not bluffing, Angie," he says. "Don't you want to hear what I want?"

I turn back at him. "I don't know what information I could possibly have that would be of any use to you. What do you want to know about? My family's history? It's posted all over the tabloids. All over the internet. I've got nothing that would give you any leverage over the Steels."

He scoffs. "Why the hell would I want information about the Steels?"

I blink. "Because we have money. Because we have power. Isn't that what you said you care about? Power and control?"

He rubs at his forehead. "Christ, you're dumber than you look. No wonder you want to go into psychiatry. You're not smart enough to be a *real* doctor."

I want to blow up at him, but that would just be giving him what he wants.

"If you don't want information about my family, then I really don't know what use I could be to you."

I'm about to turn my back to him when his words slink into my ears like a deadly viper.

"I want information on Jason Lansing."

I give him a dirty look. "All I know about Jason Lansing is that he's our anatomy professor. My knowledge of his life begins and ends with that."

Without another word, I walk out of the diner and into the cool morning air. But Ralph's words follow me like a shadow.

Power and control. And information about Jason.

What kind of information does he think I have?

BROKEN DREAM

His dick size?

And that's assuming he knows that we've slept together. Which he couldn't possibly...

Shit. We were in the anatomy lab. If he saw us kissing there, he could have...

Jason locked the door.

But not soon enough.

The chill of the morning seeps through my clothing, but it's a welcome respite from the toxic warmth of the diner. I draw in a lungful of crisp, clean air, hoping it will rid my senses of Ralph's stench.

Control. The word echoes in my mind as I start walking through the town. What control does he think I have? Yes, I could pay him off, but that's not what he wants. He wants me to feel helpless, powerless under his threats.

And he wants some kind of leverage over Jason. Leverage that he thinks I can provide.

I'm glad Aunt Mel is still here.

She said she had a meeting and then she'd be flying back to the Western Slope this afternoon.

I quickly text her.

CHAPTER THIRTY-SIX

JASON

I open my mouth, but before I say anything, a chirping sound comes from Dr. Steel's direction.

She grabs her phone out of her purse. "Sorry. I must have forgotten to put it on silent."

"No worries."

"I'll just check it later. It's my niece."

Angie.

She has other nieces, but they're not in Boulder. At least not that I know of.

"Go ahead. I don't mind."

"You sure?"

I nod. "Family is important."

Don't I fucking know it.

"Okay. This will only be a second." She taps out a message and then tucks her phone away. "My niece wants to talk before I leave later today. Now where were we?"

"Your suggestion to continue our conversation," I say, my voice steadier now despite the surge of adrenaline that the mention of Angie has triggered.

"That's right," she says, her tone softening. "I want to make it clear, Dr. Lansing, that I'm not here to pass judgment or make you feel cornered. This is about your well-being—

BROKEN DREAM

both mentally and physically."

I nod, understanding the logic behind her words but resenting them all the same. They feel like chains holding me back from something I desperately need.

"I get it," I assure her, trying to put a little warmth into my tone. "And I'll do whatever it takes. If that means talking more, then we'll talk more."

"Good. That's what I like to hear," Dr. Steel replies with a small smile.

"I believe we were discussing my potential emotional responses to the surgery," I say, my tone now a touch icier. "You were suggesting that a negative outcome might lead to a breakdown, correct?"

"Not necessarily."

"Let's cut to the chase, then." I clear my throat. "This hospital is state of the art, and Dr. Patel has privileges here. It is the closest hospital to my home, and the hospital where I began my surgical career. I want the surgery here."

"Yes, I understand all that, but—"

"Please. Let me finish."

She nods. "Of course. I'm here for you, Dr. Lansing."

Right. She's here for the hospital, not for me. "This is about money, and it's about bad PR."

"It's about your well-being, Dr. Lansing."

Yeah. That's crap and we both know it.

"Please," I say, doing my best not to roll my eyes. "It's about a lot of things, but when it comes down to it, the board is mostly concerned about money and PR. So here's my solution. I'll sign a contract not to sue the hospital or issue any negative statements should the outcome of the surgery not be as expected."

244

Dr. Steel eyes me for a moment, seemingly caught off guard. "Dr. Lansing," she begins, her voice steady and measured, "I appreciate your willingness to cooperate and protect the hospital's interests. But at the end of the day, my primary concern is your overall health."

"I understand that," I say quickly. "But what this boils down to is trust. My trust in the hospital and the world-class surgeons."

"No." She shakes her head. "My job here—what they've asked me to do—is to assess your mental health with regard to the experimental surgery. And I'm afraid a promise not to sue is not necessarily indicative of good mental health. In fact, it could very well indicate the opposite."

I fall silent, stung by her words. I expected some objection, but the idea that my willingness to protect the hospital is somehow a reflection of poor mental health... What the fuck?

"You're right," I reply slowly, lying through my teeth. "Perhaps it's not indicative of good mental health. But it is indicative of my determination and my desperation."

Dr. Steel sighs, pinching the bridge of her nose. "Life isn't about making deals, especially when it comes to your health. This isn't about contracts or promises or legalities. This is about *you*."

"Yes! Now you're making sense. This is exactly about me!" I pound a fist to my chest. "*My* life, *my* choices, *my* future!" I take a deep breath to gather myself before continuing more calmly. "And if signing away my right to complain or cause legal trouble gives me a shot at regaining what I've lost, then that's a risk I'm willing to take."

"I'm no lawyer," she says, "but I'm fairly certain that in any experimental surgery, part of the informed consent that

BROKEN DREAM

you sign will include a waiver in the consent process where the patient agrees not to hold doctors or hospitals liable for known risks of the procedure. These are of course not enforceable in the case of negligence or misconduct. And it certainly wouldn't take away your right to sue in the case of gross negligence, fraud, or intentional misconduct."

"But I'm willing to sign away those rights," I say.

She closes her eyes and takes a deep breath in. "And I'm telling *you*, Dr. Lansing, that it doesn't make a difference. No court in the world will uphold an agreement if it's deemed unconscionable or grossly unfair, which waiving your rights to sue in case of negligence or misconduct would certainly be."

I sink back into my chair. "So what does all this mean?" I ask, struggling to keep the frustration out of my voice.

"It means," she begins gently, "that we need to focus on your mental well-being first. We need to ensure that you're mentally ready and strong enough to cope with any outcome from the surgery."

"All right, then."

She presses her lips together. "And after today, Dr. Lansing, I'm not sure you are."

I flinch at her words as if I've been slapped. Her calm, steady gaze stings more than any outburst would.

"I want to help you," she continues, "but I need you to be open with me. You need to be prepared for the worst while hoping for the best."

Her words echo in my mind, yet they feel distant and unreal. *Prepared for the worst.* But what's worse than waking up every day in this broken body? What's worse than the fear that I'll never regain what I've lost?

"I appreciate your candor, Dr. Steel," I manage to say

through gritted teeth. "I am aware of the risks, and I am prepared to face them."

"Are you really, though?" She leans forward, her gaze searching mine. "Or are you just saying what you think I want to hear?"

I suppose she's got me there. "I don't need your judgment," I snap back, anger flaring up once again. "I need your support."

"And I want to give you that support. But it's my job to ensure that you're making a sound decision, not one based on desperation or the fear of being left alone in this condition."

"I am not afraid," I retort. "I'm determined."

"Determination is important," Dr. Steel says. "But so is understanding. Understanding that there are no guarantees with this surgery. Understanding that life may not return to exactly how it was before."

"I *do* understand that." The words come out more forcefully than I intend. "I understand it better than anyone, Dr. Steel. You're not talking to someone off the street. You're talking to a former surgeon." I stand. "Do you not think I've had my own failures? That mistakes I've made haven't led to terrible consequences for my patients, up to and including death? If there is one person who *does* understand the ramifications of this choice, it's me."

Her eyes flicker with something I can't quite identify. "Good," she replies. "Now we need to work on accepting it."

Acceptance. The word hangs heavy in the room. Her response to what I just said doesn't make sense. Acceptance of what exactly? The possibility that I may never regain full function of my hand?

I've already had to accept that.

Why the hell are we even having this ridiculous

BROKEN DREAM

conversation?

"You've accepted the reality of your condition, yes," she continues, "but accepting the potential outcomes of this surgery is a different matter altogether."

I let out a laugh at that, unable to mask the irritation creeping into my voice. "You're implying there's something left to lose, Dr. Steel. I think we both know that's not the case."

She remains silent a moment longer. "Dr. Lansing," she finally says, "there's always more to lose."

The room goes silent as her words settle in the air between us. I feel my resolve waning under her relentless matter-of-factness and the truth of her words. The energy to argue with her is draining away, leaving me feeling tired and old.

I've lost my child and my wife. I've lost the life I built, both at home and at work.

What more could I possibly lose?

And then I realize.

Angie.

I could lose her.

But that's stupid, isn't it? I barely know her. She's a hot little student that I've been messing around with because it's forbidden.

But even as I think those words, I know I'm lying to myself.

There's something more with Angie. Perhaps if I lost the total use of my hand, she wouldn't want to be with me anymore. People have broken off relationships for a lot less.

Already I know Angie wouldn't do something like that, but still...

I could lose her.

Or I could lose my life. Patients sometimes die on the operating table for no apparent reason.

"Maybe you're right," I finally concede, my voice barely above a whisper. "Maybe there is more to lose."

"I know this isn't easy for you," she says, her tone softer now. "But it's important that we proceed carefully. That we consider all potential outcomes and ensure that you're prepared for them."

"And what if I'm not?"

I can see the empathy in Dr. Steel's eyes as she leans forward, placing her notepad on the table beside her. "Then we work on getting you prepared," she says gently. "You'll need to go back to therapy."

I shake my head vigorously. "I won't. I won't see Dr. Morgan again."

"No, I don't recommend that you see Dr. Morgan. I'll recommend someone else."

"So you're saying no surgery."

I want to shout. Tell her I hate her. Tell her she's a bitch.

But that won't help her decide I'm mentally fit.

It will convince her that I'm not.

So I say nothing. And I wait for her to speak.

CHAPTER THIRTY-SEVEN

ANGIE

Aunt Melanie's text comes a moment after I send mine.

> Yes, I'll have time to see you. I'm at the hospital in a meeting. Meet me on the sixth floor in an hour.

Good enough.
I head on over to wait.
Funny that I haven't looked into Jason.
So I start a search.
I've seen his faculty profile, but I want to know more.
What was Ralph alluding to?
The first thing I find out is that Jason Lansing is a pretty common name.

I sigh, pushing my hair back from my face. Adjusting the search parameters, I include his profession and the city of our university.

And a link catches my eye—an obituary. My heart skips a beat as I see it's for a woman named Lindsay Lansing. The similarity of the surname is enough to pique my interest. I click on it.

The date on the obituary is three years old. The cause of

death isn't mentioned.

> *It is with profound sadness that we announce the passing of Lindsay Davis Lansing, a beloved wife, mother, and schoolteacher. Lindsay's unwavering kindness, boundless love for her students, and devotion to her family left an indelible mark on all who knew her.*
>
> *Lindsay grew up with a passion for education and a deep desire to nurture young minds. She earned her degree in education from the University of Boulder and spent her career inspiring children to learn and grow, believing every student deserved a champion. Lindsay's classroom was a haven of encouragement, creativity, and laughter, reflecting her own vibrant spirit.*
>
> *Lindsay faced unimaginable heartbreak with the loss of her cherished daughter, Julia, at the tender age of three.*
>
> *She is survived by her loving husband, Dr. Jason Lansing...*

My heart drops out from under me.

This woman was Jason's wife.

And she had a daughter, who I assume she had with Jason.

This man who I've become entangled with has faced two tremendous losses. No wonder he's been so hard to read.

It was only three years ago. He's probably moved on a little bit, but he's still grieving his wife. And I can't even imagine what he feels about his child.

They must have died only a few months apart. I read the rest of Lindsay's obit.

She is survived by her loving husband, Dr. Jason Lansing, her sister, Marla (Christopher) Delgado, her brother, Logan (Cynthia) Davis, and her parents, Mr. and Mrs. Barry (Lisa) Davis.

In lieu of flowers, the family asks that donations be made in Lindsay's name to the Boulder Food Pantry to continue her legacy of compassion and support for children and families in need.

Lindsay will be remembered for her grace, her warmth, and the love she shared with the world. She now rests alongside her beloved Julia, leaving behind a legacy of strength and love that will forever be cherished.

Finding myself immersed in this personal tragedy makes me feel uncomfortable. But then again, Ralph brought this up. He started this game, and whether I like it or not, I'm immersed in it now.

No further mention of the daughter. Another quick search uncovers her obituary, and this one truly brings me to tears.

First a photo. A beautiful child with dark hair and green eyes like her father. Ruby-red cherub cheeks and a sweet smile.

It is with broken hearts that we announce the passing of Julia Lindsay Lansing. Julia's life, though far too short, was a bright and beautiful gift to all who knew her.

Julia brought boundless joy and love into the lives

of her parents, family, and friends. Her laughter was infectious, her curiosity endless, and her smile could light up even the darkest day. She loved animals, drawing pictures with her favorite crayons, and cuddling with her cherished stuffed frog "Fwoggie."

Julia's days were filled with the simple wonders of childhood—playing in the park, singing songs with her parents, and exploring the world with wide-eyed innocence. Her sweet nature and radiant spirit touched everyone she met, leaving behind memories that will be treasured forever.

Julia is survived by her devoted parents, Dr. Jason and Lindsay Lansing, whose love for her was boundless and unwavering. Her presence in their lives was a profound blessing, and her memory will remain forever in their hearts. She is also survived by her grandparents, Mr. and Mrs. Barry (Lisa) Davis, plus an aunt and uncle on her mother's side.

In honor of Julia's love for animals, the family asks that donations be made in her name to the Boulder Animal Shelter.

Julia's brief but beautiful life will always be remembered as a testament to the power of love, joy, and innocence. Though she is gone from this world, her light will continue to shine in the hearts of those who loved her.

I grab a tissue to wipe away the tears that have accumulated on my cheeks. Jason's parents aren't mentioned, nor are any aunts and uncles from his side. Are his parents dead?

My God...

Jason lost his daughter.

Then a few months later, his wife.

It doesn't say the cause of Lindsay's death, but I'm betting she took her own life.

Any couple would seek counseling of some sort after losing a child. They were probably seeing someone. But it clearly didn't work for Lindsay.

Which explains why Jason is so skeptical of psychiatry.

I wipe the remaining tears from my eyes and blow my nose into the tissue.

Poor Jason.

Once a renowned surgeon and now a widower who lost a child and is relegated to teaching anatomy lab to first-year medical students.

Then it hits me.

The injury to his hand. Could it be related to his daughter's death? A ski accident or something? We *are* in Colorado. It's a pretty common occurrence.

I can't help myself.

I keep digging.

CHAPTER THIRTY-EIGHT

JASON

"No," Dr. Steel finally replies, the gravity of the word hitting me like a punch. "I'm not saying 'no surgery.' What I'm saying is that we need to approach this responsibly." She places a hand over her heart. "You're not just a patient, Dr. Lansing. You're a doctor. You know as well as I do that the success of any medical procedure depends as much on the patient's mental preparedness and strength as it does on their physical condition. A good support system is also necessary, and I'm not sure you have that."

Her words are reasonable. Logical. Utterly infuriating.

"Responsibly," I echo, unable to keep the bitterness from my voice. "Is that why we're sitting here, talking about therapists and court cases instead of discussing the actual procedure? Is that why you're trying to convince me that I should be content with my life as it is instead of fighting for something better?"

"I'm not suggesting anything remotely close to contentment," she replies calmly. "I'm suggesting preparedness, Dr. Lansing. Preparedness for all outcomes."

I run my hands through my hair. "It's almost like you think Dr. Patel and her team are going to fail. They're the best at this."

BROKEN DREAM

"I have every confidence in Dr. Patel and her team," Dr. Steel says firmly. "But there are no certainties in medicine. Not even with the best surgeons in the world."

"And you think I don't know that?" My anger flares again. "I'm not some naïve kid, Dr. Steel. I was a surgeon once myself, as I've told you repeatedly. I know the frustration of a bad outcome. And as for this procedure, I know the odds."

"Then you should also understand," she says, "why it's crucial to address your mental well-being before we proceed."

I fall silent at that, unable to voice my frustration without resorting to shouting. She has an answer for everything, a rational counterpoint to every argument I make. And if she says the phrase *mental well-being* one more time, I may explode.

She looks at her watch and smiles. "I'm afraid our time is up. My job here was to assess your mental and emotional well-being with regard to this experimental surgery. While I believe you understand, objectively, what could happen, I'm not convinced that, given your past trauma and loss, you are emotionally ready to handle any possible outcome. I worry about your coping abilities, about your lack of a support system. And I say this with the highest regard for you, Dr. Lansing, both as a colleague and as a human being."

I stare at her, the words sinking in like weights in water. The implication is clear—my surgery is on hold until I can prove to her, to them, that I'm mentally stable. That I can handle whatever happens next. It feels like a cruel joke.

She stands and extends her hand to me. "I'll be in touch regarding the recommended therapist," she says. "Dr. Carlos Engel is on the faculty here at the medical school. He specializes in the trauma of loss. I think he'd be a good fit."

HELEN HARDT

I look at her hand and then back at her face, my anger replaced by a cold numbness that seems to permeate my very bones.

Carlos Engel. He seems like a nice guy for a shrink, but I hardly know him.

So I guess I'll play the part. Become an actor. Pretend I think psychiatry is beneficial, though it cost me my wife.

"Fine," I say. "Thank you for your time."

"You're most welcome." She grabs her coat off the rack and wraps it around her. "Now if you'll excuse me, I have to meet my niece. She should be waiting outside."

My body goes rigid.

Angie?

Outside Pete's office? This very office?

"I'll wait here, if you don't mind," I say. "I need to think."

She frowns. "I'm sorry. I told Peter I'd lock up the office when we were finished."

Great. Just great.

I have no choice but to follow Dr. Steel out of Pete's office.

Where Angie is sitting on the floor, reading something on her phone. She looks up when she hears us.

"Aunt Mel," she says. Then her eyes widen. "And Ja— I mean, Dr. Lansing?"

"You know each other?" Aunt Mel asks.

"He's my anatomy lab professor," Angie says.

Shoot me. Just shoot me now. HIPAA be damned. It's clear I was meeting with Dr. Steel, and Dr. Steel is a renowned psychiatrist.

Yeah, shoot me now.

"Nice to see you, Angie," I say as nonchalantly as I can.

"You too, Dr. Lansing," Angie says, her voice trembling

257

BROKEN DREAM

just a touch.

"Dr. Lansing and I were just discussing some hospital board business," Dr. Steel says.

Nice save.

Problem is that no one's going to believe it.

"Thank you for your time, Dr. Lansing." She offers me her hand. "I'll be in touch."

Normally in this situation, I'd reject her handshake. But since Angie's right there, I take her hand weakly. "I appreciate it. I think we can get this all settled."

"I'm sure we can."

I nod to her and Angie, and then I walk down the hallway toward the elevator.

What a mess.

I've been living in a hole for so long.

Grieving my daughter, grieving my wife. Grief never goes away, but it does get easier to handle.

Mostly I'm angry.

Angry that the two most important people in my life were taken away from me, along with my ability to do my chosen profession.

And damn it, I was a good surgeon. I was a fucking amazing surgeon.

Now, after three years, two things have happened that made me happy.

First, Dr. Matthews and Dr. Patel gave me hope. Hope with this experimental surgery that could restore the function in my right hand.

And second, I met a woman. A woman who made me believe there is life after Lindsay. A woman who made me want to love again.

The problem? She's my student, and her aunt, a renowned psychiatrist, is the one trying to block me from my potentially career-saving surgery.

The Lord giveth and the Lord fucking taketh away.

I look up at the ceiling just as the elevator dings and the doors open.

Is the universe laughing at me?

Dangling a carrot in front of me?

Because there are two things right now that I want more than anything.

Angie and the surgery.

And the universe seems to have decided that I can't have either.

CHAPTER THIRTY-NINE

ANGIE

So Aunt Mel knows Jason.

I really wanted to confide in her about what I'm feeling for him and then also talk to her about Ralph and his threats.

But now that she knows Jason?

God, what to do?

She checks her watch. "I have an hour before I need to leave for the airport. What did you need to talk to me about, Angie?"

I draw a breath. "It's kind of difficult to talk about."

We head toward the elevators. I hold my breath but then let it out slowly when I see that Jason has already descended.

Thank God.

As much as I love being in his presence, right now is not the best time.

"We can grab a snack," Aunt Mel says.

I pat my stomach. "I'm still full from breakfast. But maybe a cup of coffee. There's a shop on the first floor of the hospital."

She laughs. "Oh, I know that. I spent a lot of time at this hospital in my day. I was on the board for a long time, and I still come in for special consultations, like I did today."

"So what's going on?" I ask. "What did you need to talk to Dr. Lansing about?"

She blinks. "Like I told you, just some board business."

"I didn't realize Ja— Dr. Lansing was on the board."

"No, he's not." She looks at me, but her eyes are not meeting mine. "He's just doing some consulting, like I am."

Aunt Mel is stuck between a rock and a hard place. She told me earlier that she was seeing a patient about an experimental procedure, making sure his past trauma wouldn't interfere with his recovery. Thanks to my internet snooping, I now know the details of said trauma.

She knows that she told me that information, and now she knows that I'm acquainted with the man who walked out of the office with her. It doesn't take a genius to figure it out.

But she doesn't want to violate doctor-patient confidentiality any more than she already indirectly has, so I'll do her a favor and lie through my teeth.

"I guess that makes sense. He's a professor at the medical school associated with the hospital, and he's a former surgeon who probably worked here."

We descend to the first floor, and when the doors open, we head straight toward the coffee shop.

"What would you like?" Aunt Mel asks. "My treat."

"Black coff— No. You know what? I'll have a skinny mocha."

She cocks an eyebrow. "Skinny? You could use a little more meat on your bones."

"Okay. A regular mocha, then." I'm never one to worry about my weight. All of us Steels seem to have the metabolisms of teenage boys.

Aunt Mel orders my mocha and a latte for herself, and we take a seat at one of the tables.

"So," she begins, "what can I do for you?"

BROKEN DREAM

I have to come up with something. I can hardly talk to her about Jason now that I've connected the dots.

Then again, this is Aunt Melanie. I talk to her about everything. I talked to her more than I talked to my own mother growing up. She and I have always been close, and she's the reason I want to go into psychiatry.

"This is between you and me," I say.

"Of course." She grabs my hand across the table, squeezes it. "Everything you say to me is always just between the two of us. You know that, Angie." She tilts her head. "Something really is wrong, isn't it?"

"Not wrong so much as..."

"You can tell me. I noticed you seemed a little off at dinner last night and breakfast this morning. What are you struggling with?"

I open my mouth to speak when the barista brings our drinks over.

Aunt Melanie smiles. "Thank you."

Once the barista leaves, Aunt Melanie meets my gaze. Her own seems troubled.

I take the lid off my mocha and swirl it, letting the steam escape.

"So this is really confidential between the two of us," I say again. "You can't tell anyone. And I mean *anyone*."

"Of course not, Angie." She furrows her brow with concern. "What is this about?"

I take a sip of my mocha.

Burn my tongue.

"A couple of things." I swallow. "This wasn't going to be easy to talk about anyway, and now it's even harder."

"Why is that?"

262

HELEN HARDT

"Because it involves... It involves Dr. Lansing."

Aunt Melanie's eyebrows nearly pop off her head. "What about Dr. Lansing?"

"Well, like I said, he's my anatomy lab professor."

"Yes. I know you're having trouble with lab. With cutting into your cadaver."

"Yeah, but that's not the problem. I..." God, my cheeks are burning.

"You can tell me," Aunt Melanie prods. "You don't have to, but if you think it will help to talk to me about it, please, tell me. This is a judgment-free zone."

I purse my lips. "Are you saying you're acting as my therapist?"

She chuckles lightly. "No, I'm acting as your aunt. Your aunt who cares very deeply about you and does not like to see you troubled."

"Can you say you're acting as my therapist? That way I know you'll be bound to keep this between us."

She laughs uneasily. "I'd do that for you anyway, Angie. You know how things are between us."

I look down at my mocha again, swirling the dark liquid in its paper cup. Aunt Melanie waits patiently, sipping her latte. She's good at hiding it, but I can tell she's worried.

"Okay," I say, taking a deep breath. "It's about Dr. Lansing... Jason."

"Jason?" Aunt Melanie repeats, surprise coloring her tone.

"He told us to call him Jason," I say. "In class, I mean."

"I see." She takes another sip of her latte.

One thing about Aunt Melanie—you can never tell exactly what she's thinking. I suppose she's had to learn to hear just

BROKEN DREAM

about anything from her patients and not react.

"We... Jason and I... We've sort of been...spending time together," I say, avoiding her eyes. "Outside of class."

Aunt Melanie doesn't immediately respond, but when I glance up at her, her expression is unreadable.

"I see," she says after a moment. "And how is this affecting you?"

"Well..." I hesitate, unsure of how to put my confusion, my longing, my fear into words. "It's...complicated."

Aunt Melanie raises an eyebrow but waits for me to continue.

"The thing is... He kissed me after the first day of anatomy lab and—"

"Wait, wait, *wait*," she says. "He *kissed* you? That's completely inappropriate."

"I know that. He knows it too. But he... He's been through a lot, and—"

She leans in, lowering her voice. "Please tell me this hasn't gone any further than a kiss, Angie."

My cheeks are on fire.

Can I lie to Aunt Mel? God, no. She'll see right through me. She's like a human lie detector.

"Well..." I start hesitantly, "We... It wasn't just a kiss."

Aunt Melanie's eyes widen. "Angie..."

"I know, Aunt Mel," I say quickly, wishing to God I could take it back. "I know it was wrong. I'm not trying to justify what happened. But it was..." I close my eyes. "It was amazing. For both of us."

She is quiet for a while, taking in my confession. The bustling coffee shop seems to melt away, and all I can see is her concerned gaze, her furrowed brows.

264

"I can see why you're so troubled."

"It's more than that."

She sighs. "All right. I'm here for you."

"This other student in the lab saw us. Then he came on to me, and when I made him stop, he said he saw the kiss in the lab—"

"Dr. Lansing kissed you in the lab?"

"Well...yeah."

She tents her fingers in front of her face. "Dear Lord..."

"Anyway, Ralph—that's the other student—threatened to go to the dean and have Jason fired."

"But he hasn't done that?"

"No. Not yet, anyway. I think he wants me to dig up information on Jason. Since we're...you know...intimately acquainted. And I... I don't know what to do," I say, my voice cracking. "I could try to pay him off, but I don't want to give that snake a penny."

"That's a difficult predicament," Aunt Mel says. "But paying him off isn't the answer. That would only be a temporary solution, and it's morally wrong."

"I know." I sigh, rubbing my forehead. "Just... I don't want to see Jason get into trouble because of me."

Aunt Mel reaches over the table and gently pats my hand. "Angela," she says softly, "I'm sure you care a lot about Dr. Lansing, but you must remember that he is an adult. He understood the consequences when he crossed that line with you. It's not just about your actions. It was *his* choice too."

Her words hit me like a punch in the gut. She's right, of course. I've been so wrapped up in my own fear and guilt that I hadn't considered that part.

"Yes," I murmur, swallowing hard against a sudden lump

BROKEN DREAM

in my throat. "You're right. I'm also an adult, even if we are thirteen years apart. My mom and dad are thirteen years apart."

Aunt Mel gives me a reassuring smile. "Age difference does not define the success or outcome of a relationship. However, the circumstances differ with your parents and you. Jason is in a position of authority."

Her words resonate with clarity. I look down at my cup, the mostly untouched mocha now cold and unappealing.

"Angie," Aunt Mel says, "this is a complicated issue. It's important to understand that this isn't just about romance or feelings. This is about ethics and professionalism too."

I nod, biting my lip. My heart sinks as I realize that we have indeed crossed lines not meant to be crossed.

Of course, I always knew that. But every time that thought popped up, I relegated it to the back of my brain. Now that I've told someone else about it, the reality of the situation has come crashing down.

"Maybe you should talk to Jason, discuss these things openly," Aunt Mel says.

"But what about Ralph?" I ask, blinking back tears. "He could ruin everything."

"Ralph is attempting to blackmail you. That's illegal. He's the one who should be fearing consequences." Aunt Mel leans back in her chair, folding her arms. "We'll figure out a plan to deal with him."

I manage a weak smile at her words. Aunt Mel always knows how to handle tricky situations with grace and tact.

"But before anything else," she continues, "you need to have an honest conversation with Jason. Understand his perspective and make sure he understands yours. This isn't just your problem. It's his too."

Tears prick my eyes as I nod. Despite everything, the weight of it all seems a little less daunting now that she knows.

"But promise me something, Angie," she adds, her gaze sharp and serious.

"Anything," I whisper, meeting her steady eyes.

"Promise me you won't lose yourself in this mess. Hold on to your values, your dreams, and your future. Don't let anyone—not Jason, not Ralph—dictate who you are or what you will become."

I blink at her. "I promise. I won't lose myself."

I only hope I can keep that promise, because all I want to do is lose myself in Jason, in what I feel when I'm with him, in the passion and desire between us.

Aunt Mel smiles. "Good girl," she murmurs.

We sit quietly together for a few moments, the hum of the coffee shop around us becoming muted background noise.

Finally, Aunt Mel breaks the silence. "And Angie," she says calmly, "you must also remember that you're not alone in this. You have a family that cares about you, a family that will help you navigate these waters."

I nod. "Okay, Aunt Mel," I say, wiping away the stray tear that has managed to escape from my eye. "But please don't tell them about this. At least not right away."

She nods. "I'll keep this between you and me as long as your safety isn't compromised. Lord knows your father and your brothers—not to mention your uncles and cousins—would speed down I-70 and kill Dr. Lansing with their bare hands if they found out about this." She gives me another comforting smile. "But don't forget. Sometimes the hardest decisions are the ones that need to be made. It may not seem like it now, but this will pass, and you'll come out stronger on the other side."

"Thank you, Aunt Mel," I reply, finally managing to give her a genuine smile.

She raises her coffee cup toward me. "To strength, courage, and tough choices."

I raise my own cup in response.

Strength.

Courage.

Tough choices.

I have to give Jason up.

And I just don't want to.

CHAPTER FORTY

JASON

Can my life get more fucked up?

I spend the rest of my Sunday drinking bourbon and feeling sorry for myself until I pass out on my couch.

I awaken to my phone buzzing.

"Yeah?" I say, not bothering to look to see who it is.

"Jason, hi. It's Louisa."

My heart lurches as I check the time. Eight a.m. Damn. It's Monday morning. "Hey. What's up?" My voice sounds groggy.

"I wanted to find out how your meeting with Dr. Steel went."

I sigh. "It sucked."

She pauses. "I...was afraid it might not go well. Dr. Steel is a tough cookie, but she knows her stuff."

"So you agree with her, then?"

"I agree she knows her stuff. I know that she wouldn't come to a conclusion without thinking it through rationally, weighing all the variables. What exactly did she say?"

"She didn't say no to the surgery." I rub at my forehead. "But she does recommend postponing it until I get some therapy. But I *really* don't want to go back to therapy, Louisa. It cost me everything I had left."

No response for a moment. Until—

BROKEN DREAM

"I may have a solution."

My heart lurches again. "Don't fuck with me, Louisa. Don't give me more false hope. I'm not in the mood."

"I'm not fucking with you. There's a state-of-the-art surgical center in Switzerland where Gita first performed the surgery with an excellent outcome. She thinks she can get you in there."

I don't respond for a second, my heart pounding. Part of me wants to get angry, to tell her to go to hell, that I don't want any more false hopes. But the other part—the part that sees the opportunity, the glimmer of hope—can't just push it away.

"You should know up front that this wouldn't be cheap," Louisa continues.

"There's always a catch," I say. "But I have money, Louisa. And what I don't have, I'll get."

"You'll have to stay local during rehabilitation. You'd have to take a sabbatical from your teaching."

I'm ready to agree now, but that's not what Louisa wants to hear. She wants to make sure I know what I'm agreeing to, that I'm not jumping in headfirst when the best psychiatrist in Colorado just told me to take more time.

"I'll think about it," I finally say, my voice hoarse with raw emotion.

"You do that," Louisa says. "Gita and I are in your corner, and so is Peter."

"Peter said that?"

"Not in so many words, but this psychiatric assessment wasn't his idea. It was the board's."

Of course it was.

"I understand. I'll be in touch."

"Good. Enjoy the rest of the weekend."

The weekend is pretty much over, and I spent it being psychoanalyzed.

When the call ends, I stare blankly at my phone's screen.

Could this be it?

Could this be the silver lining I was waiting for?

But Switzerland...

I love that place, and I always wanted to take Lindsay there. I promised her an amazing trip filled with chocolate, skiing, and those breathtaking views of the Alps. I pictured us wandering through quaint villages, hand in hand, sampling fondue in cozy little cafés, and laughing as we tumbled in the snow. It was going to be perfect—just us, away from everything, living in the moment.

But life had other plans. Cruel plans.

Perhaps Switzerland is what will save me. Give me hope.

Hope...

The thought buzzes in my brain long after I've drained the last drop of bourbon from my glass.

I have money.

I have what's left of the life insurance proceeds from Julia's death.

I didn't get anything when Lindsay died since her life insurance policy had a suicide clause.

Is it enough?

I could also wait it out. Do the therapy that Dr. Steel requires and see if I can convince the therapist that I've got good enough coping mechanisms and support in case of a negative outcome.

But the thought of therapy, of rehashing old wounds and bringing all my demons out in the open again...

It's too much to bear.

BROKEN DREAM

I slug down another shot, the burn of the bourbon providing a temporary distraction from the turmoil in my mind. I glance at the photo on the table beside me—Julia and Lindsay, their smiles frozen in time. A reminder of what I've lost, what I'll never have again.

I drag myself off the couch and walk over to my front window, gazing out at pine trees dusted with snow.

"Damn it," I mutter to myself, rubbing my temples. Thank God I don't have any classes on Mondays. I'm a freaking mess.

The phone rings again, and I have half a mind to ignore it. But when I see Louisa's name flash on the screen, I pick up without thinking.

"Jason?"

"Yes?" My voice sounds rough even to my ears, heavy with unshed tears.

"You need to know something else," she says in a rush. "About the center in Switzerland."

"What?" I ask, bracing myself for another blow.

"Gita thinks you're a great candidate...but apparently I was wrong about the timing. The facility has an unexpected opening, and one of Gita's assistants thinks he's found a cadaver nerve that would be a match. She needs your decision by tomorrow."

"Tomorrow?" I echo, my voice choked in disbelief. "How the hell am I supposed to decide by tomorrow?"

"I know it's difficult," Louisa says, her voice gentle in my ear. "But this may be the only chance you get, Jason."

I stand silent, my breath hitching as I process her words.

"So if I say yes," I begin slowly, "I'd have to leave when?"

"As soon as possible. Gita suggests within the next week."

"A week..." I repeat, staring blankly out the window.

A week to arrange a leave of absence, and if that's not possible, to quit my position at the medical school. A week to leave everything behind and take a leap of faith into the unknown.

A week.

That's it.

"Yes. Look, Jason," Louisa says. "I know it's not ideal. But sometimes life doesn't give us perfect choices."

I hold back a scoff. If anyone knows the truth of that statement, I do.

To leave my teaching position, at least for the remainder of this semester.

To leave...

Fuck.

To leave Angie.

Angie.

But I'll be back. And I won't need my teaching position if I'm a surgeon again.

To hold the scalpel back in my hand... To be a healer again...

"I'll do it," I say. "Tell Gita I'm in. I have money, and if it's more than I have, I'll get it somehow. I'll take out a loan. A mortgage on my home. I'll make it work."

"Good enough," Louisa says. "I'll email you the details tomorrow. In the meantime, get a flight booked to Bern."

"I will."

As soon as I end the call, I grab my leather jacket and walk over to Angie's where I pound on the door.

She opens the door, a look of astonishment on her face. "Jason, what is it? I have to get to campus."

I grab her, kiss her lips, and then break away.

BROKEN DREAM

"Come with me," I say. "Come with me to Switzerland."

She tilts her head slightly, eyes wide. "What?"

I wrap my arms around her waist, giving her a toothy grin. "The surgery for my hand. Long story short, I can get it done right now if I go to Switzerland. I'd have to wait a long time before they'll allow it to happen here." I cast my gaze to the ground. "If the board allows it at all."

She stands there blinking for a moment before her gorgeous lips finally part.

"But I have school... *You* have school."

I shrug. "I'll take a leave of absence. And you can take a semester off. They'll need me to stay in Switzerland for a while to follow up on the procedure. But school will be waiting for you when you get back." I cup her cheek. "You're a good student. I'll bet you could hunker down once you get back and still graduate on time."

Before she can speak again, I reel her in for another kiss.

She breaks her lips from mine. "You're talking about me going away with you. On a trip. We're not even..." She blushes. "We're not even official. We... We can't be. You'd lose your job."

I laugh at that. "I don't need my job as a professor if I'm back in surgery. And no one will care if a surgeon is dating a medical student."

She pouts her lips. "But still, Jason. *Switzerland.*"

"It's beautiful. You'll love it. I went while I was a fellow."

"I'm sure I'd love it, but—"

I cut her off with another kiss.

This woman. This beautiful, smart, young woman.

I let go of her, and she's about to speak again when I place a finger over her lips.

"Just...think about it. I'm going to leave in a week. I'd love to have you come with me."

And I turn, run back to my place, and get into my car.

I keep my passport in my desk at work. Seemed to be the smart thing to do in case I ever lost my driver's license while on the job. At least I'd have another form of ID.

Christ, I hope it hasn't expired...

No, it shouldn't be. I renewed it right before my last trip overseas, when Lindsay was pregnant. That was a little over six years ago. Passports are good for ten years, right?

God, I hope I'm right.

I drive over to the school, ignoring the speed limit the whole way, and park in the fire lane. I'm only going to be here a few minutes.

I rush into my office. I reach for my keys when I realize the door is unlocked.

Shit. Did I forget to lock this? There are sensitive documents in here.

Won't happen again. I'll make sure the door is locked securely when I leave for Switzerland.

I open the door, and my heart races.

My office looks like a storm went through it. Papers are scattered across my desk's surface and onto the floor, some crumpled. My computer monitor is tilted, and drawers hang open, their contents dumped out. On the bookshelves, textbooks and journals have been pulled out and tossed aside. The locks on my filing cabinet have been forced open. I look inside to see that several file folders are ripped.

Someone in here was looking for something, and they were doing it quickly.

What the hell could I possibly be keeping in here that would be worth ransacking my office so crudely?

BROKEN DREAM

I close the door behind me, locking it. I walk over to my desk, looking through the papers. It's mostly copies of old syllabi, lecture notes, even some old patient-related files from when I was still a surgeon. I couldn't bear to part with them when I stopped cutting. I needed some sort of connection to the past.

Speaking of connections to the past...

A single envelope, slightly wrinkled, is strewn to the side carelessly by whoever searched my office.

To Jason...

Christ. It's the note that Lindsay left behind the day she killed herself.

I've never read it.

The day she died, I stuffed it in my pocket. I gave it to one of the cops who eventually came over. He gave it one look and then returned it to me. It was pretty easy to tell what had happened.

That night, I came into the hospital and placed this envelope at the bottom of my lowest desk drawer. Far away from my everyday files and documents, but a small lifeline to the woman who was once the love of my life if I ever needed it.

I don't know why—I really should be focusing on more important things right now—but I pull the note out of the envelope. Maybe now that I'm about to get some of my life back, I can handle the letter's contents.

Then a knock on my door. "Dr. Lansing?"

"One second." I look at the first words.

Jason, I'm sorry, but I can't carry this weight any longer.

I feel a sting in my gut. But there's another feeling, one I can't quite place. Is it...wariness?

Another knock on my door, louder this time. "Dr. Lansing! Please open the door."

"Be there in a minute," I say.

Probably some student trying to get extra office hours, despite the fact that mine are by appointment only. I return to the note.

Losing her shattered me in ways I can't put into words. I've tried to be strong—for you, for us—but the pain is relentless, and I can't see a way forward.

Please know this isn't your fault. You gave me everything, but I've lost myself in the void she left behind. I hope you find peace someday, even if I couldn't.

I squint at the note. Something is wrong here. Lindsay *did* blame me. She could never say it out loud, but I could tell every moment of the rest of her short life that she harbored resentment toward me for the death of our daughter.

I'll love you forever. See you on the other side, babe.

Lindsay

Three more sharp knocks. "Open the door now, Dr. Lansing."

I whip my head back to the door. "Christ! I'll be there in a second. I'm...changing."

"You have thirty seconds, or I'll knock the door down."

Knock the door down? Definitely not a student, then.

BROKEN DREAM

Maybe it's Peter. He probably heard about how my meeting with Dr. Steel went, and he's concerned I've gone off the deep end.

"I'm fine. I'll be out in a sec."

I look back at the letter, read over it again. Once, twice, three times.

And an anvil drops in my gut as I realize...

This isn't my wife's handwriting.

CHAPTER FORTY-ONE

ANGIE

It's been an hour since Jason came to my house, and I've been sitting on the floor on the other side of my front door, thinking about what to do. I should get to campus, but I can't get myself to move.

He wants me to go away with him. To Switzerland. For God knows how long. Long enough for me to have to take a semester off school.

Aunt Melanie will disapprove, that's for sure.

My whole family will.

But Jason's right about one thing. I can come back. It's not like I'm *moving* to Switzerland.

But...we haven't even been on a date. All we've done is sleep together.

I laugh at that. There was no sleeping involved. And we've only done it in a bed once.

I rub at my forehead. Tillie scampers up to me and gives me a kiss on the cheek.

"Thanks, girl," I say to her.

I can't take Tillie overseas, either. I'd have to drive her out to the Western Slope, leave her with my family. I just adopted her. It would break my heart to leave her so soon.

But then there's Jason.

BROKEN DREAM

The chemistry we share is undeniable. I've heard my own mom and dad talk about how they fell in love. My aunts, my uncles, my cousins, too. The Steels in particular tend to fall hard and fall fast.

Is that what's happened to me?

Am I actually in *love* with Jason?

I can't stop thinking about him. About the time we've shared together. About our first kiss in the anatomy lab, how he ravaged me in my own kitchen. And then back at school, with the cadavers silently watching.

And maybe I'm the only person who can support him in this endeavor. This surgery that means so much to him. A chance for him to return to his old life.

It's only a few months. Brianna would not stop blabbering about how beautiful the UK was when she went with Jesse's band.

I've never even left the continental U.S. The Steels aren't typically big travelers, despite our wealth.

And away from the university, away from the judging eyes of our colleagues and peers, Jason and I could actually try being a couple.

In that moment, I know what my decision is.

I'm going to do it. I'm going to throw caution to the wind and see if this thing with Jason has any legs.

I run over to his house, pound on his door. "Jason. Jason!"

No answer.

His car isn't in the driveway. He must have gone somewhere. Probably to campus.

I call his cell. It rings a few times and then goes straight to his voicemail.

Weird. After asking me to go to Switzerland with him, I

would think he'd pick up pretty quickly to learn my answer.

Maybe he left his phone in his car or something.

I'll drive over to the university. I have a class in an hour anyway, and I want to tell Jason in person that I'm going to go to Switzerland with him.

I dash back to my house, let Tillie out for a quick potty break, and then get in my car.

Once I've parked, I walk up to the building.

I see Jason's car parked in the fire lane. I recognize it from the day he discovered we were neighbors.

Good. He's here.

I run to his office, nearly knocking over a few students and professors on the way.

"Excuse me, sorry."

I turn the corner to the hallway where his office is located.

Jason, my sweet Jason. The man of my dreams. The man I'm in love with. He's going to be so happy to hear what I have to say.

And I run right into someone.

I fall back on my butt. For a second everything is blurry.

I rub my eyes and look at who I've run into.

Oh, no.

Sitting on the floor across from me, rubbing his forehead, is Ralph. A few pieces of paper are scattered around him.

Great. Just great.

He looks at me and scowls. "What the hell, Angie? Would it kill you to look where you're going?"

I slowly get to my feet. "Sorry. Just excited, I guess."

He furrows his brow. "Excited about what?"

I cross my arms. "Excited about something that is none of your damn business, Ralph. Just like most things in my

BROKEN DREAM

personal life."

His ears perk up at my words. "So you're admitting it, then, that you've been fooling around with Dr. Lansing?"

I scoff. "Christ, Ralph. Do you know any other songs?"

He smirks. "That's not a denial."

"I've already denied your accusation countless times. I don't need to do it further."

"Whatever." He gathers up the documents he dropped when we ran into each other and stuffs them into his pockets. He glances over his shoulder down the hall. "But you seem in an awful rush to get to his office."

"As a matter of fact... I have an appointment with him. Office hours. About anatomy lab."

He curls his lips into a grin. "I think you're going to have to reschedule."

I roll my eyes. "Yes, I'm sure you, like everyone else, think that I'm a lost cause because my interest is in psychiatry. But I'm determined to prove you all—"

He holds up a hand. "Save it. Be a psychiatrist if you want. Be a dentist, a chiropractor. Hell, go for your yoga certification. I don't give a shit."

I lift an eyebrow. "Then why did you make that nasty comment about rescheduling my appointment?"

He chuckles softly. "Because your precious Dr. Lansing isn't in his office right now. He was escorted out about a half hour ago."

Keep reading for a sneak peek of
Healed Heart,
the conclusion of
Jason and Angie's story.

HEALED HEART SNEAK PEEK

I return to my office, sit down at my desk, and open the bottom drawer where I keep things that have no other place. I can't recall the last time I looked in there.

Damn. Right on top is an old picture of Lindsay and me at a medical conference—one of the few times she went with me. Julia stayed with Lindsay's parents. It was the last trip Lindsay and I took alone together before...

Before the accident that claimed our daughter and my livelihood...and led to my wife's suicide.

Except...

I sigh. Of course it was a suicide. I found her in the bathtub, her wrists slit...

But the note.

The note I never bothered reading until today...

As I stare at the photo, the discord of the morning grows louder in my head. What the hell is going on? An accusation from an anonymous source? Then Lindsay's note, written by someone else?

She still could have taken her life, but this opens up a huge can of worms.

I pinch the bridge of my nose and try to concentrate on what I need to do next. I look at the photo again. Lindsay's smile sends an ache through my heart. Same as it always does.

There's only one place I can go to find what I need. I pull out my cell phone and call Lindsay's parents.

After a few rings, her mother picks up. "Jason?" she says, her tone full of surprise.

Can't blame her. I rarely call them anymore. It's too painful—for all of us.

"Lisa," I say, my throat tight. "I need to ask you something."

"Of course," she says. "What is it?"

"Do you still have any of Lindsay's things?"

A pause on the other end, followed by a soft sigh. "Yes, Jason. We still have some of her things here. I...couldn't bear to let everything go."

The sadness in her voice slices through me. I hate that I'm forcing her to relive the pain of losing her daughter.

I clear my throat. "Anything that has her handwriting on it? Something other than a signature?"

"Handwriting?" Lisa's voice wavers. "I think we have some family recipes she wrote down. And maybe some old letters. But why do you want them *now*, Jason?"

I rub the back of my neck, trying to ease the aching tension. "I'm sorry, but it's important. Could I possibly come by later to look at what you have?"

Silence then.

I can almost hear her thoughts.

Why is Jason interested in this stuff now? Why is he making me relive my biggest loss?

Finally, she exhales deeply. "Sure, Jason. Come by around six. We'll have dinner ready as well if you'd like to join us."

"That's okay. You don't have to bother."

"It's no bother. It will be nice"—she chokes a bit, as if holding back a sob—"to see you. You and Lindsay used to eat here so often."

I sigh. This won't be awkward at all. "Thank you. I'll see

you for dinner then."

I end the call and place the phone face down on my desk as I let my gaze wander to the photo of Lindsay and me once more.

And then the note.

I stare at the handwriting—the slight slant to the right, the way the ink presses harder in places as if she trembled or hesitated.

I read the words again.

Jason, I'm sorry, but I can't carry this weight any longer.

Losing her shattered me in ways I can't put into words. I've tried to be strong—for you, for us—but the pain is relentless, and I can't see a way forward.

Please know this isn't your fault. You gave me everything, but I've lost myself in the void she left behind. I hope you find peace someday, even if I couldn't.

I'll love you forever. See you on the other side, babe.

Lindsay

My eyes moisten, but I don't cry.

I stopped crying long ago. I couldn't cry for my dead wife, and the guilt still plagues me. I cried out all my tears for Julia.

In fact, what I felt was anger. Anger that she couldn't bring herself to blame me outright, to give in to the rage she felt, to fucking heal.

And anger at that damned psychiatrist, Dr. Morgan, who said she could help us. Said she could help Lindsay.

Oh, God...

If Lindsay didn't take her own life...perhaps Dr. Morgan *could* have eventually helped her?

What am I doing? What do I hope to find? To prove?

Whatever the real story is, Lindsay is still dead. Our daughter is still dead.

I grip the edge of my desk, my knuckles white.

I was finally beginning to move on.

With the surgery.

With Angie.

But everything has changed.

I won't let this lie.

I can't.

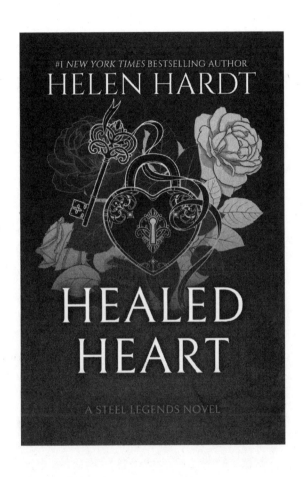

AVAILABLE OCTOBER 7, 2025

ACKNOWLEDGMENTS

Thank you for reading *Broken Dream*! Those of you who are waiting for Griffin's story, have no fear. She will return! But honestly she needs time to heal, and I needed to take a break from her trauma as well.

So what did I do? I created a doctor with his own trauma! Just how my mind works, as you know. I can't resist torturing my characters.

What better setting for romance, suspense, and character torture than medicine? I've been obsessed with medical drama—specifically *Grey's Anatomy*—for years. What's more exciting than the high-stakes world of medicine colliding with raw and complicated human emotion? So after over sixty novels, I'm finally tackling that world. I hope you enjoy this first installment of Angie and Jason's story!

Thank you to the team at Waterhouse Press for keeping this world alive. Special thanks to my editor extraordinaire, Scott Saunders, and also to the rest of the team, Jon, Jesse, Haley, Chrissie, Michele, and Amber. I appreciate all of you!

Thank you to my husband, Dean (aka Mr. Hardt), my sons, Eric and Grant, and my daughter-in-law, Cally, for your endless support. Special thanks to Eric for helping me get this manuscript in top shape before it went to Waterhouse.

To my wonderful street team, Hardt & Soul, thank you for being my cheering squad. I love you all!

And of course, to all my readers—I couldn't do any of this without each and every one of you. Special thanks go to my beta team and my Ream community.

Healed Heart will be here soon. In the meantime, don't forget to look at my extensive backlist for your next read!

ALSO BY HELEN HARDT

The Steel Brothers Saga:
Craving
Obsession
Possession
Melt
Burn
Surrender
Shattered
Twisted
Unraveled
Breathless
Ravenous
Insatiable
Fate
Legacy
Descent
Awakened
Cherished
Freed
Spark
Flame
Blaze
Smolder
Flare
Scorch
Chance
Fortune
Destiny
Melody
Harmony
Encore

Steel Legends:
I Am Sin
I Am Salvation
Broken Dream
Healed Heart

Blood Bond Saga:
Unchained
Unhinged
Undaunted
Unmasked
Undefeated

Misadventures Series:
Misadventures with a Rock Star
Misadventures of a Good Wife (with Meredith Wild)

The Temptation Saga:
Tempting Dusty
Teasing Annie
Taking Catie
Taming Angelina
Treasuring Amber
Trusting Sydney
Tantalizing Maria

The Sex and the Season Series:
Lily and the Duke
Rose in Bloom
Lady Alexandra's Lover
Sophie's Voice

Daughters of the Prairie:
The Outlaw's Angel
Lessons of the Heart
Song of the Raven

Cougar Chronicles:
The Cowboy and the Cougar
Calendar Boy